I0571880

ALWAYS A MARINE

Volume Two

By

HEATHER LONG

Featuring...

The Marine Cowboy
The Two and the Proud
A Marine and a Gentleman
Whiskey Tango Foxtrot
Combat Barbie

℃

Decadent Publishing Company
www.decadentpublishing.com

This book is a work of fiction. Names, characters, places, and incidents are the products of the author's imagination or used fictitiously. Any resemblance to actual events, locales or persons, living or dead, is entirely coincidental.

Always a Marine – Volume Two
Copyright 2013 by Heather Long
ISBN: 978-1-61333-508-6
Cover design by Mina Carter and Cribley Designs

All rights reserved. Except for use in any review, the reproduction or utilization of this work, in whole or in part, in any form by any electronic, mechanical or other means now known or hereafter invented, is forbidden without the written permission of the publisher.

Published by Decadent Publishing Company
www.decadentpublishing.com

Printed in the United States of America

"What the Critics are Saying...."

The Marine Cowboy

"Ms. Long does a wonderful job with dialogue, and I could picture the southern drawl coming from A.J.'s lips, endearing him even more than he already had." ~ Reviewed by Aster, Long and Short Reviews

"The Marine Cowboy is a truly enjoyable combination of hot, sweet, sexy and funny." ~ Sizzling Hot Books

The Two and The Proud

"The heat factor was off the charts, even in limited pages. The Always a Marine series is a crowd pleaser for sure, and *The Two and The Proud* is no exception!" ~ Reviewed by Aster, Long and Short Reviews

"For a short book it managed to work in two steamy scenes!! Really nicely written and wonderfully engaging characters." ~ K., Amazon

A Marine and a Gentleman

"Watching these two men re-connect was engaging and the chemistry between them is tangible." ~ Shh Moms Reading

"While it is the first m/m book in Heather Long's series, it is a great debut in the genre. I really hope she will write a longer m/m romance book, as I would certainly buy it!" ~ Lasha, Amazon

Whiskey Tango Foxtrot

"I don't know how Heather Long packs so much into such a short story. I laughed, I cried, and I sighed." ~ D. Antonio, Amazon

"I find this to be an almost perfect story. I didn't want it to end and now I'm ready for more." ~ Night Owl Reviews

Combat Barbie

"There's a scene where she's talking with Kyle about part of her time overseas and the dialogue is so clear and heartfelt, I couldn't help but be moved." ~ Reviewed by Shelly, Red Hot Books

"It was also great to read about females in the military and their contribution and how they view themselves." ~ Alexis Grace, Amazon

THE MARINE COWBOY

HEATHER LONG

ಐ

Chapter One

*W*ith air brakes hissing, the bus rolled to a stop. A.J. grabbed his ruck out of the seat next to him and made his way up the aisle of the Greyhound. The driver gave him a friendly smile and a wave on his way past then the sun hit him as he stepped into the open air. The old depot, about a mile outside Freewill, Wyoming, was surrounded by green grass right up to the edge of the old blacktop two-lane road.

He tilted his head back, drinking in the cool air, warm sunshine, and silence. *God bless the silence.* No men catching up on what happened on watch. No gunfire. No babble of foreign voices. Nothing to rankle nerves rubbed raw after five years with too few breaks in the blistering heat and desolation of Iraq.

Opening his eyes, he skimmed the mountains in the distance, an uninterrupted vista of lean, green, and free. Three deep breaths of fresh, clean, mountain air and he almost felt like a new man. He hefted the ruck over one shoulder and began to walk. The shape of the town's exterior sharpened with every step he took.

He pushed the door to the Blue Moon Café open and stepped inside to the jingle of the bell. Bud Gaines glanced up from behind the counter and shot him a wide-welcoming grin. "Well,

I'll be a son of a bitch! Look what the cat dragged in."

A.J. crossed the room and took the older man's outstretched hand in a firm grip. "Hey, Bud."

"Hey there, yourself. Why didn't you let me know you were coming home?"

The words carried a decade of chastisement. A.J. spent half his youth in trouble with, or being praised by, the café owner, a close friend of his father's. When his dad passed ten years before, Bud stepped up to the plate and gave A.J. an ear when he needed and left him alone when he didn't.

"Didn't want to make a fuss. Is the coffee fresh?" He slid onto a stool and set his bag down next to it.

Bud answered with a baleful expression that said 'of course' and filled a fresh mug for him. "On leave?"

"Nope. Home for good." He glanced around the café. The mid-morning lull was in full effect. His didn't recognize a dark-haired female sitting in a window booth. She read a book and didn't even glance up. *Definitely a newcomer.* All the old-timers gave him a friendly nod or at least met his eye. He turned back to Bud, eyeing him over the rim of his coffee cup.

"There will be fuss as soon as Mattie hears." Bud may not be that fond of his siblings, but A.J. was one of Mattie's favorites. He'd worked at the Misbegotten Gaines Ranch all the way through high school and two years into his studies at community college.

Before I talked to a recruiter. Before I left for Parris Island. In the seven years since, he hadn't been home, not once. But he saw the postcards stuck to Bud's corkboard on the back wall, all sent by A.J. from his training to deployment.

"Well, hopefully I'll be home before she gets wind of it. How many horses do I have left?"

There'd been a herd of over a dozen, all trained by him. Two stallions, ten mares, and a two-hundred acre spread staked out by his father that they'd shared until the man's death. It wasn't much, but it was home.

Bud wiped the counter and gave him a crooked grin. "Left?

Try about fifty head at Jamie's last count. Brady's been looking after them. He brings them into MGR when the weather turns, but otherwise, they're still running on Turner property. You had four new foals this spring."

Fifty.

A.J. smiled, the unfamiliar stretch to his mouth relaxing him for the first time since he'd signed the discharge papers and accepted his C.O.'s congratulations. He'd believed he needed to start over from scratch. Fifty meant he'd be working from dawn to dusk. Hot, sweating, honest work.

"I'll give him a call and let him know that I'm home." He finished the coffee and set the mug down. Bud slid across a keychain with the gold coin that served as a fob. Scooping them up, he rose. "Thanks for everything, Bud."

"You need a ride?"

"No, sir. I think I'll walk." Ten miles wouldn't take that long and he could use the stretch. He'd taken buses all the way from Dallas after turning down Captain Dexter's job offer and longed for the familiar sights of the mountains and valleys of home. He appreciated what the man built with Mike's Place. Helping veterans and their families was honorable work, but A.J. needed to be away from all of it—to be back where he belonged.

"Don't be a stranger, boy. You know where I am if you need me."

"Yes, sir." He slung the bag over his shoulder and found the book-reading woman staring at him when he turned. He met her sweet brown eyes with a friendly grin and touched a hand to his head, as if he wore a hat. "Ma'am."

Her startled smile punched awareness through him. It turned her solemn, thoughtful expression into something fresh and sunny. A man could appreciate a smile like that.

But he put thoughts of the new girl out of his mind as he left the café and crossed the street. He knew the route to his ranch like the back of his hand and was eager to see it again.

ↄ৪

Sheri took a fast drink of her cold coffee to cover the hiccups that shot through her when the rugged stranger stared right at her. *Holy hell in a hand basket.*

Her gaze tracked him as he left the café and crossed the street. The jeans he wore hadn't been spray painted on his ass, but they definitely gave her a great visual of hard muscle and male confidence. He walked like he owned the town, but without any hint of pretentious air. That was a man who belonged in Freewill. She didn't know who he was. She thought after six months she'd met most of the locals, but she would have remembered *him.*

"A.J. Turner." Bea poured fresh coffee into her cup, heating it up.

Sheri spent nearly every morning at the café reading before she walked one block down to open the library. Trading her job as a corporate executive at a Fortune 500 company to be a small-town librarian didn't suggest upward trajectory, but the town of Freewill healed that broken empty place inside left by her ex-husband's series of affairs.

"The war hero?" She blinked and glanced back at the window, but he'd already disappeared.

"One and the same. Boy hasn't been home since he left and didn't tell anyone he was coming back either." Bea clucked her tongue and wrote out the check. The café preferred the old pen and paper method, and since Sheri ate fruit and drank coffee every morning, the price was always the same.

"What branch did he serve in again?" Curious, she glanced at the waitress. Bea had been born, married, gave birth to her children, and buried her husband in Freewill. The town fixture wasn't going anywhere. She also took Sheri under her wing from the day she arrived, treating her like an old friend—or a daughter.

"Marines, honey. That young man is definitely one of Freewill's proudest." She winked and went back to work.

A Marine. A tremor raced over her and her stomach seemed

to bottom out.

The message waiting in her email that morning from Madame Eve made so much more sense. Biting her lip, she strained to look down the street. She wished she'd paid closer attention to him when he walked in, but she only got one good glimpse at his face when he turned and caught her staring.

Her cheeks heated at the memory. He'd caught her attention the moment he entered the café. She hadn't missed the corded muscle in his arms, tense and well defined even as he drank a cup of coffee. The man was gorgeous and wore his masculinity like a second skin.

But his smile.

Her heart squeezed. The polite smile creasing his rugged face transformed him from handsome to a full-blown heartthrob. Her body hummed in reaction. *To a smile.*

Wow. He just got home, Sheri. Dial down the hormones. Not even a mental lecture could dilute the man's effect. She closed her book and counted out a few bills to pay the check. Waving to Bea and Bud, she headed out. An hour until the library opened, but she wanted to use the computer to answer Madame Eve's email.

Ms. Vaughn,

After careful consideration and research, your request for a 1Night Stand has been approved and a match to your specific requirements identified. Please respond via email if you are still interested.

That was it. No signature, no 'be well,' no phone number to call and ask the woman questions. She'd applied to the dating service with an exceptionally specific list of requirements.

Exceptionally.

In fact, so specific Sheri thought no one could fulfill them. Her keys trembled in her hand as she unlocked the door and let herself into the quiet, one floor building. Her office and the front desk sat right next to the door. The stacks were quiet and dark with about twenty-five rows curving around the corner desk. She booted up the computer and set her purse, keys, and book next to it.

"C'mon," she urged it. The machine connected with the speed of a 300-baud modem. The slower pace didn't usually aggravate her. Logging in, she opened a webpage and typed in her email info. Three minutes later, she read the note from Madame Eve again.

It still asked her if she was interested. Clicking the mail above it, she reviewed her application.

I am looking for a unique man, one who is both hero and hometown. He must be honorable, courageous, and forthright in his activities. He must be single. It's okay if he is divorced, but not if the divorce was his fault. No adulterers need apply. He should have served his country as a Marine, but be a cowboy at heart. This is the man I want to spend a one-night stand with.

It took a whole bottle of wine to write that list and she hadn't sent it until she'd read it sober the next morning. She wanted a paperback hero, a man from a romance novel, and she wanted to find him in the small town of Freewill. Certain the service would never be able to deliver on that fantasy, she'd submitted it.

And then she forgot it, because she never expected anything to happen. The whimsical application came from a moment of weakness and profound loneliness. She wanted a man who would kiss her like he meant it, hold her like she mattered, and make love to her like she was the only woman for him.

Biting her lip, she scrolled back to the question. An image of A.J. Turner's sexy grin filled her mind and her stomach flip-flopped. She glanced at the tiny stuffed buffalo sitting on top of the monitor as if it would give her the answer she needed.

With shaking fingers she typed one word.

Yes.

And hit send before she could change her mind.

Chapter Two

One week later....

A.J. nailed the board with three swift hits of the hammer and moved on to the next nail. Overall, the Spotted Horse Ranch wasn't even a fifth the size of the Gaines' place, but it was home. His grandfather, and later his father, kept it up, growing it only as much as a body could handle. They didn't bring in employees or contractors, preferring to do the work themselves.

He'd stripped off his sweat-soaked shirt an hour before. A tool belt rode low on his hips, the weight a comfortable thing. The work gloves hugged his hands, and the cowboy hat he favored rode low over his eyes, keeping the sun out. Rising before dawn, he was determined to finish the new paddock so he could bring the younglings in closer to start working them.

A whinny from the pasture pulled his gaze up. A truck rolled up his long drive. He sighed, his seven days of blissful silence, the beer with Brady notwithstanding, was about to be interrupted. The decade-old truck bounced slowly over the ruts in the drive. He needed to grade that drive before winter.

"A.J.!" Mitch Cramer, the ancient town postman waved from the open window of the vehicle. The wrinkles in the man's face and baldpate were a testament to his longevity. "How you doing, boy?"

To him, like so many of the old timers, A.J. would always be just a boy. Hanging the hammer on his belt, he stripped off his work gloves and walked over to the truck. "I'm good, Mr. Cramer. Real good. How is Mrs. Cramer?"

Rosey Cramer had been teaching kindergarten at the local school for nearly forty-five years and, at last count, didn't seem to have any plans to stop.

"Retiring." Cramer grinned broadly. "We've got us some great-grandbabies down in Jackson Hole and she wants to spend more time with them."

"Great-grand-babies?" That was news to him. He'd gone to high school with Veronica and Chet, the Cramer grandkids.

"Ayup. Ronnie had herself some triplets." The man's smile seemed to grow three feet. "Two girls and a boy. Lots of quilting, knitting, and spoiling to be done."

"Congratulations." He shook his hand again. "Please pass on my regards to Ronnie."

"Will do. Oh, and before I forget...." He picked up a bundle of mail on the seat next to him. Tied together by a thick cord, the top letter showed an Allen, Texas, return address. "I wouldn't be running this out here, but the letter here was marked urgent. You remember to come into town on Saturdays to get your mail. My Rosey still makes up brownies for the Saturday pick up."

Accepting the stack, he nodded. "Yes, sir. I remember."

Task done, Mr. Cramer gave him another wave and drove away. He didn't linger to be social; he took his job as a postal worker seriously. Driving all the way out to the Spotted Horse was a favor, not one he'd likely repeat unless another 'urgent' delivery came in.

Mopping the sweat off his face with a bandana, A.J. headed up to the sprawling porch with its slanted roof. He grabbed a bottle of water from the cooler and took a long pull then cut the tie holding the letters together. Recognizing the Captain's writing, he slit his letter open first. The rest could wait. A sheet of paper slipped out with a single line.

Turn on your damn phone. – L.

A.J. sighed. He'd shut off his cell phone his first day back in town. He hadn't missed having it. In fact, save for two trips into town to pick up supplies and a beer with Brady, he avoided talking to anyone. Not even the pretty librarian whose name he learned was Sheri. Ms. Potts at the grocery told him a lot about Freewill's transplant when she caught him watching her over the produce. Guy Wilks from the gas station mentioned her. Her car needed an oil change and she'd been there, too. In fact, both times he'd gone to town, he'd seen her everywhere.

Maybe he'd swing by the library and check out a book on his next trip. He laid the letter on the porch table and secured it with a rock. The cell phone sat inside, dropped into a drawer in the entry hall and forgotten. He tracked dirt across the entry floor, but he could sweep that out later. The interior of the house needed more work than the exterior. But winter came early in Wyoming, and he could strip and refinish the floors when the snow fell too deep to do anything else.

Holding down the power button, he carried his cell back outside, and dropped to sit on the porch swing. A yawn stretched his jaw. The phone vibrated as text message after text message hit the screen.

Logan's name popped up. So did James's. Then Luke's scrolled three or four times. He'd missed over a dozen calls and nearly that many voice mails. Grimacing at the screen, he fought the temptation to turn the damn thing off again. But the Captain wouldn't send a letter if he didn't need something.

All the voicemails were from Luke. Tossing back another swig of water, he checked the text messages first. Luke's were straightforward. Answer his phone or call him back. Pick one. They were shorter and more terse toward the end, but essentially the same message. An unfamiliar number sent him two text messages as well.

Your 1Night Stand has been arranged. Please review email for details.

His what?

He dialed Luke's number from memory and drained the bottle of water while the phone rang on the other end.

"Dexter."

"Captain. What's up?"

"You turned on your phone. Good. Madame Eve has been trying to get a hold of you." He heard a woman laugh and murmur something and an equally muffled response from the Captain. Probably talking to his fiancée.

"Who?"

"Madame Eve—Evangeline—the lady who runs the 1Night Stand service?"

Pushing his hat back, A.J. scratched his head. "Not to sound stupid, but what the hell are you talking about?"

Luke laughed. "Don't play dumb. We talked about this, about eighteen months ago now? We all signed up."

He wasn't playing dumb. Tossing the empty bottle into the recycling bin, he grabbed another one out of the cooler and pressed the coldness to the back of his neck. "Seriously, Captain? Eighteen months ago, I was running munitions and supplies between Mosul and Baghdad."

"Perkins wanted to sign up for a service that matches couples looking for one night together. He didn't want to date, didn't think he was ready to do it. When he backtracked on the idea, we all said we'd do it, the whole unit."

Vague recollection itched in the back of his mind. "Dating service."

"Something like that. Sound familiar now?" Luke's easy humor relaxed the tension knotting A.J.'s shoulders.

"Vaguely. But I was still in the sandbox." He'd signed up, but didn't think anything of it. He was away, without a leave date in sight, but solidarity held them together.

"I know. We put that on your application and when you sent word that you'd signed your discharge papers, I updated the profile to active."

If any other man told him that, A.J. would be hard pressed not to break his nose.

"You did what?" His voice went soft and quiet.

"I marked you active. You agreed, A.J. We all did." The

gentle humor fled, replaced by the hard tone of a commanding officer, one he'd followed for years.

"Luke, I appreciate it. But I just got home. I have a lot of work here, and I don't have time to fly back to Dallas." Maybe he had an out after all.

"You don't have to. Check your messages. Madame Eve's been trying to get in touch with you. Seems someone in Freewill might be seeking a little free loving."

An image of the sexy librarian popped into his head. He'd gotten a good look at a pair of lean, long legs at the grocery store and even more generous breasts when he'd seen her at the gas station. Her russet hair refused to stay confined to a braid and escaped in little tendrils he wanted to see spread out on a pillow while he sank into her body.

"You're not backing out are you, Sergeant?" Luke's voice carried just enough of a dare in it to get A.J.'s back up.

"No, sir. I'm not. I'll check the messages." If for no other reason than he had made a commitment to his unit, whether he remembered it or not. Another image of the sweet curve of her ass as the librarian turned away from him solidified in his head.

"Enjoy it, A.J. Enjoy being alive and home. It's one night, right?"

"Yes, sir." He hung up a couple of minutes later and stared at the phone. He thought about shutting it off, but he was a man of his word. And it was good to talk to Luke, to catch up on what the others were up to. He still couldn't believe the captain was engaged.

He checked the text from the unfamiliar number. It asked him about his availability. It was Wednesday now. He glanced at the paddock and the fourteen sections where he still needed to put boards up.

If he finished today and took care of the one-night stand thing on the weekend, he could go see his librarian after church. Did she go to church?

Saturday. Afternoon or evening preferred, he typed. That would give him time to get a haircut and feed the horses before he went.

He hesitated. Was it really fair to whomever they were hooking him up with that he was interested in another woman?

It's just one night, A.J.. What can happen in one night?

He hit send and tossed the phone on top of the letters then pushed himself off the porch swing and went back to work. The fence boards weren't going to hammer themselves into place.

ભ

Saturday afternoon? Panic locked up the air in her lungs like an allergy attack. She grabbed her brown sack lunch and dumped the food out before putting the paper up to breath into it. It crumpled and rattled with every forced inhale and exhale.

Why did I say yes? What had she been thinking? Her teeth dragged over her lower lip as the pounding of her heart finally slowed. She stole a glance around the library. The chatter of children playing in the back with their mothers was the only noise of the day. Fortunately, no one was close enough to see her near freak out.

She leaned back in the chair and stared up at the ceiling. Saturday afternoon she had a date to get laid. Should she add that to her appointment calendar? A wildly inappropriate giggle stole through her.

This is assuming my date is with A.J. Turner...what if it's not? It's Freewill, how many cowboys have you seen in this town?

The sound choked off and she swallowed hard. *But no Marines.* A.J. was the only Marine she knew there—well correction—the only Marine under the age of sixty.

A ding on her computer signaled a new email. She clicked it open. The date was set for four p.m. at a private cabin at the Misbegotten Gaines Ranch. Heat crept into her cheeks. The location hadn't even occurred to her. A private cabin meant she could avoid the main house and maybe any whisper of her date.

But it was Freewill...how discreet could she manage to be?

Oh my God. What do I wear?

Chapter Three

*I*t was after three before A.J. hit the shower. After a quick sluice of water to rinse away the sweat and a shampoo to get the grit out first, he took his time to shave. He'd pushed himself to finish the paddock and guided the first of three yearlings in there an hour before. The barn sported fresh paint and all the damaged boards had been replaced. First thing Monday, he would start working the yearlings out, getting them used to lunging with mild weight and more. As he scraped away the stubble, he considered ordering a hot walker. He could build one, but that would cut into the time he wanted to spend on the horses.

Washing off the traces of shaving cream, he rinsed his hair one more time and then shut the shower off. Fifteen minutes later, he pulled on boots and settled a black Stetson on his head. Nothing a little spit and polish couldn't clean up.

He went over the mental list of chores. Horses fed. Water troughs full. Young stallion in the paddock getting used to his new workout space. House lights shut off. Truck keys in hand, he considered indulging himself and riding one of the horses over to the MGR Cabin where he was supposed to meet his 'date,' but a truck required less care and no stabling.

Not that he minded if the Gaines noticed his presence or not, but the lady in question might. Freewill offered a lot of freedom to its residents. Unfortunately, an absence of gossip was not one of those freedoms.

He left the front door unlocked and strolled over to classic 1950's pickup truck. It sat parked in the U-shaped drive in front of the main house. The vehicle had belonged to his grandfather and father before him. The day after he arrived, he went over the engine with a fine-tooth comb, replacing rotted belts and changing the oil, glad that Guy came out every season to warm her up, run some fresh fuel through her lines and adjust the belts. He'd washed it up that morning first thing, polishing away seven years of dust and firing up the engine. He liked the smooth lines and comfortable ride.

He also enjoyed repairing it and there was a heavier duty SUV and modern pickup in the garage if he needed them. The car didn't boast a CD or tape player much less anywhere to plug in a phone with MP3s, just an old radio that picked up two stations, country or news.

A.J. chose neither. He cranked the window down, fixed his hat and pulled out of the drive and up the long, bumpy gravel toward the road at three-thirty straight up. He would be early, but that suited him fine, too. The ride to the cabin took less than fifteen minutes. He parked the truck and trotted inside to check the lay of the land.

The cold dinner he'd requested sat packed neatly in sacks on the small bar separating the kitchen from the main room. Firewood stacked in the hearth would let him light a fire if they wanted it. The bearskin rug lay invitingly in front of the stone hearth. The sheets on the queen-sized bed were turned down and waiting and a bottle of champagne, wine, and case of beer chilled in the fridge.

All his bases were covered. He hadn't heard a peep from the service since agreeing to the night, save for acknowledging the plans he made. Tipping his hat back, he ignored the beer for a moment and walked out to the porch to wait. A breeze came in from the mountains. The scent of pine, green grass, and a hint of water drifted through the air. In the distance, horses whinnied, but the trees muffled the sound. If he didn't know the old log cabin sat in one of the most exclusive and coveted spots of the MGR, he could almost believe he was alone.

The sounds of nature washed over him, relaxing nerves that, even after a week at home and back breaking labor working on the ranch, remained raw. An engine purred through the silence, but it didn't turn onto the gravel road leading up to the cabin. At one minute to four, a twig snapped, and he opened his eyes to look to his left.

I'll be damned.

The librarian stood next to one of the trees at the edge of the cabin's clearing, her smile shy and her sunglasses pushed up to reveal wide, almost nervous eyes. She wore a cherry-colored sundress, baring creamy white shoulders and long arms. The skirt brushed her knees, and where he expected sandals, she wore a pair of sturdy, low-ankled boots.

He approved. Feminine, but smart. Sexy, but sensible. Trailing his gaze back upward, he met her sweet brown eyes with a grin. "Afternoon, ma'am."

"Hi." Her voice was sweet.

Funny, I've seen her all over town and this is the first time I've actually heard her.

Crossing the yard slowly, she minded where she put her feet. She must have walked down from a main point on the property. If he'd known she needed one, he would have offered her a ride.

Hell, if he'd known she was his date, he would have put more effort into the planning. This promised to be a hell of a lot more interesting than trying to see her after church.

"I'm A.J. Turner." He removed his hat and held out his hand. One-night stand or not, and he preferred more than one, she was a lady.

"I know." She slid her hand against his, caressing his palm ever so briefly before closing her grasp and accepting the handshake. "Sheri Vaughn."

"You're the librarian." He grinned. Her skin was soft, warm, and almost as sweet as her smile. He closed his grip on her hand

and held it.

She lifted her eyebrows, but didn't protest. "And you're the Marine."

"It's a pleasure to finally make your acquaintance. I'm really glad I turned my phone back on."

A pretty, pale pink suffused her cheeks, and she lowered her lashes, shielding her brown eyes. "I'm sorry?" She laughed and tugged her hand. He let her go, reluctantly. She smoothed her hand over her dress and then up to touch her hair. The awkward nervousness was endearing.

"I came home and shut off my phone. I had a lot of work to do on the ranch and liked the thought of the quiet. Almost forgot about the service." He winked, enjoying the blush that deepened on her cheeks. "Would you like to join me on the porch? And maybe a drink?"

"I would, thank you." She walked toward the cabin, hands clasped behind her back. "I guess that explains why it took a week for me to hear back."

He settled the hat back on his head and pulled out one of the handcrafted oak chairs for her to sit on. Fortunately the porch was wide enough to boast a small table and chairs.

"My apologies, ma'am." He brushed his fingers across her shoulder as she sat. "If I'd realized, I would have called a lot sooner."

She looked up at him. "Why is that?"

It was too soon. They'd just met—officially at least. But the urge to kiss her swung through his system like a well-aimed hammer. He leaned down and brushed his mouth against hers. Her breath tasted of mint and her lips were like petals.

Her swift inhale emboldened him, and he massaged her lips slowly, teasing them apart until his tongue could taste hers. Locking his hands on the chair, he focused only on the kiss and the sweet hesitation that evaporated with a low, groan. She kissed like a summer breeze, warm and inviting. Desire burst through him, and he wanted to sink into her and linger a while, but he'd promised her a drink.

With even greater reluctance than he felt when he let go of her hand, he pulled back. Her brown eyes were dark and dreamy when she met his gaze. "Because I've wanted to do that since I first saw you in the café."

cs

Sheri's heart ping-ponged against her ribs at the wash of masculine scent wrapping around her. A.J. winked as he stood and disappeared into the cabin. It gave her time to gather her scattered brain cells back into some semblance of thought.

Dear God, the man can kiss. Heat flushed through her, cascading with awareness that left her tingling. She rubbed her thumb against her lower lip. It was like she could still feel him touching her.

"What do you want to drink?" His voice drifted out through the open door.

"Um...." She twisted toward the sound of his voice, trying to find her composure again. "Beer is fine, if you have it."

The pop of a bottle cap made her jump.

"I definitely have that."

Excitement skated over her nerves. She hadn't been able to think of anything else since details for the evening arrived in her inbox. She spent all day at the library half-expecting comments about the sign she posted stating the library would close at three on Saturday and not reopen until Monday. But nope, not a word.

A.J.'s boots thumped the wood floor of the porch as he strolled back out and set the bottle in front of her. He started to sit and frowned. "Did you want it in a glass?"

"Nope. Bottle's fine." She took a long pull to demonstrate just how fine she was with it. He sat and stretched his legs out in front of him.

Dragging her gaze up from the way his jeans molded to the thick muscles of his thighs, she found him staring at her with a hint of amusement. "Good evening."

"Good evening." Self-conscious laughter bubbled up. The

23

habit was one of her least favorite; the inability to control the nervous chuckle. "Welcome home."

"Thank you. Welcome to Freewill." He grinned, tipping his bottle toward her.

"Thank you." They clinked the bottlenecks together and she followed his cue with another swallow. She was a cheap date, the alcohol in the beer relaxing the butterflies flapping through her belly.

"How long have you been here?" He shifted in the seat and crossed one ankle over the other, settling in for the long haul. Everything about him rang true to her wish—everything. God, even his black Stetson complemented his tanned skin and true blue eyes.

"Six months, give or take a week. I arrived in the middle of winter." An unpleasant time to show up considering how deep the snow had been, but she'd found no shortage of helpful hands, and it didn't take her long to find an apartment in town and get the job at the library. In fact, the town council was thrilled to have the library open six days a week.

"You seem right at home now." He tipped the bottle up for another drink.

"I like it. I like it a lot. I thought after Los Angeles, I wouldn't want to live in the middle of nowhere. But it's quiet. There are no gunshots in the middle of the night. No worries about drive-bys. No ex-husbands to run into." She grimaced. She hadn't intended to bring him up.

"Most of the town shuts down at nine. The quiet is good." The emphasis he placed on quiet seemed significant.

"Did you grow up here?"

"Born and raised."

She relaxed more, leaning back in the chair and toying with her beer bottle. A.J. oozed a definite masculine sensuality, but peaceful, too. All the ruffles and worries seemed to smooth away.

A hundred different questions scrolled through her mind, but his favorite sexual position might not be appropriate. Yet. "How long were you gone?"

"You don't already know?" He lifted his eyebrows, skepticism sliding under the words.

"Well, yes, I do know. Seven years. You enlisted right out of junior college, and you served overseas for most of your contract. You made sergeant fairly early and showed great promise. You're a credit to Freewill, and they are exceptionally proud of you." She wrinkled her nose. "Even if you did sneak home and not let them throw you a parade."

He threw his head back and laughed, a warm, throaty sound that sent tingles zinging all the way from her breasts to her toes and back up again. "Not many secrets in Freewill."

"True. I had noticed that. Bea at the café got my whole life story out of me before Christmas."

"She's good at that. So's Bud and Brady and Jamie and Guy...." He winked again. "We're all very good at knowing everyone else's business."

"It's kind of sweet." In a town like Freewill, her ex-husband wouldn't have been able to get away with affair after affair. In fact, he wouldn't have gotten away with a passing interest in one without her hearing about it.

"Sweet's one word, nuisance is another." He sat forward and tipped his hat up, his expression serious and somber. "Tonight, for example. Folks know my truck. You came down from the big house. They'll know. They may not say anything to you directly, but they're going to know we were here—together. Is that a problem for you?"

The thought had occurred to her when she parked up at the MGR. She didn't know the layout that well and the smaller roads that twisted and turned on the ranch confused her. Walking down seemed simpler, and she had no reason to be embarrassed about her attraction to the man sitting across from her.

Hell, her only regret at the moment was they weren't already naked. Her body hummed with anticipation and had since she realized he had to be the man Madame Eve set her up with.

"Nope. You?" She watched him, looking for a reaction, a tell that might suggest he had something to hide.

"I don't mind one bit. But I do have two questions, and I'd like honest answers, before this goes any further." His expression remained serious.

"All right." She sat up, posture straightening and clasped her hands around the bottle.

"How long have you been divorced?" He didn't move, but the steadiness of his gaze told her he wouldn't miss a nuance of her answer.

"Eight months, four days, ten hours and maybe fifteen minutes." Not that she counted. But every day she'd remained married to the sleaze after learning the truth, a little piece of her soul died. The final papers cut the jesses tying her to that crumbling lie. *Thank God.*

A.J. nodded slowly, lifting his bottle and watching her as he took a long swallow. "Are you still in love with him?"

She frowned, even the thought was distasteful. "No."

"Good." He leaned back again, still watching her. Every glance warmed her skin like a physical caress.

"Why?" *Where is he going with this?* Adultery was definitely a trigger for her—so maybe it was the same for him.

"Because I don't poach and I don't share." A smile curled up one corner of his firm mouth. "And tonight, I plan to kiss every inch of your body, find out what makes your nipples tight, and just how many orgasms I can tease from between your thighs. If I do my job right, you won't remember his name tomorrow."

Her stomach flip-flopped. Lust swarmed through her like an invading army. She moistened her lips, her mouth dry and her heart pounding. "Do we have to wait for tonight?"

Chapter Four

*W*rapping his arms around her middle, he lifted her up out of the chair. His lips were on hers before the final syllable of the question ended. The slow burn in his blood, ignited the first time he'd seen her, roared full force. Their mouths fused and his tongue darted between her lips, lapping up the simple taste of her, sweeter than candy. Her knees hitched around his hips, and she twined her arms around his neck. His hat fell as her fingers thrust into his hair and bounced down to rest in the chair he abandoned.

He didn't release her mouth, enjoying the tentative stroke of her cherry-flavored lips. She didn't remain passive under the assault, thank God. Fisting her fingers in his hair, she tugged his head and slanted the kiss. He crossed into the cabin and caught the door with his heel to shut it. Against her, his body turned into a hard, hot wall of need. His cock stiffened painfully behind his zipper, begging for release.

A low moan vibrated in her throat, and he chuckled at the sound of raw desire that matched his own. At the edge of the bed, he stroked his hands down her back to cup her bottom. Her gasp jerked her head back. Her eyes were wild with the fever, the sweet, brown-eyed girl transformed into the luscious, hungry lover.

He traced the column of her throat with a series of open-mouthed kisses, lapping at the thundering pulse point. Massaging the roundness of her ass, he loved how the curves filled his hands, soft, and responsive. Like the first strong winds of spring, she pushed away the cold loneliness he barely noticed anymore. Alive and wild in his arms, she drove away any thought of taking it slow, getting to know her, and easing into sex.

When she pulled at his shirt, he swept up and caught her mouth again before she could do more than suck in a breath of air. The urge to strip her naked, slide down her body and lick every part of her until she begged to come rolled through him like an unrelenting storm. These were the moments he fought for in the service—the freedom to be where he wanted, when he wanted, and by God, be with who he wanted.

"A.J....." His name rode past her lips on a soft moan and she peppered kisses across his jaw. Her teeth grazed the soft spot behind his ear and a low groan vibrated his throat. He lowered her onto the bed. With another teasing brush of her lips, she sucked on his lobe, and a rush of pleasure stole through him. He pulled free, staring at her tousled hair, dilated eyes and sweet mouth, swollen from his kiss.

"I'm right here, darling." He went for the buttons on his shirt, stripping down because he wanted no more interruptions. Her hot gaze scorched his skin, and dammit, he should have gotten her naked first. He toed off his boots, pulled out the condoms from his back pocket and grinned at her wide-eyed stare as he dropped three on the bed. "Don't worry, sweetheart. I have plenty more in the truck."

Sheri threw her head back and laughed.

His hands were on his belt buckle when she reached up to untie her dress. "No, ma'am." He pinned her with a look. "You leave my present wrapped. I'll take care of that in just a moment."

Playfulness flashed beneath the fire in her eyes. "Why sir, I do believe you say the most provocative things." She cupped her breasts through the dress, and her fingers flicked where he imagined her dusky nipples would be. His dick hardened like corded steel. If he grew any stiffer, he risked permanent injury.

"You've got a wicked streak in you, librarian." The zipper's release gave him a momentary relief, but his cock thrummed against his belly as he peeled the jeans down.

Her low whistle of appreciation stroked his masculine pride. "You're about to make a fantasy come true. I don't think I'm anywhere near wicked enough." Her confession scraped sparks through him. He nudged her hands aside, replacing them with his own. Her breasts were full, a solid handful, and he massaged them through the dress. Sure enough, her nipples stabbed at his palms.

"Is that so?" He continued to trace her shape, almost arguing with himself over where to start. Urging the hem of her dress up, he revealed a lovely crescent moon tattoo on the curve of her right hip. Rubbing his thumb over the shape, he glanced up at her.

"Yes, it is definitely so. My one other impulsive decision."

"What was the other one?" Curiosity filled him.

She stretched out a hand and stroked it across his abdomen, the muscles contracting at the feathery touch. "This date—you."

"Nice." Lust peaked inside of him. Continuing his quest upward, he teased the gentle mound of her sex through the damp panties. Thank God she seemed as aroused as he. Her breath came in fast little gasps as he explored her reactions. He increased the pressure, searching for her clit. She caught his cock in a gentle fist as he swirled his thumb.

"I want to be naked."

"You will be." He slid his hand under the edge of the fabric and dipped his fingers between her slick folds. She gripped his cock and stroked up and down. His eyes nearly crossed. With reluctance he caught her hand in his and urged it away from him. He didn't want to blow too early.

She growled, almost baring her teeth at his action and he laughed. Damn, she was fun. He caught the side of her panties, right at the seam and tore them. Her eyes widened at the rending of the fabric, but she arched her hips and he pulled them free.

"Better?" He murmured, nudging her thighs further apart so he could enjoy the view of the soft, damp pink flesh. Her shaven pussy damn near did in him. He groaned at the single, neat strip of curls stretching up almost like an arrow. Did she do that just for him? So much more to his sexy little librarian than he knew.

"Almost." Rolling her head back, she lifted her hips in entreaty again. "But I think I'm overdressed for the occasion."

"Me, too." All of a sudden, he felt very agreeable. Playing with her was a joy, but he wanted her naked and all those soft, delicious curves beneath him. He didn't even mind when she stripped the dress upward in one long, sensual tug and tossed it off the bed. "No bra."

He approved.

"It's a sundress." She crooked a finger at him and he came down on top of her, catching her mouth in another hot, wet kiss. He let his hands roam down her sides, stroking her silky, soft skin and enjoying the warmth as his cock slid against her damp heat. She was sugar and spice and everything a woman promised.

Dragging himself away, he grabbed a condom and rolled it on. Lying at her side, he turned to look at her, meeting the sharp intelligence in her brown eyes.

"Do you remember what I told you on the porch?" His voice, tight with need, rose no higher than a whisper. At her slow nod, A.J. let go of the control reining him in. "Good. Consider yourself warned."

Rolling over, he kissed a path down to her breasts. He'd forgotten how much he missed this—touching a woman, exploring her body, feeding her pleasure. As much as he'd wanted to be alone when he returned to Freewill, he craved the contact with her—with Sheri. He swirled his tongue around one hard-pointed nipple and increased the pressure of his thumb against her clit. The dual actions sent her breathing into jagged little spikes. She fisted the bed sheets in her hands. Already imagining the feel of her gloving his cock, he fought for that final step, tormenting himself on the sweet sensation of her pleasure.

Closing his mouth over one turgid point, he slid a single finger inside her, urging her release. Her first shout spurred him to add a second finger. He delved into the sensuous heat, thrilled with her wild response and steadily increased the pressure with his tongue until her body clenched, spasming around him. She cried out, hips bucking up to meet his hand, and he abandoned her breast to swallow her cries of pleasure.

She let go of the bed sheets to thread her fingers through his hair, and he slipped his hand free to adjust her hips. He groaned, fighting to control his pace and entered her slowly, inch by fantastic inch, her sweet heat enveloping him as he thrust. Lifting his head, he stilled and waited for her eyes to open.

"I'm going to come hard and I'm going to come fast." He wanted her to know what she did to him, how it felt to have her pussy wrapped so tight around his cock that he saw stars. He wanted to fly off that ledge with her and pound into her until he emptied all the pent up passion dragging his balls taut. He didn't usually favor dirty talk. Some of the guys mentioned it now and again, but he liked to treat a lady like a lady. Odd that he wanted to talk dirty to Sheri, the beautiful librarian with the sweet brown eyes.

My brown-eyed girl. She tightened her grip on him, wrapping her legs around his waist, her wild smile sparkling with challenge. His body tired of his thoughts.

"Bring it, Marine."

She didn't have to tell him twice. He surged forward, promising himself they'd go slower next time. He pistoned into her, his cock sinking deeper with every stroke. The velvet glove of her sex locked him in, squeezing him tighter. She made the sweetest noises; all gasps and sighs, and caressed his spine, urging him closer to the edge. They writhed together and there was no stopping his orgasm. It blew through him, swelling until every cell in his body converged and burst with pleasure.

She jolted against him and bit down on his shoulder. "A.J."

He came in a burst of hard, hot liquid release. Sheri trembled against him, skin quivering, pussy clamping and unclamping. He dragged her closer, rolling onto his side and held her tight as they shook together.

Gradually, his pulse quieted and breathing returned to a semblance of normalcy. Glancing at the clock, he grinned. They had hours.

Hours left to play.

CB

Two orgasms. Two. Back to back and she was full, stretched, and sore in all the right places. She couldn't get over the feel of him, the hard steadiness of his muscles and the contrast of his demanding passion to his utter gentleness. Head pillowed on his shoulder, she rubbed her palm against his chest. His heart thundered and her mind raced. A.J. Turner was made for sex. She couldn't remember the last time she'd felt so good.

The soothing stroke of his hand running up and down her arm helped to quiet the pleasurable aftershocks tingling through her with every breath. She pushed herself up on an elbow, studying how their bodies tangled together. A small smile hovered against his lips.

"Hey." He exhaled the greeting soft, slow, and sexy as hell.

"Hey back." She walked two fingers across the firm abdominals and smoothed her palm against his chest, half exploring, half petting. Eddies of pleasure radiated from all over—between her legs, hell, even her toes seemed to quiver in satisfaction. "Thank you."

He chuckled, continuing to stroke her arm, her side and down over her hip bone. "You're welcome and thank you." His stomach growled into the silence and they both burst out laughing.

It pained her to pull away, to feel the last of him slip free, but when her stomach gurgled nearly as loud as his, the giggles struck again. He trailed a caress down to her thigh and watched her with solemn, almost too bright, blue eyes.

"I had dinner delivered for us. It's a cold supper—sandwiches, drinks, potato salad."

She turned her attention to the kitchenette, spotting the white bags with the MGR logo on the side. "Hungry?"

He cupped her breast and rolled a calloused thumb across her nipple. It stiffened in appreciation and pleasure tingled everywhere. "Starving."

Blissful desire sighed through her. A.J. sat up and kissed a lazy path across each breast, pausing only to nip and suck at the distended nipples crowning each one. She skimmed her nails across his scalp, torn between the urges to watch his dark head move back and forth and pushing him back until she could impale herself on his cock again. She wanted to be on top next time. Her thighs quivered at the images popping into her head. He slipped a hand around the back of her neck and fed her erotic fantasy with a long, lingering kiss. God, the man knew how to kiss. He took control, slanting his mouth against hers, demanding access with his tongue, and twining it sensuously with her own.

With foreheads resting together, he broke the kiss. It was almost too much intimacy. They touched everywhere. It wasn't just the physical contact, but the way his entire being seemed to pour into hers, searching, seeking, captivating.

"I want to get up and feed you. But that means I have to stop touching you and feasting myself." The throaty admission turned her insides to jelly. It was an almost corny line, but the raw emotion in his voice made it echo with sincerity.

"We can do both." She grinned, a streak of naughtiness stealing through her. "You can clean up. I'll get the food. We meet back here in two minutes."

"Right here?" He swept his gaze down to where his spent cock nestled between her legs and her knees framed his thighs.

Surprising herself, she pushed up and kissed him, licking the seam of his lips until he allowed her to take possession of his mouth. He tasted a little of salt and beer and totally man. His scent filled her nostrils. "Right. Here." She murmured.

"Okay." He massaged her ass, exploring her curves. The heat of his body had to be leaving imprints on her soul. Everywhere they met, a new forest fire of sensation broke out.

Their mouths parted and came together with every sentence. "But we have to move to do that."

"I know." He swept his hand up her spine, tangled it in her hair, and thrust his tongue into her mouth. He took control of the kiss, pursuing her tongue and claiming it. She groaned and moisture flooded between her legs. The aftershocks turned to foreshocks and she wanted him, right now.

"Tell me," she let out between bursts of air, tasting him with every stroke of his lips against hers, "When."

He surged upward, holding her straddled on his lap. Breast to chest, the friction heightened every point their bodies made contact. "Okay."

Damn, he knows how to kiss. The slant of his mouth demanded, promised, engaged, and held her at his mercy. She clung to him, starved for the contact. The one-night stand offered her a fresh start, a clean slate, and delivered so much more. Her mind whirled with the possibilities. The slow stiffening of his cock pushed between them and she pulled back, laughter bubbling up.

"Okay, two minutes." He grinned and brushed his thumb against her lower lip but made no move to let her go.

"Two minutes," she agreed, her heart pounding behind her ribs. And still, they didn't move. If anything her knees tightened against him, and she wanted to rub herself all over him like a cat in heat.

Gripping her hips, he stole another kiss and murmured against her mouth. "On three...."

"Wait." Nipping his lower lip between each word, she asked, "On three-three or after three?"

"Hmm." He flexed his fingers against her skin, the touch scalding her, as though branding it through her flesh. It was like she could feel him everywhere, every place he caressed with his fingers or kissed with his mouth, tingles of sensation continued to eddy. "On three."

"Okay." She sighed, opening her mouth to his tongue. The brush of his sweat-slicked chest glided sensuously across her almost too-sensitive nipples. Dragging her palms against his back, she explored the flexing muscles, tensing and teasing together.

"One...." he muttered, trailing hot kisses across her cheek. His traced the whorls of her ear and sucked on the lobe. "Two."

Coils of pleasure tightened in her belly, winding up like some old-fashioned toy clicking past the point where she needed to let go, the tension holding her captive almost too much.

"Three." He lifted her off him like she weighed no more than a feather and set her on the bed. Her body cried out at the absence of his, but he levered himself upward and paused long enough to give her a hand. "Go."

Her mind hummed with eroticism. It took her a moment to even remember what they were supposed to do on three. He strode over to the bathroom, the muscles of his ass flexing with every step. Her insides quivered as the promise of his jean-clad ass on the street that day was delivered in spades.

Shaking off her self-indulgent, carnal stupor, she wandered over to the bags on the bar. Opening them one at a time, she unloaded the sandwiches, cold drinks, and tin of potato salad. She'd barely unwrapped one sandwich when he boxed his masculine body against her, the rigid length of his cock pressed against her ass and his hands slipped up to cover and massage her breasts.

She shuddered, hungry for him again, needing to feel him filling her.

"You like?" He laughed softly. How could he not know what he did to her?

"Yes." She sighed. But that wasn't where she wanted him. The riot storming through her system blotted out coherent thought.

"You mentioned fantasies earlier." He bit down on the soft

juncture between her shoulder and her neck. "Do you have any others?"

Oh. You. You. And for good measure more you. The wild, unrepentant need rushing through her should be embarrassing. Some, small rational part of her urged her to remember this was one night, nothing more, nothing less. She shut off the devilish little voice and refused to think about it. Their one moment was right now and tomorrow could damn well take care of itself.

"I have so many." And it was true. She wanted to do him up against a wall, on the floor, take his cock into her mouth and swallow him as he came. She wanted him to push inside her, ride her until she went limp.

She never wanted him to stop.

"Tell me," he ordered and continued the sensual torture.

"Take me now, like this." Heat burned in her cheeks, and she rubbed back against him. He nudged her legs further apart, and his fingers dipped between her legs. The sweet friction against her sensitive folds was almost too much. *I'm going to die like this, dissolving into pure desire....*

"Like this?" he asked, his husky voice turning her inside out. His thumb grazed over her clit, the light brush ratcheted up the pressure inside and she arched. If she were a cat, she would purr with the pleasure of it.

She licked her lips and held onto the counter. "Just like...that." But he nudged her thighs apart further and guided her hips back until she stretched, fingers locked onto the counter.

"Hmm...this looks good enough to eat." The delight in his words threatened to undo her right then and there. She clenched her butt, fighting the urge to rub her thighs together. "Don't move. I'll be right back." He abandoned her, retreating toward the bed. Her thighs quivered and her feet shifted. "Stay just like that...." The order throbbed through her.

The promise of his touch eroded her control. *What control? Who are you kidding?* Laughter rose up out of her again. She twisted at the sound of foil tearing. A.J. stood next to the bed and rolled the condom down his cock. He glanced up, meeting her eyes with a slow grin of his own.

"Did I mention what a genuine pleasure is to meet you, ma'am?" The slow, languorous cowboy drawl whispered from the rugged, hard Marine mouth. All of her sexual fantasies were rolled into one, living breathing—and thank God—hard man.

"You might have skipped that part." *These things only happen in books—real life romance is so much messier than this...why the hell am I analyzing?*

His eyebrows lifted as he strode toward her, purpose and determination radiating from every step. He guided his cock to the entrance of her sex and pushed in a tantalizing inch. "Then let me correct that oversight right now."

She didn't need any urging to lean her upper body forward and push back until he filled her. The trembling inside increased three-fold.

"It is my genuine pleasure," he teased her, thrusting with each word. "To meet you." He retraced his path down her front and found her clit, and she forgot anything as he drove her over the edge into a climax.

Chapter Five

"So why the Marines?" She sat cross-legged on the bed, nibbling a sandwich. Her cheeks were rosy, a beautiful shade against all that creamy skin.

A.J. thought they were done after the bar, but she pushed him back toward the bed, food forgotten and teased his cock with her mouth until he came in self-defense. Three rounds in five hours and he wanted her again. He reached over to wipe a spot of mustard from the corner of her mouth with his thumb and sucked the spicy flavor between his lips.

"It was the right thing to do." He shrugged. "My grandfather served, and his father and his father before him. Far as I know, it's been a family tradition since the French and Indian wars. The only reason my dad didn't was his asthma."

The food spread out between them, like a picnic on the bed. They were both naked, and he appreciated the unabashed freedom to look at her breasts. They rose and fell with every breath. Her full, dusky nipples beckoned him, but he forced himself to let her eat before he took his time exploring every reaction.

She'd mentioned fantasies, and he had the inexplicable urge to fulfill every single one of them.

"That's kind of sweet, to have a family legacy like that." She leaned sideways, stretching out to reach for her bottle of water. His cock twitched, rousing slowly. She was a lovely woman, soft and curvy in all the right places.

"It is what it is, Sheri. It was the right thing to do. I enlisted, I trained, I served, and now I'm home." And that summed up his military life. Granted, it didn't mention the guys or the friendships, but his grandfather told him once that the men he served with in Korea were men he could rely on. He could call them anytime he needed something—whether it was a favor or just someone to jaw with—and they would be there. A.J. had attended a reunion with his grandfather in the early nineties. All those men in their sixties and seventies tossed back beers, laughing, reminiscing, and picking up right where they'd left off forty years before as though it were yesterday rather than decades in the past.

Brotherhood, his grandfather told him, didn't end with a war or an honorable discharge. He hadn't truly appreciated what that meant until now. But like his grandfather, A.J. knew the men in his unit were a phone call away. If he needed them, they would come. The same was true for him.

"And you were done. That's why you came home?"

"More or less. I left to defend this way of life and now I'm home to enjoy it. Work on my ranch, fix it up and go back to training horses. If the guys need me, they know where I am." He accepted the water bottle she offered him, washing down his own meal. Content, he sprawled on his side and propped his head on his hand, studying her.

"Can I ask you a question?" Shyness surrounded the question; she could ask him anything she wanted. He would have to show her that.

"Anything."

"What was it like? Afghanistan...Iraq?"

"Hot. Monotonous most days, and lonely, and it could all change in a moment. You could go from routine to hellish in the space of a few seconds." Odd to think he missed it, the routine of the unexpected firefights. But he didn't miss the injuries or the surge of adrenaline pumping fear out of his system, knowing it only took one stray bullet—one misstep—and he would be in the coffin they saluted or the stretcher they carried off the field.

He was one of the lucky ones. His scars were all on the inside.

"Were you in both?"

"Mostly Iraq. I did a lot of supply runs, boring job, but necessary. Well, boring until it wasn't." He tipped the bottle of water up and took a drink.

"I'm sorry you had to go."

Capping the bottle, he set it aside and caught her hand in his, Interlacing their fingers, he squeezed comfortingly. "I'm not. I met some great people—I learned a little Farsi. I learned what it's like to truly have nothing and to hold a family together in spite of political and militant turmoil everywhere."

Sadness etched into the lines around her eyes. He didn't want her to only think of the bad, he saw some of the news stories reported from overseas. They barely skimmed the surface of everyday life.

Lifting her fingers to his lips, he pressed a kiss to her knuckles. "Last year, I was running supplies from Baghdad to Mosul. On the route, there's this really small town—I mean small—like five-houses-and-some-goats small. They didn't have any businesses or even a real road besides the main stretch we drove. But every time we went through, we saw the kids out there playing. They had this really ratty soccer ball, and they kicked it, laughed, and played. They always cleared the road when we came through, staring at us with these wide, solemn eyes. Except for the kid with the ball, he waved. I got used to seeing him." He could almost feel the searing heat, the fifty pounds of gear weighing him down and taste the sand and sunshine like grit on his tongue.

"We didn't always drive the exact same route, better to avoid insurgents if we're unpredictable, but we went through often enough, I recognized the kid. About seven months ago—maybe eight—we're going through one day and I don't see the kids out there, they aren't playing like normal. It's all a little hinky, too quiet—and we go on alert. Out of the ordinary is a warning. Out of nowhere, I see the kid with the ball—he races out of one of the houses and puts his ball in the middle of the road and just sits on it. We have three choices, stop, go around, or back up."

He tensed, living in that moment again, remembering the rawness of wonder as they stared at the kid. Sheri squeezed his hand. "What happened?"

"We went with our gut, the lead car moved around us and we slowed the convoy. I got out with four others and one of the guys who spoke the language, told him to move." A.J. laughed a little. "This kid says no. Tells us that men came through the night before and made lots of noise up the road—they were digging and shifting and they were strangers. Not U.S., not friendly to the village. They shot one of the other kids' fathers—that's why the kids weren't out playing. They were mourning, but this kid with the ball—he didn't want us going up the road."

"Oh my God. What did you do?"

"Called it in, backed off, and let the sweepers go through—they found five—maybe eight charges—all planted on our route. Kid saved our lives." A.J. grinned up at her, her tension deepened and he wanted her to see this was the good kind of story—the one with a decent ending. "So I got that kid a new ball—and gave him and his family enough money to leave that dirty little village if they want, too."

"Ohhh...." She dragged the word out and tears sparkled in her eyes. "Did they?"

"Don't know. But they can. Kid didn't have to help us—we're just the guys driving past every few days or so. He could have gotten shot, blocking our truck that way—but he took a chance and did what he thought was right. Kids like him—and his family—they make it worth it."

"You're amazing."

A little uncomfortable with the praise, he shrugged it off. "I'm just a Marine who did his job."

"No one in my family served, I don't think. I didn't know my dad's parents, but my mom's dad had a club foot. He worked as a machinist, built equipment, provided supplies, and volunteered. My mom spent time studying to be a nurse, but then she got married and preferred popping out babies." Sheri made a face, letting go of his hand to swipe at the trace of tears on her cheeks. He hadn't meant for the story to make her sad.

"Nothing wrong with babies." He couldn't resist trailing a finger over her thigh. He liked the flush pinkening her cheeks.

"I know. I was just thinking that it's a great legacy and I don't have anything like that. Just plain, vanilla, stay-at-home folks."

"Hey, we like the vanilla stay-at-home folks, they give us something to defend and better—someone to come home to." He squeezed her leg.

"I can't believe you're real." She dropped her gaze to the sandwich in her hands. "And that you're here...in Freewill...with me."

"Why?" He drew a pattern against her skin, just lazy circles, swirling over and over on her thigh.

"I told you I was divorced." Her smile turned self-deprecating. "Well that marriage was definitely not one of my proudest moments. I married him while we were still in college, but we were both busy. I wanted to be an attorney, so did he. When I got accepted to Stanford Law, and he didn't, I should have seen it coming—but I didn't. We lived apart, visiting only on weekends all the way through law school. I hit the books, he hit the sheets." She shifted, her expression darkening, and A.J. had the urge to go and punch the son of a bitch.

"It's stupid, I mean all the signs were there, but I didn't want to believe them. It's easy to be blind to someone else's faults—especially if admitting they have them makes you question your own judgment. Course, I couldn't it ignore it when the paternity suit came in and he didn't try to deny it." Her mouth twisted. "What's worse, not only did he have one woman suing him because she had his kid, but he'd knocked up two others. I think he had affairs *on* his affairs. I didn't think I'd been so humiliated in my life—only I was wrong. Because one of the women he knocked up worked in my law office. She was one of the investigators I used and hung out with all the time."

"I'm sorry. He sounds like a real jackass." A.J. was glad she'd unloaded that waste of air.

"He was—hell, he probably still is. He didn't actually want a divorce. He thought we had an ideal situation and actually looked surprised when I had him served. But as soon as the divorce was finalized, I just couldn't stay there anymore. I needed a fresh start. A clean one, away from all the lies I told myself to get through the days."

"And now you're here, in Freewill." He could wish her ex hadn't done that to her, but he couldn't fault the result. If she hadn't come to his Wyoming town, he might not have met the sexiest librarian he'd ever seen.

And that would have been a crying shame.

"Yep, now I'm here with you...on a one-night stand." Her smile chased away the shadows lingering in her eyes. "And I have to ask, maybe it's not PC, but why did you sign up? I mean—you're gorgeous, sweet, and a fabulous kisser. Why would you need a service to find a woman?"

"All the single guys in my unit signed up. Not everyone made the transition home easily and they had a hard time reconnecting with their civilian life. So, the captain encouraged us all to commit to a one-night stand. It helped out our buddies who really needed the assistance to just go for it. I kind of forgot that I did it." His turn for confession. "It's why the Captain had to nudge me."

"Oops."

"Yeah. Oops. He probably won't let me live that one down, but it's all right. I deserved it." He didn't mind friendly ribbing and he owed the man a case of beer for taking the time to send him that note. "But I planned to ask you out after church on Sunday anyway."

"Oh?" She lifted her brows and to his immense pleasure, her face pinkened again.

"Hmm-hmm." He caressed the curve of her knee. "I kept seeing you around town every time I had to run in for supplies. So I promised myself after I finished fixing the barn and the paddock I needed for training, I'd see about buying you some fried chicken and a cold beer. So tell me, Miss Sheri, if I came up to you after church on Sunday and invited you out for some dinner and a beer, what would you say?"

"I don't know. Why don't you ask me on Sunday, and find out?"

A.J. grinned and swept the food aside to roll her onto her back; he nuzzled her cheek. Her eyes widened, and he delighted in her innocent wonder. "I think I'll have to do that, but right now, I want dessert...."

With her sigh echoing in his ears, he kissed a path down her breasts, to her belly, and her thighs spread obediently.

Damn, it's good to be home....

THE TWO AND THE PROUD

HEATHER LONG

಄

Chapter One

$\mathscr{R}$ain poured in great sheets as thunder rumbled and the occasional flash of lightning burnt his retinas. Rowdy checked the GPS for the third time when he swung into the carport outside the hotel. The Castillo Washington was a five-star luxury hotel parked squarely in downtown D.C. Fifteen minutes behind schedule; he was still thirty minutes early for his date. He preferred early to late. Handing his keys to the valet along with a tip, he took the claim ticket.

The interior of the hotel appeared as luxurious as all the advertisements boasted. Parquet floors, vaulted ceilings, crystal chandeliers, and a dozen intimately arranged seating areas. Shops lined one wall, offering designer clothes, shoes, purses, and souvenirs for hotel guests. Signs pointed in the direction of the front desk and the hotel's various lounges.

Rowdy bypassed all of them and took a seat on a comfortable sofa outside the dark, moody *Aces*. It was after happy hour, but the business crowd inside remained thick.

A waitress scooted over to him. "What can I get for you?"

He blew out a breath. He'd debated this on the drive over. He enjoyed a good glass of wine, having grown up drinking his family's personal vintage. But years in the Corps turned him on to various types of beer—and he enjoyed those even more. "Sam

Adams. Bottle." He added the last before she asked.

"Of course." She set a napkin down on the table next to him and strode off, her hips swaying despite the briskness of her pace. Unbuttoning his jacket, he pulled out his phone, thumbing it over to the email box. He checked his watch and nodded. Still early, which gave him time to scan the crowd and observe his date as she arrived.

The waitress returned with his beer, and he gave her a credit card to open a tab. He was on his second swallow when a woman in a dark blue dress sashayed in. She surveyed the lobby, and the tables around him. For the briefest of moments, their gazes collided, but she moved on and waved at someone behind him. He washed back his amusement with another drink.

A trickle of female arrivals streamed past—they glanced at him or gave him a flirtatious smile but continued on to other destinations and plans. At five minutes past the appointed date time, annoyance crept in. Fifteen minutes passed and annoyance settled in his gut along with his beer.

He checked his phone for other messages—still nothing. The tables around him filled. But he wasn't the only one sitting alone. Two tables over, a devastating redhead with relaxed posture studied the crowd. Dressed in a pair of jeans, suit jacket, and white button down shirt, she faded into the setting—which made no damn sense. She was one hell of a looker. Rowdy's eyes narrowed—she wasn't watching the crowd.

She stared at him.

The corners of her mouth curved into a mysterious smile and she saluted him with her beer.

He nodded and glanced down at his phone when it vibrated.

The mail flag signaled and he thumbed it open.

Feel free to join me.

His eyebrows climbed. It was a forwarded message—from the 1Night Stand service.

Slanting another look at the redhead, he lifted his eyebrows and she grinned. Intrigued, he grabbed his bottle and walked over to the sofa she claimed. "Good evening."

"Good evening." Amusement twisted between the words. She stood and stretched out her hand. "And let me begin this introduction with an apology...Kim Wakefield."

"Hello, Kim Wakefield. Rowdy Easton."

Her firm grip was warm, soft, and perfunctory. A lot like the woman herself. Despite her attempt to cover up her femininity, she only emphasized it. Of course, maybe she hadn't attempted to disguise it. Women didn't have to wear dresses on dates.

"You look a little confused." She held his hand longer than was necessary, but he didn't mind.

"Curious. Not confused."

She released her grip and disappointment surged through him. A second curiosity, but he set it aside for the time being. She motioned to the sofa next to her, and he waited for her to sit before taking the center cushion. It put him right in her space—and what an alluring space it was.

"What's got you curious?" She leaned back, crossing one leg over the other. She wore boots, laced tight, low heeled, and sensible. He knew expensive shoes and he knew combat boots—hers looked like a combination of the two.

"You." He studied her face. Surprisingly, she didn't have green eyes so traditionally associated with red hair. Instead, her eyes were almost the color of amber. Under the low overhead lighting, they gleamed like polished gemstones.

"Me?" She lifted her brows.

"Oh, yeah. You." The waitress paused next to them and he held up two fingers. "Another Sam Adams and whatever the lady is having."

"Corona Extra, two limes please," Kim supplied and gave an amused snort after the waitress walked away. "I am not her favorite person."

"Why is that?" *Did she know the waitress personally?* He glanced briefly in the other woman's direction.

"She stared at you the whole time and you didn't look away from me. Thank you, by the way. It's a very nice compliment." Kim moved with the bare minimum of excess. Her relaxed expression couldn't hide the sharp assessment in her eyes or the air of expectancy wrapped around her.

"You're welcome." He linked his fingers together. The date arrangements they'd agreed on said drinks first. They could take their conversation to their reserved room after. Cocktails and conversation seemed a good way to kick off the night. So where did the sudden impatience curling through his gut come from?

"You still look...what was the word you used? Curious?" The low, smoky quality to her voice teased the hell out of him. But then so did her mysterious amusement.

"Definitely curious." The waitress returned with their fresh beer bottles, served them, and he waited for her to leave before continuing. "Why does a woman like you need a service like this?"

"It's not about need." She met his question with complete candor. "It's about want. We don't really live in a society where you can walk up to someone and say, 'nice shoes, want to fuck?'"

He damn near choked on his beer. Coughing once, he slid a sideways look at her. The amusement in her expression increased. "No?"

"Nope." She leaned forward and looked at his shoes pointedly. "By the way, nice shoes."

He laughed.

Kim Wakefield was an enigma—but damn, what a sexy one. He lifted his bottle, and they clinked bottlenecks in salute. "I like yours, too."

It was her turn to chuckle and the sound rippled over him, a sensuous caress like nails stroking his spine. He took a long pull of the drink and settled back against the sofa. "So what do you do?"

"The boring work conversation. Hmm. Not the best opening play." She winked and took a long drink.

"Hard to top the shoes," he countered.

"True. But you could at least try...."

Is she challenging me? All right. "Does the rug match the drapes?" Embarrassment pricked him, but he ignored it and tossed the gauntlet down brazenly. She threw her head back and laughed again, the rich sound applauding his effort, but he didn't count it a success until her amused amber gaze met his again.

"I could answer—but I get the sense you're the kind of man who likes to fact check."

Bold. Brassy. Brilliant.

He liked her.

"Yes, ma'am. I do."

"Good, I prefer a man willing to work for what he wants." She rolled her tongue over her lower lip. "Moment of truth time."

"Oh?" After their rather bawdy, albeit bizarre, conversation—she wanted truth?

"I work for NCIS. Is that going to be a problem for you?"

The Naval Criminal Investigative Service. She was a cop.

His whole body revved.

Rowdy's nostrils flared and his pupils dilated. His visible, physical reaction to where she worked and what she did for a living zinged her like a shock of static electricity. The clenched fist in her gut relaxed. Too often when men found what she did, they retreated or worse, they looked patronizing. The Marine sergeant did neither. He leaned closer.

"How long?" Even better, he didn't ask the typical follow-up question.

"A few years. I got friendly with the agent onboard during my float on the Tortuga." She cradled her beer bottle in her hands, twisting it back and forth. The cold moisture cooled the sudden warmth in her palms.

"No way you were a sailor." The corners of his mouth curved.

"Hell, no. We stole the eagle from the Air Force, the anchor from the Navy, and the rope from the Army." She lifted her eyebrows and waited. He didn't need long.

"On the seventh day when God rested, we took the perimeter and stole the globe and we've been running the show ever since." Their bottles clinked together in a toast. "Fighters by day...."

"Lovers by night. Drunkards by choice." She finished it, joining him in the final act of the refrain. "And a United States Marine by an act of God."

They tipped their bottles back and drained them before setting them aside. Her face almost ached from the smile, but she was right. All the background info she dug through on the 1Night Stand service and the security clearance request she filed were worth it. They hadn't made it out of the lounge and for the first time in months, she relaxed.

"Seriously, why NCIS?"

"Counterterrorism, investigation, keeping the Navy and the Marines safe here and abroad—it worked for me." She licked her lips. "I like being a Marine. I liked serving, but I wanted to do more, too. The funny thing was, the agent afloat was this real player. He was forever taking women out when we were in port and he knew even more...but he never hit on us."

"'Cause you'd probably have hit him back." Rowdy's astute summation pegged it.

"Probably." She shrugged. "Still, he gave me an opportunity. A couple of years later when I cycled out, I gave him a call. He hooked me up and I got a job."

"That's awesome. No seriously." He raised a hand as if she'd protested the compliment. "Been thinking about what I want to do—got the letter a few weeks ago offering me an out. Don't want to go back to the family business. Didn't think about law enforcement."

"I work cold cases, mostly, but everyone deserves to have answers. What does your family do?"

The waitress swung through and she didn't bother with the flirt or come hither looks this time, replacing their beers with fresh ones. Rowdy waited till she left and turned sideways, their knees brushed and another finger of tension tightened inside of Kim.

A deliciously provocative tension.

"Military contractors. The family is Navy through and through. I'm the black sheep. I went Marines. Didn't want to hoist the yardarm as it were." His self-deprecation disguised the conflict his choice must have caused for his family. "Don't get me wrong—they're proud—but I'm not a nine-to-five paper pusher who enjoys blocking out the day with back-to-back meetings, inspections, and compliance reports."

She promised herself she wouldn't make a face, but couldn't help sticking her tongue out in a grimace. "Bleh."

"Exactly."

The third beer would be her last. The warm and fuzzy radiating out from her belly didn't need any alcohol to fuel it.

"I can appreciate that. I work for a living, and it's not going to change." She enjoyed his swift wit. "So why did you join?"

"For the Marines? Or...." He lifted his eyebrows teasingly.

"Both."

"Well there's a long reason and a short one—"

She arched her eyebrows at his dramatic pause, and laughed. "Please tell me you didn't."

"Hey, you like my shoes—that's the long reason." He added salt to the tease with a wink, and she shook her head, laughter vibrating through her. "The short reason is I wanted to. I know a guy who knows a guy—as it were—and he said it was worth the experience."

"Yeah?" Curiosity aroused, she leaned toward him. They were close enough and the heat of him seemed to warm the air between them.

"Yup. There's this unit—have you heard of Mike's Place?" He brushed a hand across the back of hers, a light touch—exploring.

She liked it.

"Rehabilitation facility in Dallas." She'd heard of it. She'd even written a check the month before to the fund the men and women in her former unit who were planning to donate. They were fortunate, they hadn't lost any on their team...but not everyone was lucky.

"Exactly. Friend of a friend is there, and he said a number of the Marines who got the operation started used this service. Some were pretty damn successful." He stroked the back of her hand, light casual touches. Each brush of his skin on hers created another tickle of sensation to skate through her.

He spoke with a beautiful cadence, every word measured and enunciated clearly. She'd thought his eyes were brown, but they were a distinct hazel—a sparkle of green against the earthier shade. When he tipped his head back to laugh, they darkened, but when he stared at her intently—like he did now—they seemed to gather the ambient light. Like glitter embedded in paving stones.

Slow down before you gush that he glitters in sunlight. She shook her head a little trying to shake the mooning, girly swoon out of her. Realistically, Rowdy was a good-looking man with even features, a slightly crooked nose and a strong jaw. His lips were firm and his eyes captivating. He was no cover model, but everything, from his manner to his speech, pulled at her and the desire curling through her belly had nothing to do with sunshine or sparkles.

"You okay?" Concern edged out his amusement.

"I'm fine. I'm just imagining you naked and it's very distracting." Once upon a time, her commanding officer warned her about being too candid. But Rowdy didn't seem to mind.

Two heartbeats followed her statement and his humor resurfaced. "Well now, if you're done with your beer, we can take care of your imagination with a reality check."

She put the half-full bottle down, not really caring if she finished it. He motioned to the waitress. The action pulled her gaze to the way his shirt tightened over his chest.

Oh, yeah.

She definitely preferred reality.

Chapter Two

Rowdy noticed the resemblance in the elevator on the ride to the fifteenth floor. He glanced sideways at Kim. Like him, she stood next to the back wall of the elevator, posture ramrod straight, hands relaxed at her sides, feet parallel and perfectly pointed forward. At his chuckle, she aimed a questioning glance in his direction.

He opened his mouth to answer, but the elevator dinged and the doors swished open. They both started forward, right foot first. His chuckle turned into a full laugh. She paused and pivoted to face him while he struggled to get himself under control. He laughed like some sixteen year-old, certain he would make it to third base before the date was over.

The humiliating, if humbling thought, sobered him.

"Dare I ask?" Her eyebrows arched in a delicious curve and the corners of her mouth flattened. Fortunately, she didn't look annoyed, only curious.

"Just noticing some similarities. Had I seen you walk in, I would have pegged you Marine from the get go." He glanced at the wall sign and gestured for her to precede him down the hall.

"Ahh, then you have discovered why I staged it to watch you arrive." The teasing look she tossed him evaporated the rest of his humor and sent awareness flaming through his blood.

"Not really sure I care who got here first...." Admittedly, there was a hell of a lot about the lady he didn't know yet and—if he thought about it for any length of time—too many unasked questions.

At the door of their reserved room, he pulled out the electronic keycard that he'd gotten earlier from the dating service, along with the address and the confirmation of their date. The lock flicked from red to green and he opened it.

The suite was far more sumptuous than his utilitarian apartment on base. From the plush, thick carpet, cheerful fireplace and candles waiting to be lit set romantically about the room to the champagne chilling on ice...it cried out luxury and hedonism. He held the door until Kim entered. She let out a low whistle, but her expression didn't say impressed.

The room's low lighting didn't mute the storm's increased force outside. Sheets of rain coated the windows and lightning flashed in the distance.

"I'm thinking you've been holding out on me, Marine." The entry way descended three steps into the main suite. It was a luxurious room, but the sitting room was framed around the fireplace, with the bed tucked into the corner. It was cozy, romantic, and everything a couple needed for a night of passion.

He flipped the security bar shut and followed her casual path through the room. *Does she just see the affluence?* The Castillos did a fantastic job of blending wealth and comfort. The expense didn't matter, but the effect did.

"It's a nice room in a nice hotel in the capitol." The deflection rang hollow and he could only imagine she heard the same emptiness. Kim walked over to the windows as though watching the storm, but he sensed the weight of her regard via the reflection in the glass. "Champagne?"

"You're suddenly uncomfortable." It wasn't a question. "What changed between downstairs and now?"

He'd had alcohol downstairs. Considering the options, he bypassed the champagne and rummaged around the small wet bar until he found a bottle of tequila. He ignored the price tag, pulled it out and held it up.

She turned. "We need salt and lime to do it justice."

"Yes we do." He couldn't agree more. Setting the bottle on the table, he dialed room service. "You want anything to eat?"

"Whatever is fine."

When they answered on the second ring, he blew out a breath and managed a calm that did not reflect his inner turmoil. Something was off in the whole situation and he couldn't put his finger on it. His instincts screamed, however, and he chose to listen to them right then.

"Hey can you send a couple of sampler platters and a pair of limes cut up for drinking and some salt? You can deliver the limes and salt early." He replaced the phone in the cradle, pulled off his jacket, and rolled up his sleeves.

"Okay, now you're really not comfortable." She studied him with a faint frown.

"You're right. I'm not. Never thought I'd be the guy who said an empty one-night stand didn't appeal to me." He threw the jacket on the bed and stared back at her. She was even more beautiful in the room than in the low light in the lounge downstairs or the fluorescent in the elevator. Her skin was like fine porcelain, pale enough to make the freckles—freckles she tried to cover with makeup—stand out. But she didn't look washed out. Far from it. She was peaches and cream, a fine white wine, a rich sauce. Her amber eyes reflected the light occasionally and her red hair, tucked back into a neat ponytail, needed to be let loose.

"Okay, I'm usually pretty good at following a train of thought, but I think yours got off somewhere and caught a cab to the next station. You're not interested in the one-night stand after all?" The first sentence came out as sassy as any she delivered downstairs, but the question echoed with a quiet vulnerability. It revealed a chink in her armor, an utter femininity. It attracted and baffled in the same breath.

"Didn't say that." A knock on the door interrupted and he answered it long enough to accept the lime and salt, passing the waiter a quick five and a "thank you" before shutting the door in his face. He carried the condiments over to the bar, opened the tequila and filled two shot glasses. "Lose the jacket and come have a drink with me."

Her lips pursed and for a moment, the barest of moments, he thought she might refuse. She stripped off her jacket and hung it over the back of a chair next to the window. She wore a shoulder holster with a nine millimeter strapped under her arm.

Eyeing the gun, he waited.

"No one leaves the office unarmed. Standard procedure." Her explanation made sense, but rang as hollow as his earlier deflection.

Hollow.

He snapped mental fingers. *She's been deflecting since the opening bit downstairs with the shoes.* He could almost hear his libido release a low groan. Agent Kim Wakefield was no more comfortable with this night than he was—she simply played it better—keeping him off center and distracted until....

What? She fucks my brains out?

Not sure how those results could be a bad thing, he tapped the side of the shot glass. "Put the piece in the safe. They have the kind you can program here. I'll keep my eye on the tequila." He wouldn't have tried to memorize her combination anyway, but he didn't miss the minute relaxation around her eyes when he told her he'd watch the drinks.

True to his word, he kept his attention on the alcohol while she stowed the gun. When she leaned against the bar next to him, he pushed a shot glass over to her. "Let me preface this by saying I absolutely want to have sex...but I don't want to be limited by the one-night stand."

She hesitated in mid-reach for the glass and stared at it, not him. "Clarify?"

"I like you. You're smart—which is both good and bad."

"How can it be good and bad?" Her chin came up and she swung a hard gaze at him. Temper flared beneath the surface, bright as the lightning outside, enhancing the outrage in her eyes.

Gotcha. One little nudge to crack the cool façade and the passionate woman beneath glared at him. *Yeah, that's more like it.* A second knock on the door interrupted, and he let her think about it while he took the tray from room service and sent them away. He set the food on the luggage stand and ignored it for the moment.

Sprinkling salt onto the side of his hand, he said, "It's good, because it's sexy." He licked the salt, tossed back the tequila, and finished the ritual by sucking one of the lime wedges. "It's bad because you're playing a game with me." He poured another shot since the first had warmed his gut and loosened more of the tension. He'd barely added more salt to his wrist when she caught his hand and stroked her tongue over his pulse point before gliding along the side of his hand to take the salt.

All the blood in his head rushed south and he let out a low whistle. "Damn."

She slammed back her own drink and sucked on a lime, her gaze never leaving his. "Courage isn't doing something because you know you can do it." She moistened her lips and he couldn't look away. "It's doing what you're not sure you can be successful at."

Rowdy poured another shot and damn near swallowed his tongue when she offered her hand, the salt waiting for him. Taking the bull by the horns—or the agent by the wrist, as it were—he sampled the sweet flavor of her skin under the condiment.

"We don't have to do anything," he assured her. Hell, the last time he'd forced a woman was never, and he had no intentions of starting now.

They took turns with the ritual, her tongue laved against his palm and his balls went tight. He pressed the lime wedge to her lips after she finished her drink. He could almost see the hard tips of her nipples through her shirt when he bent down to lick salt from her fingers.

Her free hand glided under his chin, tipped his face to look at her, and their mouths collided. He wasn't entirely sure which of them initiated the kiss, but their tongues dueled for dominance. Cupping his hands on her ass, he lifted her. She locked her legs on his hips, and it took four steps to get to the bed. They landed together, on their sides, facing each other and he delved deeper into her mouth, tasting the traces of their drinks.

Impatient with the ponytail, he slid two fingers beneath the band and worked it free. Her hair spilled in a glorious mass against the white comforter. In addition to the red, there were several streaks of gold, either kissed by the sun or on purpose—he didn't know and didn't care. "Talk to me," he murmured against the corner of her mouth, nibbling a couple of kisses, which led to a series of them. He wanted to nuzzle her ear and feel her hair against his skin.

She arched her back and laughed when he closed his lips on the pulse point behind her ear. Always one to exploit a weakness, he paid particular attention until she squealed in breathless laughter and then lifted his head to look down at her. Her cheeks were a ruddy pink, flushed with passion and laughter. "Tell me—what's got you so wound?"

"You just met me. You don't want my life story." She dragged him back down for another kiss. Admittedly, the soft satin and velvet of her lips were like a drug to his system, he could spend hours sampling the different types of kisses—the long, hot wet one—the sweet, almost chaste teasing one—and the hard-tongue-sucking-teeth-nibbling-drive-his-cock-wild one.

But as stiff and painful as his dick grew, he wanted more than a quick bang in the dark—he wanted all the passion and fire beneath the thin veil of ice. He rolled her over and pinned her hands above her head. Lifting his head, he stared down at her. *Fuck, she's gorgeous.*

The buttons on her shirt had come loose in their tussle to reveal a lacy-cupped bra hugging her breasts. The light sprinkling of freckles on her nose stretched down to decorate the gentle swell of flesh straining against the bra. The pupils in her eyes widened and her breath came in gasps to match his own.

"You know the best part of a one-night stand?" He traced his fingers down the column of her throat to her chest and shifted to circle the outline of one stiff nipple. "You don't ever have to see me again...we can say whatever the hell we feel like and there's no judging, no strings, no consequences—"

One minute he was on top and the next, he was flat on his back with the titian-haired goddess straddling him. She flicked open each button of his shirt until she could tug it out of his pants and drag her nails lightly down his chest. "Has anyone ever told you that you talk too much?"

Laughing, he curled upward and locked his lips around the nipple he'd been teasing, nibbling it lightly through her bra until her back arched and she hissed out a long breath through her teeth.

"We can talk about it after," he unbuttoned her blouse the rest of the way and slid a hand around to unhook her bra.

"Good plan."

Chapter Three

Kim didn't know whether to scream in frustration or shout with joy. Of all the men the mysterious Madame Eve might have picked for her, she'd chosen a man who actually cared what she thought. Her breasts ached with every delicious caress he lavished on her nipples. He took turns, trailing hot kisses between each. His teeth scraped and electricity zapped through her. Tenderness snuck under the wave of passion with every stroke of his tongue. She cradled his head in her arms, holding him to her.

Emergency flags waved in her mind, but she ignored them. Rowdy's hands slipped around her ass and flipped her over onto her back again. He traced a path across her belly to unbutton her jeans. His pupils flared until they swallowed the hazel irises. Dragging a zipper open never seemed to take so long or sound so loud. He slid off the bed and peeled the denim downward, sweeping her panties with them, but had to pause when he arrived at her boots.

Lifting up on her elbows, she grinned at him. Toe to heel on one and she kicked it free. He pulled the other off and then her jeans hit the floor and he stared at her, his eyes dark with desire.

"You're beautiful, Kim." He rubbed a hand along the calf of

her leg.

"And you're overdressed." The temperature in the room couldn't cool the heat raging over her skin. He stood at the foot of the bed, his shirt hanging open to reveal the ripped muscles stretched tight across his pecs and the sturdy four-pack of his abdominals. Lean and mean, like a Marine should be. She loved what she could see...but damn she wanted more.

He stripped off his shirt and dropped to wrap his arms around her. His kiss took her mouth, hard and demanding. His tongue invaded like a surgical strike, taking the perimeter and claiming it for his own. The rough fabric of his jeans glided against her legs, harsh and sensuous in the same breath.

Breaking the kiss, he nuzzled a path to her ear and tugged at the lobe. "Put your hands over your head."

Her brain struggled to interpret the order beneath the fog of pleasure clouding her thoughts. She dug her fingers into his back, but he shifted until she pulled her hands free reluctantly. Shackling her wrists lightly, he drew them over her head and tucked them beneath a pillow.

"Keep them there." He drew her earlobe back into his mouth and sucked on it. Shivers raced over her body and her nipples tightened further. He licked and nipped a path down the column of her throat, punctuating each stop with a word. "Don't. Let. Go."

He kissed her nipples again, licking swirling circles of pleasure around them then nibbled a bit at the curves of her breasts and dipped down to her belly button. Her belly quivered at the feathery touches of his lips to her flesh. She dug her fingers into the pillow, gripping it tighter the lower he traveled. When he slid his hands beneath her thighs and lifted her legs, she groaned.

Warm breath tickled the inside of her thigh. "Not letting go, are we?"

"No." The single word came out as a growl between her teeth. He chuckled and showered warm, wet kisses along the inside of her thigh. He took his time, lingering at sensitive areas each time her hips bucked in an invitation. Her sex clenched in anticipation. Fumbling with the pillow, she nearly pulled her hands free, but he looked up the length of her body as though sensing the decision and their gazes clashed.

"Don't." *One word.*

One order.

And her body went liquid with need. She unclenched her hands and forced them to stay beneath the pillow. He slid forward and draped her legs over his shoulders and cupped her ass. It was torture, sheer, unmitigated torture—his hot mouth closed over her clit and she moaned. He sucked, drove her insane as the unbearable tension mounted inside her. Stroking his tongue along the length of her labia, he stabbed it inside her once in a provocative tease.

"You're killing me," she complained. She couldn't hold still, even as he dug his fingers into her ass, firming his grip.

"Shh...." He whispered the command, but thrummed her clit until she nearly pitched over the edge. When he pulled back at the last moment, she got pissed. Tipping her head up, she glared down at him.

"Dammit, Marine. If you don't put something inside me in a minute, I'll scream."

Rowdy grinned at her, a lazy, heart-flopping smile, bathing her passion in sweetness. "Is this what you want?" He drew one hand from beneath her ass and then a finger slid inside of her. It wasn't much, but her eager body jerked to meet it, clamping down greedily as he gently thrust in and out.

"How's that?" The droll humor barely disguised the husky need in his voice, but she writhed against the tension pulling at her.

"Yes." *Close...so close.*

He bit down on the inside of her thigh—a sensitive spot and electricity zapped through her. She came in a rush, riding his fingers as he continued the rhythmic thrusts. When the lightning dimmed to quivers of pleasure, he slowed his fingers. She looked up to find him watching her, his sweet lips curved into the most beautiful smile.

The low light from the lamp haloed behind his head and the gaze locked on hers felt dark and hot. A fresh shiver of anticipation raced through her. "Better?" he murmured.

"Almost."

"Oh, only almost?" He drew his fingers out, dragging them over the sensitive flesh, stroking around her clit, but not quite touching it. "Did I forget something?"

She gripped the pillow, tempted to throw it at him. The hard points of her nipples ached. Pleasure still danced through her blood and as good as an orgasm.... "More, please."

"More." His grin curved higher. "And you said please."

"Yes, sir. Now give me more." She feasted on the sight of his chest, surprised—and delighted—to see the sheen of sweat on his brow and glistening on his arms. He was nowhere near as unaffected and calm as he played it. "Unless we're done with the keep-my-hands-still part?"

He slid off the bed and free of her legs. She couldn't quite read the expression on his face, but his chest rose and fell rapidly. The veins in his arms popped above the muscles. She dragged one foot up the bed lazily, thighs parted. When his gaze fell to her sex and he moistened his lips, she smiled.

Definitely not in as much control as he wants me to think. He wanted her and the naked heat of his desire nudged her own need back into overdrive. Long seconds passed while he stared at her. A muscle ticked in his jaw and his breath echoed noisily as he exhaled. Finally, he shook his head as though breaking a trance. He pulled a foil-wrapped condom out of his pocket and his jeans hit the floor. It was her turn to lick her lips. His erection was full and a droplet decorated the tip. She wanted to lick her way from base to tip—what a tequila chaser he would make.

He slid the condom on slowly and, the hell of it was, the action only served to turn her on more. She rubbed her thighs together and lifted her hips, half in invitation and the other half in demand. But he didn't rush. Smoothing the condom into place, he gave himself a firm stroke and her pulse seemed to double.

"Rowdy...." She pursed her lips, the heat scorching her insides climbing from slow boil to flaming sizzle. "Get your ass on this bed."

He laughed. "You are very impatient for a Marine...."

"And even more so as a woman, but you have until three—" She didn't have to finish the sentence because he crawled onto the bed and fused his mouth to hers, settling into the cradle of her legs, rubbing his cock against her sex. She dragged her hands out from under the pillow but he shackled her wrists with his hands.

Groaning, she gave a playful struggle and he laughed against her mouth. "Patience, very Special Agent Wakefield, or I'm going to come and then we're back to square one."

Catching his lower lip in her teeth, she rubbed her chest to his, the friction driving her nuts and his erection bumped her clit. She broke the kiss. "Rowdy...."

"Fuck it," he groaned again, released her wrists, and drove into her.

Kim exhaled hard. He filled her, stretching her out in all the right places and seating so deep it melted her restlessness like sugar in the rain. She locked her ankles behind his hips. She didn't want gentle, and based on the struggle in his face, he didn't have it in him to give it to her anymore. He drove into her with hard, impatient strokes.

She welcomed the pounding, exulting at each exquisite glide of his cock against her inner walls. Her sex clenched around him, greedily holding on. He thrust his tongue into her mouth, a conqueror this time, mirroring every push of his lower body, driving her toward the blissful edge. With her hands free, she was finally able to let them roam over his body. She explored every ripple of muscle along his back, stroking them as they strained, and when she dug her nails into his ass, he swore and slammed into her harder.

The tension in her middle coiled tighter and tighter. She

arched her hips, meeting every pounding thrust and her lungs burned. Oxygen became optional as she clung to him.

"Come," he ordered, his voice low, and urgent. "I need you to come."

Understanding that he struggled to hold off his own satisfaction while fulfilling hers burst the dam inside and she spiraled right over the edge. The climax struck her like a tidal wave, and she let out a cry, clinging to him. A second wave of pleasure burst over the first, and he tightened his arms, driving all the way to the hilt until a third wave robbed her of thought and he came with a shout. The tension rippled through him and down, and the waves eddied around her, drenching her in bliss. He collapsed slowly, and they clung to each other, slippery with sweat and sweet release.

He buried his face against her throat, and they panted for air.

"Better?" He asked when his breathing calmed, and she laughed.

Chapter Four

*H*e pulled two bottles of cold water out of the mini fridge and trailed a caress along her bare leg with one when he sat back down on the bed.

Kim lifted her head and shot him a dry look. "Not nice."

Looking at the length of her warm leg, superbly shaped muscle, and her very firm ass, he disagreed. "You said you were hot."

Unabashed at her nudity, she rolled onto her side and snatched the bottle from his hand. He barely twisted the top off his when she pushed the ice cold bottle against his own ass.

"Damn, that's cold." He didn't flinch, but only barely. Her laughter was reward enough. He tipped the bottle back and nearly drained it. His heart was finally beating a normal rhythm and he didn't have to pant for air. Yet, every time he glanced at her, his cock stirred again—making its intentions known. It would recover as soon as it was able.

"Thank you."

The odd sentiment turned him around, and he twisted to meet her gaze. "For what?"

"For not opening it." She twisted the cap off. "Sounds stupid, but guys do it all the time. It's sweet and thoughtful—and you are both of those things—but you still let me open my own bottle."

Stretching out next to her, he flung an arm behind his head and used it for a pillow. "I would have opened it, but you grabbed it out of my hand." He could have accepted the compliment, but why bother with false platitudes? Kim fascinated him, the layers of vulnerability hidden safely behind impenetrable body armor.

She took a drink, as thirsty as he was from the way her throat convulsed with each swallow. "It's a bitch sometimes, being female."

Yeah, he wasn't going to walk into a landmine-laden field without a map and a guide—in fact, why not just go right around it? "I can't imagine it's any easier being an agent."

"You'd be surprised." She rolled over and leaned against the pillows. Her head was higher than his, but he liked the angle. He liked to see her face when she spoke. He'd ripped away some of the veil she kept over her expressions, and she stared into the distance.

"Shock me." He ran his fingers over her thigh. Her skin was still warm and flushed from their lovemaking. The musk of sex lingered in the air, underscoring the sweeter fragrance she wore. Odd how he hadn't even noticed it earlier, too captivated by the power of presence she cultivated. Bare ass naked and flush from sex, she still held him in rapt attention.

"A case doesn't give a crap who solves it, and most of the time when I'm on an investigation, they don't see me. They see the badge. Of course being a woman affects it sometimes—some people will tell me more because I'm female and some will tell me less." She shrugged. "But it's not maneuvers to see who gets to the door first or who picks up the check, or maybe I want to pick out my own damn wine."

The chafing at being treated like a lady bothered him. He couldn't put a finger on why, so he said nothing and tried to look at it from her viewpoint. She was a Marine. She served at least four years, the standard contract, and she didn't have officer written on her, which meant she took the grunt route—like he did. She worked for NCIS, so she stayed involved even after stepping back from active duty.

Tough. Resourceful. Smart. The labels all applied. So why chafe at being treated with respect?

"You're thinking awfully hard down there." The lines between her brows wrinkled into a frown. "We're supposed to be having a good time."

"I am having a good time. I'm getting to know you—just haven't quite figured it all out." Rowdy sat and scooted down the bed to grab another water bottle. The fridge only had four when he opened it. He could call room service—again—but he didn't want any other interruptions. Not to mention they still had food to eat and more exploration to do.

"Figure me out?" The dangerously soft question suggested he reconsider his phrasing.

"Yeah. I like you. I want to do right by you, and I was brought up to show a lady respect. It could be awkward if you're offended by the same ideas." He watched her chew the thought over while he drank.

Her expression barely rippled, but one corner of her mouth twitched. "It's not that it offends me...."

"No? If we walked out right now, would you get upset if I held the door for you?" He finished the second bottle in three full gulps. Dammit, he would have to order some more.

"Probably, but then it would have more to do with being naked than you holding the door." The logic and her grin combined to unravel his argument and he laughed. Tossing the empty bottle into the trash, he dropped down on the bed next to her and slid a possessive hand around her breast.

"So I think your feminine power argument is bullshit."

"Yeah?" Her eyebrows lifted.

"Yeah. Okay, if you want to shovel the manure, I'm a big boy. I can take it. But you have something else going on and I want to hear it." He stroked her nipple, firm little brushes—meant to be more comforting than tantalizing. But the water and the rest did the job. His energy returned.

She sighed and all the amusement in her face evaporated. Looking at the bottle in her hands, indecision shifted in her eyes.

"Sweetheart...I'm serious. You tell me anything you want. I'm a vault, it won't come back out. But I know a little something about needing a friend. You need one right now." He pushed. It was in his nature to push, something his superiors reminded him of each time they suggested officer training, but he didn't want to lead. Knowing how to lead and having a desire to were two different things. But he also knew how to listen and to be a friend.

The silence stretched out and he waited. Her expression rippled, darkening like the storm outside. "You know Camp Whitehorse?"

Everyone knew about Camp Whitehorse. Some stains didn't get washed out. They didn't talk about it, and most didn't fault it. War was hell and it was ugly. He shut down the train of thought and focused on Kim. "Yes."

"So you know about Nagem Hatab." It wasn't exactly a question, more of a statement, but she glanced at him anyway. He knew the name, an Iraqi implicated in the capture and torture of a female Marine private. His subsequent death and the abuse involved had generated scandal—it was war—war was hell.

He nodded once, waiting.

"It wasn't the only incident being investigated. Reports of— of others came to light during a different investigation." She sighed and started to roll away from him, but he locked his arm and pinned her. Anger flared in her eyes, but he met it steadily.

"Not going anywhere. You don't want to talk about it—you don't have to."

"It's not about want—it's about can't. It's an ongoing investigation. Legally, I can't really comment on it."

He dragged her back toward him and wrapped his arms around her. It was awkward—her body stiffened— but gradually she relaxed. He rubbed her shoulder gently. "Investigating Marines has to suck."

"Yep." One word, but so ripe with meaning. She traced a path along his arm with one nail. "Sometimes, it sucks worse than others. I don't mind busting idiots who think running drugs is a good idea or boosting cars—or my personal favorite—importing liquor and cigarettes."

He coughed. Sneaking cigarettes now and then wasn't as unusual as one might expect. She glanced at him and he pasted on an innocent smile. Laughter bubbled through the stern expression and her body loosened, softening and cuddling against him.

Better.

"I'm not going to ask," she promised.

"I'm not going to tell." He winked.

The rain continued to hammer against the windows outside and she sighed deeper. "I like this," she said, her voice hushed as though she worried about disturbing him.

"Me, too." And he did, he liked having her leg tucked between his, and her body wrapped up tight. He liked not being alone. "Not going to bore you with some poor little rich boy story, but I've got options a lot of the guys in my unit don't. So when they gave me the letter, I had to think about who it might benefit if I left—you know making room for those who don't have choices they can make."

"But you don't want out." Again, it wasn't a question and he pressed a kiss to her temple. Her mind was a beautiful thing.

"No. Not really."

She turned in his arms, shifting until he reclined back against the pillows and she could lay with her arms and hands on his chest, staring at him. It wasn't as nice as holding her close, but he appreciated the eye contact.

"Then don't."

Good advice. Advice he'd considered and discarded the same night he received the letter. They needed to trim back to the active force—lots of guys left for injuries or at the end of their contracts. Lots couldn't afford to go home to climbing costs in an economy that didn't promise them a job. He didn't have those worries. Financially, he could actually afford to be out of work. So, better it be him than a buddy with a wife, two kids, and a mortgage. He could take the hit for his men.

"It's not so simple." He would never allow it to be simple.

"It never is." She bit her lip and it took about a decade of dilemma off her shoulders. He could imagine her as a young Marine, full of piss and vinegar and ready to take on the world. She could probably shoulder the world better now, ripe with experience and tempered by time. But he preferred the smile to the frown—the sharp, albeit acerbic, wit to the consternation and struggle. "The worst part of this investigation is I know one of the guys—personally."

It was a fight to keep his tone calm. *How personally did she know him?* "Can you recuse yourself?"

"If it really becomes an issue—yes. Right now—I have a senior agent overseeing it. If it becomes one, we agreed he will step in and take the lead." But she obviously didn't want to surrender the case or worse, need to surrender it. There it was—the rock and a hard place.

"It pisses you off." He couldn't help the wonder in his voice, and the flash of annoyance on her face was cute—not that he planned to tell her anytime soon.

"Hell yes, it pisses me off." Passion erupted and she started to rise. He pinched her ass and she collapsed against him.

"Stop trying to get away. We're comfortable, naked, and I'm planning to lick my way down your body after our little get to know each other *tête-à-tête*." He pressed a kiss to her slack lips, and her laughter vibrated through him. Her tongue tangled with his, and his cock gave a twitch. Oh yeah, he was definitely rested enough to start planning round two.

She broke away and dipped her head down to kiss his chest. "It pisses me off because it makes me feel weak—like I need someone to do my job."

IIc appreciated her honesty and really hoped she didn't blow up at him when he tucked his legs around hers and secured his position. "Well, I'm sorry, but that is just stupid."

Chapter Five

*H*ad he seriously called her stupid? Narrowing her eyes, she studied his too-calm expression. "What?"

"You heard me. That's stupid." Repeating it didn't endear the word to her further nor did the kiss he pressed to the tip of her nose. "Come on. You're stubborn, but you're brilliant, too. Work through everything you told me and tell me you don't think being pissed off because a senior agent has your back is dumb."

The word grated, but she compressed her lips and considered his words. The senior agent hadn't said she couldn't pursue the investigation. He hadn't tried to talk her out of it. He asked her three, salient, pointed questions and then ordered her to run all her reports through him for review. The first order didn't bother her as much as the second. *"If you discover a conflict—don't care what it is or why you feel it—just tell me and I'll take it from there. No questions asked."*

Rowdy's eyebrows raised, his expression daring her to deny his words. She opened her mouth to refute it, but the words wouldn't come out.

He leaned a little closer. "I'm sorry, what?"

The snicker escaped before she could contain it. "You must drive your commanding officers batshit crazy with your attitude."

"Nah, they love me." He grinned. "But I'm right—aren't I?"

"Yes." She sighed and relaxed into his embrace. He never let her go, never let her push him away or shut him out. Odd, less than three hours acquaintance and he had her number. Scary, too.

And really freaking attractive.

He nuzzled another kiss along her jaw, melting the stubborn tension and anxiety. "So what are you unhappy about now?"

"I'm not unhappy." But she couldn't stop the half grin from taking up residence on her lips.

"Okay, pensive, then." He let her go, but not far, propping himself up on one elbow. He used his free hand to trace light patterns against her skin—the action relaxing and intoxicating at the same time. "Do you ever stop thinking?"

"Do you?" She retorted, grinning wider now. He hadn't gone for officer and it surprised her. The man kept chipping away at her resistance.

"Yes." He slid his hand down to her hip and tapped it lightly. "I'd love to stop thinking anytime you're ready."

Snorting, she rolled onto her side, and faced him. "Why did you sign up for a one-night stand?"

"I was lonely." The frank answer startled and pleased her. "You?"

"Yeah...I get tunnel vision sometimes. I like to do a good job, and I forget that it's okay to feel things even when they suck." No shame or embarrassment accompanied the admission. Her pride didn't twinge either. "I wanted to feel something good for a change."

"And do you feel good now?" Despite his playful leer, an undercurrent of seriousness flowed along the words.

"Hmm. Not bad." She cut her gaze down, studying the length of him.

"Not bad," he repeated. "Not sure whether to be offended or challenged."

"Would you like a hint?"

"No." He nudged her onto her back and slid down to kiss her belly button. Her body tightened in anticipation. "I'm going to go with challenged."

Her retort strangled on pleasure when he locked his mouth on her clit and sucked. It wasn't long before she forgot to think, too.

ങ

It was after midnight. They'd eaten their food cold and laughed all the way through it. The storm continued to pound against the windows. Kim curled against him, her red hair spilling over his chest, her gentlest of snores telling him she slept deeply. All the lines of worry erased from her face. Comfortable and replete, he watched the flashes of lightning. Sleep, however, remained elusive.

"You're doing it again," her drowsy voice purred against him.

"I blame the high-minded company I keep." He could almost feel her smile. Running his fingers through the silken length of her hair, he combed it away from her face. "Go back to sleep."

She sighed and her breath tickled his chest. "Sleeping makes the night go by too fast."

He didn't disagree with the sentiment. "But you're tired."

"So are you." Lifting her head, she looked toward the window. "It's still raining."

"Yeah." What a gorgeous sound it created. Rain spattering the glass, the steady drum of it—he could almost imagine the smell and hear the wind.

"How long were you in the desert?" Of course, she'd clued right in.

"On and off—three deployments." He liked the desert with its dry heat, golden sand, and merciless sun. But he missed the rain, the sound and the smell of it. "You?"

"No, I was afloat for most of my time in—we were on standby, but...." She shrugged.

"Good." He liked the thought of her anywhere but the

sandbox—the brutal, unforgiving, and, often as not, deadly-on-a-daily-basis sandbox.

"You're perilously close to patronizing." The lightness in her tone softened the edge on the word.

"No, it's spot-on pleasure and protective instincts. Me, man. You, woman." He mimicked a Tarzan tone.

Her snort amused him even more. "Okay he-man, she-hulk is glad she not have to smash, too."

Humor chased away the melancholy, and he threw his head back and laughed. They shook together, giggling like a pair of adolescents on a naughty sleepover. The laughter was a cool autumn breeze, chasing away the sticky heat of summer. She shifted next to him. Her teeth grazed his nipple and his mind locked up.

Roaming a hand over his chest, she elicited tingling sensations with every teasing caress of her nails. She rolled over him, her damp kisses teasing across to the other pectoral while her hair slid across him like a sensuous blanket. Cupping a hand around his cock, she stroked a finger to the tip and slid down to sit against his thighs.

"Since we're awake...."

The darkness in the room hid her smile, but he heard it. The flashes of lightning backlit her, a storm goddess come out to play.

"If you insist." He grinned.

"Oh, I absolutely do." She stroked him again, tracing her thumb over the head. No other part of her moved. Her head tilted, as though she watched him. Her hair glided over her shoulders, the length of it reached her breasts. He envied her hair—he wanted to play with her nipples, too.

She gripped the base of his cock and pumped a few times. He coiled, tension gathering at the edge of his nerve endings. His balls tightened and his humor evaporated. Like oil crackling on a super-heated pan, he was hungry for her again.

She released him and he bit back an oath. Instead of taking him in her hand again, she slid off his legs and balanced with a palm against each thigh. Without a word, she touched her tongue to the base of his cock and licked up one side to the crown, swirled her tongue around the slit and down the other side.

His body clamored, all the blood rushing to his groin, and his eyes crossed. *Holy shit....* She repeated the lazy exploration with her tongue and pulled him into her mouth. His thoughts scrambled. She set to work, kissing, licking, sucking and driving him crazy. The tension in his tight balls surged, and he dug his fingers into the sheets, fighting the urge to roll her over and pound into her. She tried to take all of him, her hand increasing the pressure at the base.

Clenching his buttocks, he refused to buck, letting her drive the rhythm. His cock bumped the back of her throat. Her nails caressed his balls—a feather light touch—but he exploded, release swamping over him like a wild tempest sweeping away his control. She didn't pull away, caressing him through the orgasm. Long minutes passed before coherent thought began to surface from the waves. She slipped away and came back with another water bottle and snuggled right to his side.

And the damn thing was he could sleep now, doused in the warmth of her embrace. He fought the closing of his eyelids, wrapping an arm around her to hold her closer.

What a perfect fit....

☙

Dawn came too soon. She stood in front of the windows and stared out over the city. The storm had blown itself out sometime in the early hours of the morning. The sun turned the eastern sky a rich azure with streaks of pink and hints of orange. Rowdy's warm, masculine arms slid around her, and she leaned back against his chest. He enveloped her in his clean, shower-fresh scent and she sighed.

"Real world time." She fought to keep her tone light. The last thing she'd expected was reluctance to leave.

"Five more minutes." His arms tightened and she closed her eyes.

"Okay."

They stood until her phone buzzed, reminding her about a meeting. He let her go and she pulled it out, thumbing off the alarm. Steeling her courage, she turned to meet his gaze. "Thank you."

"Thank you." He smiled and her lips curved in response. "If you ever need to talk...." The invitation trailed off.

"You, too." She forced herself to walk over to the safe. Unlocking her gun and strapping on her holster made it official. She tugged on her jacket then reached into her wallet and extracted a business card. She held it out between two fingers. "Seriously—you know, if you need anything—call."

He accepted the card and slid an arm around her waist before she could slip back, tugging her close. He leaned down and pressed the sweetest kiss to her lips—no demand, no hard need—a tender gift. Forehead to forehead, his gaze locked with hers. "Cut yourself some slack, Special Agent Wakefield, and let your men watch your back."

"I'll do my best."

And she was off, wrapping her soul in the body armor it would need to push on through the investigation. The loneliness dogging her steps for the last few months was gone—erased in one night. She left Rowdy in the room, but when she walked off the elevator and into the lobby—she whistled.

Oorah, Sergeant. Oorah.

Epilogue

Three Months Later...

Kim checked her watch on the way in the door for the briefing. She had two interrogations to complete and a stack of reports on her desk to file. Hopefully the meeting wouldn't take longer than the allotted thirty minutes. Several agents crowded into the room, and as one of the last to arrive, she took a spot against the back wall and used her phone to review her email.

Giles Mann, the section chief, strode in to take position at the podium. He didn't even have to clear his throat to silence the chatter. "Good morning, I know we're all busy, so I'll keep this brief. We have five new probies starting with us this week."

New probies—probationary agents in need of on the job training—reassignments and an updated case load. Standard meeting material. Tuning out the conversation, she finished responding to the email from an agent afloat about a shared investigation and missed the names on the roster as well as the parsing of assignments since her name wasn't called. The meeting ended as swiftly as it began. Escaping the room, she strode to her desk to gather her case files.

"Wakefield."

The section chief stood a few steps away, but he wasn't the person Kim focused on. Right behind the chief stood Rowdy.

Her stomach plummeted, and her breath clogged in her throat, but she swallowed the reaction.

"Sir?" Flicking her gaze from one man to the other, she gave Mann her full attention.

"Special Agent Wakefield, this is Agent Easton. He'll be doing rotations through the different sections for training. Your first probie, as it were." Mann gave her a quick grin.

Rowdy stepped forward and offered his hand. "Pleased to meet you, ma'am." His eyes twinkled with suppressed humor, and she smothered an answering smile. Electricity zinged through her with one quick handshake.

"It's nice to meet you, too—Agent Easton." She played along.

"I have a meeting with the director. Easton, you're in good hands. Wakefield, make sure I have a copy of your interrogation notes this afternoon, I'd like to wrap up the Jensen case." Mann left glancing at his watch, leaving her with Rowdy—alone save for the half-dozen other agents working at their desks in the bullpen.

"So, Probie...why don't you get to work triaging these files." She patted the fifteen new additions to the stack of thirty already fighting for space on her desk. Maybe by the time she was done with the suspect interview, she could figure out how to deal with having Rowdy there.

In her office.

The prospect thrilled and worried her.

"Okay." He nodded slowly, the corners of his mouth curving. "Agent Wakefield?"

She paused. "Yes?"

"I'm really looking forward to working with you."

Awareness pulsed through her blood. But this wasn't the time...or the place.

"I hope you still feel that way when you're done sorting those files. I have two interviews planned today. Get that done before I finish the first one and you can observe the second." She pursed her lips thoughtfully, fighting a smile. "And if you're really efficient, I'll let you spring for coffee later."

"Done and done." He grinned.

She walked away, letting her smile out of captivity. *I have a feeling life is about to get very interesting....* At the corner, she glanced back. Rowdy stood at her desk, files in hand, and he winked.

Yep. Really interesting. She blew out a breath. *Oorah.*

A MARINE AND A GENTLEMAN

HEATHER LONG

৪৩

Chapter One

Second Lieutenant Brenden Fitzpatrick didn't pace. He didn't fidget. He demonstrated none of the physical tics of discomfort—but he was uncomfortable. Three deployments to the Middle East—and an upcoming assignment to the Consulate in Yemen—gave him plenty of time to consider his options while standing in the psychologist's office.

"You can sit down, you know." James Westwood leaned back in a chair, a notepad resting untouched on one knee and a pen in his hand.

Of all the people he'd expected to run into during his interview with Captain Dexter, the doc hadn't been on the list. Hell, he only accepted the captain's invitation because they were old friends. Seeing what Luke built in Mike's Place and visiting with retired members of his unit were more than worth the trip.

"I know. I prefer standing. I've been on planes for two days." Not a lot to do on a plane but clench his ass and hope the flyboys kept the damn thing in the air. He preferred boats for travel, not that anyone asked. He could swim ten miles if the occasion called for it.

"We haven't talked in a while. How is it working out with your new chaplain?"

"Oh, she's good." Brenden looked away from the courtyard atrium and at the doc. "She can't hold her liquor worth a damn, but she's good at getting me to talk." Corporal Abby Dunlap, the company chaplain, was as middle-American mom's-hot-apple-pie as they came. But she knew how to listen—that counted for a lot among the guys.

"Good. You're taking the diplomatic assignments now?" James only asked questions he knew the answers to, or at least it seemed that way.

"Yemen. One year at the consulate there."

"That's a tough assignment."

Neither commented on the recent surge of violence aimed at American embassies and diplomatic missions around the world. They were both aware.

"It needs to be done." Frankly, he didn't worry about the violence or the potential for it. His unit was more than capable of dealing with hot tempers and disgruntled political reactions and maintaining the safety of the civilian diplomatic mission assigned to their location.

"It does, but you've been off your assignment in Iraq for just a few weeks, and now you're heading into another hot zone. That takes its toll."

Again, no questions, only facts, and James didn't fuss or try to force him to talk—one of the doc's best attributes. Brenden would or he wouldn't talk. They could get a drink or shoot hoops, and Brenden would feel better by the end of it.

"So I have a question for you, Doc." He clasped his hands behind his back. Years ago, he would probably have slid his hands into his pockets or hooked his thumbs into his belt loops. But even dressed in jeans and a polo shirt, his training didn't allow for sloppy, relaxed postures.

"Hit me." The psychologist sat forward, interest filling his expression. Brenden rarely asked questions.

"The 1Night Stand service that you and the guys talked about last night...." He considered how to phrase his question precisely. "Is it really as good as you make it sound?"

"Better, I think. The average dating service takes the edge of uncertainty off of the participants because both are aware that the other is *looking* for something more. The 1Night Stand service eliminates it further by providing immediate gratification and certainty of how a night will go." James exhaled. "Don't get me wrong, I've seen more relationships develop out of the arranged evenings than I have seen them simply be about one night of passion—but the pressure is off. You can enjoy yourself, and go back to your life, no questions asked."

"So you recommend it?" He had already booked a date based on other's recommendations. Still, he valued Doc's opinion.

The psychologist studied him. "If you're looking for companionship, absolutely...."

"But?" The unspoken word at the end of his sentence blared.

"But be prepared that the fantasy may be closer to true reality than you know. You sign up thinking you want one thing, but the reality is you want more."

"And more isn't guaranteed." That thought had already occurred to him. Hell, it was the only thing he could think about.

"I have the website information. It could take some time...."

"I signed up four months ago." The confession rolled out easier than he'd expected. "I knew I had leave, so I figured what the hell." Actually he figured a great deal more than that—the decision far from blasé.

James nodded. "Do you mind if I ask you a question?"

"Nope." He'd expected at least one.

"Did you request the kind of night you really want?" The psychologist cut right to the heart of the matter.

"Do you think it matters?" Brenden returned the challenge.

"Yes, I do." He set aside the notepad and pen and clasped his hands together. "*Don't ask, don't tell* doesn't apply anymore. You serve your country with distinction. You walk into harm's way without regard for your own personal safety. You deserve to enjoy yourself—and not to have to worry about how you get to do that."

Brenden grinned. "Thanks, Doc. I appreciate the concern."

"Lieutenant...."

"Easy, Doc." He held up a placating hand, halting the reassurance the doc would certainly offer. "I asked for something pretty specific...a guy that I used to know in another life."

Leaning back, James' expression relaxed. "Good."

"Not sure how that will work out, or even if it will, but the email came in this morning. He's agreed to it." He blew out a breath. "Just—sounds weird to say it out loud."

"It's your business, it's your life. Take it easy. Don't pile on the pressure. This isn't a suppression mission or a surgical strike...."

"It's intelligence gathering. Yeah, I know." Unclasping his hands, he flexed his fingers and paced over to the glass. "I have one more question." When the psychologist said nothing, he glanced back and found James waiting with a patient expression. "I filed the request and filled out the forms. I knew this guy in high school. He's open and gay, and wildly proud of it. He never let anyone else dictate his sexuality to him—and we had some real bastards at the school. He took a lot of shit for it, but he didn't change who he was." Brenden exhaled a deep breath. "I always had a thing for him, but it became a mission to make sure he didn't know."

"Were you embarrassed by it?" James prompted after he lapsed into silence.

He shook his head. "No. But the Marines were my future. My dad, my grandfather, my great-grandfather—hell, all the way back to Tun Tavern—Fitzpatricks have all been Marines. I couldn't be the gay one. I really couldn't."

"So you chose the military over your affection for...."

He didn't quite fish for a name, but Brenden gave it to him anyway. "Liam. And I don't know that I chose one over the other. The Marines—foregone conclusion. A commitment. A dream. I knew that's where I wanted to be. Liam—he was a great guy, the best friend I've ever had, and a real pain in the ass. His mouth got my nose broken twice in high school. But he wouldn't have accepted a quiet, on-the-side, discreet relationship. That wasn't him."

"And now? Could you handle an indiscreet, direct relationship with him?"

A fair question, one Brenden had asked every day since sending in the application.

"I don't know that I even know him anymore. I've seen him maybe twice in ten years and always in a bigger group. But he agreed to meet me." Anxiety buzzed in his ears like a lazy bumblebee in the hot summer sun. "So that's good, right?"

"He agreed to more than meeting you." A hint of a frown wrinkled James' forehead. "A lot more. You realize that, right?"

"Yeah, just not focusing so much on that part. Kind of like to cross that bridge with him, if it doesn't collapse." Maybe he should have called Liam ahead of time, but if he said no to the 1Night Stand offer, chances were Brenden wouldn't even have known. Not in the same way he did that he said yes. Because he would be in the field, doing his job, and not worrying about the *what if* of it all.

"Not to be indelicate, but this won't be your first...."

Brenden's brows shot up and he laughed. "Yeah. No. We're good, Doc, and you don't need to give me any safe sex lectures."

"Good. Look, Lieutenant you've got a good head on your shoulders. You're a solid Marine. You've thought this out. Go for it. Have a good time."

"Thanks, Doc, seriously. I...just wanted to make sure the screws were tight." He couldn't count on anything tonight. Hell, it would be good to just sit down and get a beer with Liam. God, he hoped he drank beer. In high school, Liam went through a wine cooler phase. Buying that embarrassing shit fell to Brenden—he'd looked older and rarely got carded.

James rose and they clasped hands briefly. "One word of caution." He gave Brenden his serious, no-nonsense face. "Don't make any promises you don't intend to keep, and be honest with him about your career."

"Yes, sir. That is my intention." It didn't matter that James didn't wear a uniform or that he only carried the rank of private to Brenden's lieutenant, the doc possessed presence and dedicated his professional life to helping Marines—on and off active duty. That alone earned him respect.

"Good." James patted his shoulder. "Lauren and I will see you for dinner with the guys on Friday, yes?"

"Yep, I'll be there. I can't wait to meet the woman turning Logan into mush."

They both grinned at that. Logan Cavanaugh, a rough and tough leatherneck with a bad ass reputation, tamed by the woman he and Zach shared. A sight Brenden would pay money to see. The pair were closer than brothers. They'd grown up together, served together, and when Logan's career shattered in an attack, Zach followed him out of the service and worked to keep his recovery on track. That they fell for the same woman didn't surprise him. That they were making a go of their unconventional relationship—it impressed him and deserved his respect.

"If you end up having a plus one, just shoot me a text so I can let Lauren know. God help us if we disturb the *feng shui* of her seating arrangement."

They laughed again and Brenden headed out. He debated wearing his uniform, the classiest thing he owned for the dinner with Liam, or just going comfortable.

Comfortable won out. He had some stops to make before his date and just a few hours to get it all done, but he whistled all the way to the borrowed truck.

ᴄᴈ

Liam stepped out of the rental car and handed the keys to the valet. The Dallas nightclub was not at all what he'd expected. Heavy wooden doors offered a gothic touch to the façade. A red canopy stretched out to the circular drive, matching carpet that led to the doors. A doorman dressed in a nineteenth century, double-breasted coat, top hat, and tails held out his hand for the card from the mysterious 1Night Stand service.

"I think I'm going to wait out here. It's a beautiful night." Sliding the card back into his wallet, he walked along the curb to a quieter spot away from the foot traffic and arrivals—and, unsurprisingly, no departures. It was just after six-thirty in the evening, local time. After renting the car at the airport, he'd bypassed his hotel to come straight to the club. He hadn't decided whether he planned to stay the night or not, no matter what he agreed to with the 1Night Stand service.

Even the name brought a half-smile to his lips. The woman who sent him the three emails offered an uncanny and accurate assessment of his situation. At the end of the day, the forwarded request from Brenden prompted him to say yes.

Extracting a cigar from a case in his inner pocket, he trimmed the end off of one and lit it. The fragrant tobacco filled the air and calmed his mind. He handled power lunches and dinners every night of the week. As a professional banker, he knew when businessmen tried to bullshit him or when they had a plan.

He knew how to say no.

He always knew when to say yes. Reading people for a living wasn't pretty work, but it proved lucrative.

Another couple arrived, huddled together and dashing up the steps as if it were cold. The forty-five degree temperature and dead still air were hardly cold to his Boston-forged blood.

Why Dallas? Liam would've preferred to meet Brenden at home, at the Tipperary on the Green, to toss back a pint for old times. But no, Brenden invited him to the cow town in the middle of the country where big boots, big steaks, and big boobs seemed to be everywhere.

Big hair, too. He eyed the next couple arriving. *It looks like the 80s threw up on her.* He puffed the cigar and kept his acerbic opinion quiet, but the distraction helped.

Thirty-two years old and on the ropes over an invitation to drinks. The drinks aren't the problem. Come meet the guy I've lusted after for over half my life and spend the night with him?

Yeah, nothing to be nervous about.

He'd never suspected Brenden was gay—he never exhibited any 'signs' or 'traits' as the locals used to call them. The Marine didn't behave queer, effeminate, or different from any other jock in their heavily Catholic neighborhood. But they had moments— a handshake here, a laugh there—always too ephemeral for Liam to grasp onto.

My best friend....

Frankly, Brenden Fitzpatrick was a best friend, savior, and bodyguard all rolled into one sexy as hell, fit package. But he'd never responded to the flirtatious gestures, negatively or positively. He gave him shit. He watched his back, and he beat the hell out of guys who gave him a hard time.

He stood up for him—even to his Marine father who didn't approve of his son hanging out with a queer. He'd been there whenever Liam needed him—until the day he went for OCR training and left their Boston neighborhood.

He came back. The mental argument didn't sell. He came back a handful of times. They ran into each other at a block party and again during their high school reunion. And, damn, if the man didn't look good in a uniform. Liam never thought he would go for all the brass buttons, spit and polish, but Brenden made it sexy, so he kept his distance.

Puffing halfway through the cigar didn't do a damn thing for his nerves. He couldn't figure out why Brenden made the request. *Unless he thinks he might be gay and I'm a good experiment.*

Grimacing at the thought, he decided against falling for that line. He'd walked down that road a few times in and around college—guys who wanted to experiment, thought they might be gay—and then freaked the fuck out.

Yeah, no thanks.

Alerted by a scuff of shoe behind him, Liam turned around. His heart fisted and punched against his ribcage. He blew out a hard breath of smoke and shook his head. Brenden looked even better at thirty-two than he had the last time he'd seen him four years before.

"I was really hoping for the dress blues." Liam switched the cigar to his left hand and extended his right.

Always tall, Brenden had filled out nicely. The dark green polo shirt he wore stretched over his wide shoulders. His arms were corded muscle, and his hands thick and well developed—hell, even his fingers looked like they pumped iron.

Brenden gripped Liam's hand in a firm, quick handshake that ended with Brenden pulling him forward. The hug startled the hell out of him, and he patted his shoulder awkwardly.

"Thank you for coming." The Marine stepped back and gave him a smile. A faint scar sliced through the flesh of his lip and up to the crease of his smile, one corner of his mouth didn't quite curve up as much as the other. His black hair, cut in a high and tight fashion, framed his fine bone structure from chiseled cheekbones to his broad forehead. Of course, the double knot in his nose ruined the Michelangelo's David effect, but Liam preferred the raw man to the marble.

"You're welcome. Wasn't expecting the invitation."

Understatement of the year. Backing off another step, Liam tapped some ash into the nearby tray. Thankfully, the cigar gave him something to do.

"Yeah, well, I wasn't sure I would ever issue it." The blunt, forward honesty gave him another reason to respect his oldest friend. Brenden Fitzpatrick never said anything he didn't mean. He used words sparingly and with much greater effect.

An awkward silence ballooned around them. Liam compressed his lips, biting his tongue against the acidic question burning the end of it.

"Spit it out before you choke on it." Brenden advised with an easy grin. His hard, gorgeous face looked a lot more comfortable with this situation than Liam felt, shocking since he normally took everything in stride.

But this was Brenden.

He jammed the cigar between his lips, grasping at the mundane activity. "Why?" He exhaled the smoke. "Why now?

Why me?"

"Fair questions." Brenden glanced over his shoulder as more newcomers arrived, handing off their keys and cars to the valets and making their way inside. They were alone on their little patch of sidewalk. "I missed you."

It was a good answer.

"You ever hear of picking up a phone?" Liam lifted his brows and snuffed out the cigar in the sandy circular tray.

"I wanted to see you."

Everything about him radiated control. He didn't slide his hands into his pockets, lean, or slouch. His back remained ramrod straight, legs firmly planted—and Liam shouldn't have thought about his legs because, even encased in denim, their shape and musculature drew the eye. He almost couldn't wait to see if his ass matched the rest of the package, but he forced his attention back to Brenden's face.

"Are you giving me shit because you can? Or is the invitation serious?" He braced to hear a joke or even a lame excuse.

"Serious as a missile strike. I've waited a long time to ask you out. I'm done waiting. But I figure you might need some time, you know, to adjust to the idea. So...drink?" Brenden gestured to the club. "I bet they have wine coolers."

The droll humor at the end of his invitation and the crooked grin warming his already kind eyes tipped the scales. Liam had prepared for every eventuality except Brenden being serious.

"Yeah, I think I might need something a little stronger than a wine cooler."

Laughing, Brenden gave his shoulder a firm squeeze. "Then the drinks are on me."

Liam was still trying to wrap his mind around the whole concept when he led him into the club.

Chapter Two

*B*renden leaned back in the chair. They chose a table near a wall and, as if by long habit, he and Liam chose opposite sides, both turning their chairs back against the wall. It gave them a better view and they could still talk. A waitress greeted them and when Brenden ordered a beer, Liam held up two fingers.

"Make it two."

"Since when do you drink beer?" The man had hated it in high school—called it dog piss and refused to touch the stuff. He preferred his buzz to come from fine wines and expensive liquor.

"Things change." His easy, generous smile suggested his sense of humor remained intact. "You do realize it's been a while, right?"

"Yeah, smartass. I'm aware. Thanks for the update."

He studied the man across the table from him. Always the leaner of the two of them in high school, Liam once claimed he would never look like a man, but that meant he could play his baby face for all it was worth. Somewhere between graduation and now, he'd become a man—his baby face had developed a roguish charm right down to the twinkle in his eyes.

Despite the easy smile, sexy dimples and humor—wariness lurked beneath the gleam in his gaze. *Doubt? Irritation?*

Brenden couldn't put his finger on it. The waitress brought over their beers and offered food, but they both declined. Alone again, the silence stretched.

"Look, Liam...."

"I wanted to say...."

The words collided and rolled over each other. For the first time since arriving, self-consciousness tangled with Brenden's tongue. "Go ahead."

"Okay. It's good to see you—and I mean that—and I hope you'll pardon the bluntness...." Despite the careless fall of hair across his forehead and the startling blue of his eyes, Liam pinned him with a hard look. "But since when are you gay?"

"Since always." He'd expected the question. Frankly, he would have been shocked if the other man hadn't asked.

"Bullshit." His old friend took a long pull from the beer and shook his head slowly. "I've known you too long to buy that. You pretty much nailed every available tail in high school."

"Because I was supposed to." Brenden sighed. He'd made his peace with his actions a long time ago. "That's what people expected—what my Dad expected—and I'm sure on some level what I expected. Be good at sports, like girls, graduate, enlist, and serve my country with distinction. Four out of five isn't bad." His attempt at humor fell flat.

"If you want to be flippant—fine. I'll just finish the beer and head out." But he put the beer down and pushed it away. Brenden's hand snapped out to take his before Liam could rise.

"Stay." The order came out harsher than he meant and he blew out a breath. "Please." They stared at each other and the tension in Liam's posture relaxed. He sat back, but Brenden didn't release his hand. "I'm not being flippant. I've always known—just like I always knew I couldn't act on it."

Liam turned his hand over beneath Brenden's and interlaced their fingers, obviously testing him. "Okay, I'll skip the cliché of asking why you thought you had to hide it from everyone else and ask the really pointed question of why did you hide it from me?"

"Because you were as subtle as a brick shithouse." Holding hands felt right. It snapped on a light inside of him that'd burned dim for too long. "And far too fucking charming. Not telling you meant I didn't have to act on any crazy impulses, or worse, have to break it off when I wouldn't change who I am."

"That's almost too good to be true." He let go of Brenden's hand, and reached for his beer again. "You know, magazine material. I had a crush on you all the way through high school and actually toned down so I wouldn't scare my one decent straight friend off."

Snorting, the Marine gave him a skeptical look. "Wearing a full-on evening dress to prom to make a political statement is not toning it down."

"I said I toned down my crush. Not toned down my behavior. You were who you were and so was I."

"True enough." Brenden laughed. The taffeta nightmare had looked both ridiculous and adorable at the same time. Liam may have been lean, but he stood tall, only an inch shy of Brenden's six foot three frame. The dress stopped at his calves, shaved for the occasion. "I just thank God you didn't wear heels."

"Not my finest hour. Those flats did nothing for my figure." The wry cattiness made Brenden laugh. Liam drew a circle on the table with condensation from his bottle. "You know, they don't ban gay couples at the dances anymore."

"No, I didn't know. That's cool." He mulled the idea over. He couldn't imagine it. The world didn't judge as harshly anymore, but it still judged. "That's actually really cool. Must take some brave kids to do that."

"Yeah. You know, sometimes I think it was easier to be that flaming queer, out to make everyone uncomfortable. I could go as far over the top as I wanted because that's what others expected." He shrugged. "But my dress-wearing days are over. I prefer power suits and comfortable shoes."

Shaking his head, Brenden caught the waitress's gaze and pointed to their beers and held up two fingers. She nodded and gave him a quick wink. He let the flirt pass and glanced back at

Liam. "I think you just liked making everyone else uncomfortable before they did it to you."

"I may be guilty of some of that." Liam admitted. "So what about you? Still playing G.I. Joe?"

"Yes. Are you playing the prick because I'm making you uncomfortable?" Brenden stretched his legs out, and they paused as the waitress cleared away the finished beers and delivered two more. She gave him another flirtatious smile, and he ignored it again.

"Hell yes, you make me uncomfortable." Liam sat forward and stripped off his coat, setting the jacket on the back of the chair next to him. He'd filled out since high school, his broad shoulders stretching the fabric. The dress shirt beneath the exact shade of his eyes. "You're not supposed to be gay and so easy about it."

Lowering his beer, Brenden squinted at his friend. "And you're not supposed to be so...whatever the hell this is. Nervous?"

The abrupt change of subject obviously bothered Liam. "You know, let's talk about the Marines. How is that going for you? Moving up the ranks?"

"Dude—relax. We're just having a beer." He held his hand out in invitation. "Catching up. It's okay. Really."

He brought it up again. "Oddly enough, that doesn't make me feel better. You're supposed to be straight."

"Why am I *supposed* to be?" Brenden refused to let the rejection bother him. He'd expected some resistance, but nothing like this.

"Because you're *that guy*. Top of your class, great athlete, smart, sexy, funny, and stand-up guy. You didn't let bullies get away with shit, and you were the first to volunteer for every Tom, Dick or Sally social cause someone came to you about. You were perfect. The perfect guy to dream about—perfect and untouchable."

The fervent declaration took Brenden back. "I was not perfect," he argued.

"Yeah, you were. Tiffany Hutcherson comes to you and says the varsity cheerleading squad lost at district every year because all the other teams had guys on them. You signed up to help her out. And as soon as word got out, four more guys signed up, including two of the school's top jocks. Matty Peterson lost her house in that freak storm, but she lacked popularity and no one really signed up for that fundraiser and rebuild project until you did." Liam ticked off his list on his fingers. "Jaime Zales flipped out at school because a local shelter closing meant two hundred animals would be put down, and you led a school walkout to pound pavement and get every dog adopted and took the last three ugly ass mutts home to your mom when you couldn't find them a place." He leaned forward and pointed his fingers right at him. "Perfect. You were *that guy* the one every girl dreamed about...."

It was Brenden's turn to feel uncomfortable. "They all needed to be done. It wasn't about trying to impress anyone."

The other man threw his hands up and laughed, seeming to settle down for the first time since they'd walked into the club. "And that, my friend, proves my point. You stated, categorically, at every career day, that you were headed for the Marines. You knew who you were and where you wanted to be. The rest of us flopped around like fish on a shore while you parted the waters with smooth sailing, demonstrating how it should be done." He pinched the bridge of his nose, sobered and finally took the hand Brenden offered. "You liked me for me, you watched my back, and you didn't get all weird when I did. You were my hero...."

"Yeah?" He locked his grip on Liam's. "You were mine."

Speechless, Liam couldn't pull his gaze away from the intensity in the Marine's expression.

"I thought that would shut you up." Brenden's slow grin took a devastating toll on his self-control. "You see, I knew where I wanted to go, and I knew what was right, but it didn't always mean I could be all I am and achieve both. You took risks and said, 'fuck you world if you don't like it.'"

"I actually don't know what to say to that." The last traces of wariness released his soul and he squeezed Brenden's hand.

"Okay. Then how about we just catch up? Talk about today—or, better—talk about tonight."

The flirtatious comment threatened to leave Liam without words once more, so he laughed. "You start." That seemed safer than flipping open the toy box on all the things he'd thought about doing with Brenden over the years.

"All right." Music filtered through the speakers and the din of the crowd rose in a soothing hum. Letting go of Liam's hand, Brenden turned in the chair so he could sit forward and rest his elbows on the table. "What do you want to know?"

"Everything." Oddly enough, he really did. "Boot camp. Deployment. We see a lot on the news. My mom still talks to yours so she throws me dribs and drabs of when you're out of country—well, as much as your mother shares."

Hard to ask for more without tipping to a deeper interest, so he tucked that part away—locking it up into the closet of might-have-beens where it lingered, dusty and half-remembered—till the invitation arrived.

"Are you seeing anybody?" The giddy bubble of feeling popped and his smile faded. "Are you seeing anyone?" He repeated, trying not to stare at Brenden's hands, but he hadn't noticed a ring. Of course, not all men wore them.

"Telling you everything might take a while and no, I'm not seeing anyone. I have had a few nights here and there over the years. But nothing long-term, nothing concrete. You?" The steady answer did more to soothe the knee jerk, gut reaction than anything else.

"I was. We broke up last year." Thankfully, answering didn't open that wound, the disappointment and regret of the relationship having healed into a scar. He could appreciate the good times and not dwell on the bad.

"Bad breakup?" Concern filled Brenden's face, and that was the chokepoint where Liam's feelings for the man always bottled up. He cared. He always cared—if the Marine could do something about it, he would.

"Not bad, not great." *Do I really want to tell him about this?* "We were—*were* being the key phrase, here—pretty solid for five years and so one night, over wine, celebrating our anniversary, I asked him to marry me."

Brenden said nothing, just watched and waited with a patient calm Liam envied.

"As you may have guessed from the broken up comment, that didn't go over well. So—we parted on acrimonious terms—more on my part than his. But I'm over it. It wasn't the right call for him, but it is for me." Something shuttered in Brenden's expression and Liam leaned forward. "Don't worry. I'm not sizing you up for a tux." He let him soak in that relief for the barest of moments and softened the blow with a teasing, "Yet."

"Nice." Brenden scratched his jaw and shook his head.

"Yeah, well if you saw the momentary flash of pure panic in your eyes, you'd be laughing right now, too." He wouldn't be asking the marriage question again anytime soon—not unless he could be damn sure of the answer. "Besides, I don't know that you're my type."

"Oh, I'm definitely your type. But my life doesn't lend itself to long nights hanging out on the sofa and football games every Sunday. I'm a lifer, Liam. I go where the Corps send me, and I don't intend to change that."

"I figured. The haircut, the attitude, everything—it suits you." Oddly, it did. He would never take his own hair that short, but the high and tight accented Brenden's strong features and gave him an almost dangerous, yet comforting air. It defied description.

"I'm not going to lead you on. It's what I do. I'm on leave now, but I'll be pulling up stakes in a couple of weeks for a new assignment."

Gut twisting at the thought of where those assignments might take him, Liam retreated from that topic. "So...when did you know—that you were gay?"

"Oh, during prom—junior year."

"No fucking way. You nailed Jenny Lang that night." Liam held his tongue as the waitress delivered another round.

"You want food?" Brenden glanced at him. "I need a burger, fries, whatever you have. American cheese."

"I'll take the same." He didn't care what he ordered. The waitress needed to leave so he could ask the question burning in his mind. She wasn't five steps away when he rounded on Brenden. "You fucked her. I know—I ran into you walking out of her hotel room during the after-party looking really pleased with yourself."

"For a guy as comfortable with his sexuality as you've always been, why are you having such a hard time wrapping your head around this?"

A great question, one Liam had wondered from the moment he received the invitation. He decided to forgo the sweet talk. "Because, frankly, when your teenage wet dream calls you for a date and you realize that you might actually score—it's intimidating as hell. Why aren't you nervous?"

"I was." Brenden didn't sound ashamed to admit it. "But here's the deal. *Don't ask, don't tell* was a fact of my life. Sure, lots of the guys knew and most of them didn't give two shits. I'm not going to lie to you—I've had relationships over the years, but they were nothing more than two ships passing in the night. I knew I didn't plan on staying. I had a good time and I got out. But I've had years to accept the only pants I wanted to get into in high school were yours and yours were the only ones I couldn't allow myself."

Poleaxed didn't begin to describe Liam's reaction. "I wish I'd known." Years of repeating the mantra that it didn't matter seemed to crash in on him. But he didn't feel angry...just sad.

"I'm sorry, man. You know what it was like. I—"

"No." Liam tapped his fingers against the table, the hard knot of anxiety cramping his gut relaxed. "Don't be. You're right. I do know. You didn't lead me on and you weren't a douche. I wish I knew so I could have been a real friend instead of the dick you had to rescue because it couldn't have been easy." He thought he couldn't respect the Marine any more.

He was wrong.

"So we're good?" Brenden tested.

"Oh, honey, we're better than good. In fact, tell me, sailor—do you come here often?"

"Marine, sweetheart. Learn it. Live it. Love it."

The low growl in his voice sent a shiver down Liam's spine and he laughed. "You know, I think I just might."

Chapter Three

*B*renden skipped a fourth beer. Three gave him enough of a buzz and the food helped. They ordered coffee when the waitress came to clear their plates. Music played, couples danced, laughter rose and fell in gentle swells from the diners around them, the sedate atmosphere adding to their comfort level.

The tension thawed between them and Liam grew more animated over the burgers. "I can't believe I let you talk me into a heart attack for dinner." The man dipped a salt-and-pepper-loaded fry into the ketchup.

"Hey, you're the one who added all the salt." Brenden doctored his coffee with a couple of creamers. "Besides, one of the few things I really miss when I'm not stateside is a damn good burger."

"Out of curiosity, if you're on leave, why are you in Texas and not home seeing your folks?"

"They went on a cruise." He grinned.

"Are you serious?" Liam's brows rose, amusement tilting the corners of his mouth. Brenden's father was a work-a-holic and it took a lot of work to get him to agree to the vacation.

"Yup. Mom twisted his arm. Kaleigh and I gave them tickets for their thirty-ninth anniversary. So, I took advantage of the leave to come see some friends here—members of my unit—before I rolled over to another." The coffee added a pleasant heat burning inside. Good food, good company, good coffee. He couldn't ask for more.

"So, you ready to get out of here?" Relaxed, Liam grew far more flirtatious than stressed out and wary. More like the guy he remembered.

"Sure. Did you check in at your hotel yet?" Brenden pulled out a credit card and held it up for the waitress. Liam reached for his but he waved him off. "My treat."

"Okay. I'll get breakfast."

The teasing reply tripped a ripple through the Marine's nervous system. They were really going to do this. He half expected second thoughts to assault him, but his internal security system didn't sound any alarms. Check paid, waitress tipped, and Liam's coat gathered, they walked back out into the crisp Dallas winter evening. After the warmth inside, he welcomed the cooler air washing over him. "Want to walk to the car?"

"I parked mine with the valet." Liam's words held the smallest of hesitations, but they were still there. *If they drove separately would they end the evening before it started? Did he want to drive alone? Is this a good time to call it an evening— before either of them were disappointed?* The unspoken questions hung in the air.

"Get your keys. We'll pick it up on the way to breakfast in the morning." Brenden wanted to answer all those questions and halt their trip down doubt alley before they veered off the path.

After settling with the valet, they had him bring up Liam's overnight bag. The walk to the truck was a short one. Around the corner and, just like that, they were alone. They didn't say anything, walking in a companionable enough silence, but Brenden could almost feel Liam twitching.

When they arrived at the truck, Brenden took the bag and tossed it into the bed.

Liam dragged a hand through his hair. "Would you mind if I

grabbed a smoke before we headed out?"

"Actually, one thing's been bothering me since I got here." Brenden stared at him.

"Look, smoking's a bad habit and all of that...."

Brenden pivoted and caught his old friend up against the door of the truck. His body stretched long and hard against him, taut with coiled energy inside. *Coiled and ready to strike.* Liam's eyes widened.

"I've wanted to do this for years." He exhaled the words, pressed forward, and kissed him. Liam's lips were hot and smooth. Brenden sank into the kiss, using his teeth in gentle nips to get the man's mouth to open and teased him with gentle thrusts of his tongue. He held him captive, but one real sense of rejection and he would let him go.

Liam's passivity came to an abrupt end. He slid his arms around Brenden and gripped him just above his ass, and he returned the ferocious kiss, tangling their tongues together. Their closeness in height aligned their hips and Brenden's cock swelled at the contact.

Holy hell...I'm finally kissing him.... He hadn't been kidding when he said he wanted to do it all night long. But they were still getting reacquainted; overcoming preconceptions. Liam bit down on his lower lip and ground their pelvises together in a slow, almost languorous motion, and Brenden's train of thought derailed right into the ocean.

With more than a little reluctance, he let go of his mouth and kissed his jaw.

Liam tipped his head back to suck in a noisy breath of air, and Brenden pressed his lips over the pulse point. He drew on the skin carefully, sucking it. Liam's dug his fingers in and he let out a low, "Fuck...."

Laughing, Brenden leaned back. "Right here?"

"Ten years ago that answer would have been hell yeah. Right here." His eyelids were half lowered. "But I'm an old man and I like a comfortable bed."

"Old." Brenden gave him another hard kiss, thrilled with the simple act of doing it. "Hardly."

"Some of us don't run up mountains every day for the sheer sport of it, and everyone over thirty is one foot away from the grave," Liam deadpanned and cupped Brenden's ass. "Not that I'm complaining about the running. This is solid steel."

"If you like that, wait till you see what else I have for you." The line fell off his lips easily and tempted Liam, just the way he knew it would. Liam slipped a hand between them and rubbed the bulge in Brenden's jeans.

"Look at the time. We need to go."

"I thought you wanted to smoke?" He teased, leaning into the touch even as it forced the tension coiling in his muscles to tighten. If his dick got much harder, the zipper would leave an imprint on it.

"I think I just quit." Liam nodded solemnly.

Though reluctant, they let go of each other and Liam circled around to get in the passenger side. Brenden took a moment to adjust himself before climbing into the driver's seat.

"I know why we never did this in high school," Liam declared as Brenden backed the truck out.

"Oh?" Amusement rolled under the word as he straightened the vehicle and headed for the parking lot exit. Liam's hot gaze on him felt like a physical caress and forced his hands to stay on the steering wheel and his attention on the road.

"Oh, yeah. We'd never have made it to a hotel."

"Keep looking at me like that and we won't now...."

08

Liam enjoyed the ride to the hotel, tormenting Brenden. He probably shouldn't have taken so much glee at sliding his hand along his thigh or the fact that twice he had to swerve back into his own lane. *But making the man growl?*

Yeah, that got his motor running. Brenden all but dumped him at the front drive to get their room while he took care of parking the truck. When he suggested they get a valet, Brenden shook his head. "Borrowed truck. I park it. I take it back. It goes home in the same shape I took it in."

Marines were weird. *Adorable. But weird.* It took all of five minutes to get the room card and by the time Brenden strode into the lobby, he waited by the elevator. It gave him the perfect view to admire the man's stride. He moved with the grace of a large animal, but the determination of a man confident in his own skin.

The kind of guy who will break my heart if I'm not careful.... But Liam had no intention of being careful. Maybe they only got this one night and he planned to make the most of it.

He knew the moment Brenden's gaze landed on him. His mouth spread into that delicious, heart-pounding, know-something-you-don't smile.

Yeah. *Fuck careful.*

Liam hit the elevator button and it opened with a ding just as Brenden arrived, as though it knew to be prompt. They rode up in silence, but every time Liam cut a look toward him, the Marine watched him with that same smile.

"Dude, you're freaking me out." He laughed as the doors opened and they strode out side by side.

"Just happy." Brenden carried the overnight bag along with a lighter backpack Liam hadn't noticed before.

"Yeah?" Their room was at the end of the hall. He'd upgraded to a nice suite—king size bed, Jacuzzi tub, private balcony—the works. He made enough money to splurge on luxury and spoil his man—that thought gave him pause. *He's not my anything...not yet.*

He closed the door and Brenden's arms came around him from behind, pulling him against his chest.

"You're doing it again." The low words murmured against his ear sent a shiver of awareness racing down his spine.

"Doing what?"

"Thinking. We don't have to do anything tonight." Brenden exhaled the words, not quite managing to mask the note of disappointment the offer must have prompted.

"Oh yes we do...and I'm allowed to think. It's part of my process."

"Yeah? How many steps ahead are we?" Brenden's hands slid up and down his chest, rubbing small circles from Liam's pectorals to his hips.

The teasing left his own cock aching, but the delicious sensations kept him from bitching about it. "Questions—how many times? How many positions? How experienced? What do you want to touch? And I'm betting my soul you're a top." His voice lowered, husky with need. "How much conversation do we need before I find out?"

Brenden chuckled against his ear and caught Liam's earlobe in a kiss that was both sweet and intensely erotic. His erection pressed against Liam's ass, their clothes doing nothing to disguise the Marine's arousal. "Do you want me to tell you or show you?"

Oh, God.... His heart double-timed it. *What did he want?* He liked being in control, romancing his partners, soothing them, seducing them—but when he passed a hand over the front of Liam's dress pants and stroked his dick through the material, his brain clicked off. "Show." And that order held no trace of hesitation.

Brenden pushed Liam against the wall, gently, but without any room for argument. "Hands on the wall." He murmured the order, delivered it with his tongue, tracing the whorls in Liam's ear.

Yeah. He's a top. Deep inside, Liam sighed—relaxing to the command and pressing his hands to the wall. It was a vulnerable position for someone used to being in control, but not with Brenden. He'd always held the power in their relationship.

He liked that Brenden knew what he wanted. Liked even more that he wasn't shy about telling him, and adrenaline thrilled through him. Brenden reached around to unbutton his pants, tugging the zipper open with aggravating slowness. Liam wanted to shake his hips, but Brenden shoved his hands into the pants and slid them down, dropping to his knees behind him and taking the pants to the ground. He loosened the ties on his shoes and they came off, with the pants following.

"I would never have picked you for commando." Brenden hummed in appreciation before kissing the back of one thigh and then the other.

Liam gritted his teeth. It was like being tortured by a feather. Brenden rubbed his palms over his ass and teased a finger down between the cheeks, spreading them.

"You're killing me." He rethought his position at the wall—he wanted to watch Brenden. *Did they have a mirror?*

"You said to *show* you what I wanted." The words didn't prepare Liam for the feel of his lips against his rim, the soft touch and the caress driving him crazy or the delicious sensation of his tongue against the hard ridge of clenched muscles. Brenden's hand slid up the inside of his thigh and stroked the soft skin behind his balls. Between the mouth on his pucker and the fingers stroking his nuts, Liam's legs locked up.

Holy crap. Brenden Fitzpatrick touched him—

He shook in anticipation, unable to contain the crash when the other man moved away. He started to turn, but Brenden pointed a finger at him. "Stay."

He rifled through the bags a moment and then returned. Liam couldn't bring himself to disobey again and glance over—the need for obedience adding to the delicious sense of abandon and rightness in the moment. It took only a moment before his partner came back. He brushed a kiss to the back of Liam's neck, palmed his ass and rubbed a cheek. "Good man."

He wanted to preen under the attention.

"Now, you tell me if this is too much." Brenden stroked two fingers against his anus. He'd slicked them with some kind of lubricant. The vibration of excitement shivered through Liam again.

"I'm good. Fuck that...." He exhaled the last words in a rush as Brenden stroked the hard ring of muscles, easing his finger inside. Brenden paused at the gasp, but Liam shook his head.

"No—keep going—better than good." He couldn't seem to catch his breath. It was intense, intimate and so gentle that he could barely control his own reactions. His cock stiffened out like a flag, and his balls ached.

What the hell would he do if Brenden shoved his dick into him?

A low laugh wheezed out when Brenden worked a second finger past the rim and Liam leaned back, bending into the touch. They so should have gotten naked first...the world narrowed down to the strokes and insistent stretching. Brenden added gentle caresses from his hip to his balls, and back up along his spine, sending electricity surging out to every nerve.

"I'm going to come if you don't hurry the fuck up...." Liam warned. He hadn't been so ready to explode just from someone fingering his ass since before college. He was a man who liked to play, but Brenden had him wound up.

The Marine kissed the back of his neck and maneuvered his free hand around to stroke Liam's hard cock, starting at the base and gliding up to the tip.

"Oh, shit." Liam's balls drew up tight and with his second stroke, Brenden added a third finger, stretching him full. Between the hand stroking him and the fingers pushing inside him, Liam's eyes crossed. "I want us to come together...." He could hardly make his tongue cooperate to form the words. "Suit up."

With another chuckle against his throat, Brenden pulled his hands away. Liam leaned on the wall for support, every limb trembling. The sound of a zipper skated over his senses followed by the tear of foil. "I don't want to hurry."

Brenden was at his back and his cock slid between Liam's cheeks, resting there.

His heart pounded, his breathing shallow, and his body primed. He'd never been so ready for another man—and not just any man. Brenden's palm glided down the length of his cock, and pre-cum beaded along the head. He molded to Liam's hips and then pressed his cock in, shallow, teasing pumps past the ring of muscles already stretched from his fingers.

Thank God for whoever taught him that.... Some man, somewhere in the world, took the time to teach Brenden those little tricks, and Liam welcomed every single one as they turned him inside out. The sting of the initial entry gave way to the seductive burn that sent him tumbling to a good place. The warm strokes of Brenden's hand pitched him right toward orgasm. He shifted his legs, stretching to accommodate the wonderful thickness filling him and pushed back, impaled on Brenden's cock and taking him deeper.

It was Brenden's turn to let out a hard, harsh breath. Testing the man's control, Liam rocked forward, thrusting into Brenden's hand and back onto his dick. They were short pumps, the positioning awkward for Brenden, but Liam writhed in the sensation, pressure fucking him from both sides.

Somehow, they went from being at the wall to the bed and he fell against the edge of it without breaking the connection. He would lose everything shortly. "Be close...." He mouthed the words and breathed out hard.

It was already too late for Liam, his balls dragged up tight and he came in a hard, shooting jet.

Brenden's thrusts increased, the fire lighting him up—Liam swore he could almost feel his cock expand, hardening, until he came with a shout and collapsed against Liam's back. He tried to hold them both up—but damn the man was an iron weight dragging him down into a pit of pleasure and he flattened against the bed, exulting in the wicked connection between them.

His eyes drifted closed as he rode the sensations right into oblivion. He always slept right after a good orgasm, and exhaustion dragged him down too swiftly. *Best fuck ever....*

Chapter Four

*B*renden rolled over, careful to not to wake the sound asleep Liam. He brushed the man's cheek indulgently. He'd heard of guys who passed out in those few moments after orgasm— orgasm-induced narcolepsy was what the guys called it. But he'd never met one. His muscles trembled from the release, a euphoric lethargy creeping through his blood. Disposing of the condom, he washed his hands and grabbed a couple of bottles of water. He took the time to strip off the rest of his clothes before sprawling on the bed and watching his old friend sleep.

The few steps it took Brenden to carry Liam to the bed swamped him in exquisite agony. It took everything he had to hold off the orgasm. Replete exhaustion filled him. The ecstasy and agony had been worth it.

He drank the entire bottle of water and saved the second one for when the other man woke. Everything—from his tousled hair, to his smooshed face lying right cheek down against the bedspread, to the barely-there snore—tugged at Brenden's heart. So far beyond a casual lay.

And I didn't think it would be.... Somewhere inside, he'd acknowledged it would be that way when he'd asked for this specific scenario—capturing a moment he'd denied himself for so long.

"Hey." Liam's voice slurred with drowsy pleasure, sounding almost drunk.

"Hey." Brenden smiled. "Welcome back."

"If this is a dream or that was...don't wake me." Liam shifted to cross his arms and pillow his head against them.

"Not a dream...but sleep if you need it." Energy sizzled through him. Sex served as a release—he understood the physical and mental effects. God knew, he'd kept his horniness in check till they made it to the room, but touching Liam threatened every part of his self-control, shredding it like tissue paper with a grenade.

"Don't wanna." The almost petulant tone in his lover's—his *lover's*—voice sent a thrill racing up Brenden's spine. "Want this to last."

"I'm not going anywhere." Nowhere else he wanted to be. The luxury to lay there and watch him drift in and out of sleep satisfied some deeply hidden emotional need.

"But you will." Liam lifted his head, his sleepy gaze sharpening. "You're going back out there—over there—somewhere. Aren't you?"

Brenden sighed, girding for a battle—if one happened. He'd hoped they would have longer to soak in the afterglow before crossing that rough and tumble bridge. "Yeah. Like I said, I have a couple of weeks before I report for duty."

With effort, Liam pushed upward. His gaze swept Brenden from head to toe and he grinned. "Damn—"

"You like?" He wasn't above using sex to distract him, particularly when Liam wore that smile.

"You are solid." He ran his palm over Brenden's chest, down to his abdominals and dipping lower to stroke his thighs. The touch aroused, but it also soothed. "And I figured that, but—holy crap. I've only seen sculptures with this kind of definition. In fact—" All traces of tiredness fled Liam's expression. He traced his finger along the well-defined muscles and Brenden's dick twitched in response. "I saw one at an exhibit in Boston just a few weeks ago. Don't remember the artist, but...."

To Brenden's amusement, Liam slid off the bed. He moved slowly and found his pants. Then he pulled out a phone and flipped through the screens. "Check this out. " He held it out to Brenden. "I need to go clean up." He walked into the bathroom and the water turned on.

Brenden studied the picture. "I know this guy."

"Seriously?" Liam's voice drifted out from the bathroom.

"Oh yeah. He's in my old unit. He knows this artist, too." He thought the piece might be titled 'My Marine' or 'Her Marine.' The guys razzed Brody about it, but several were envious. The work provoked an emotional response though, a visceral admiration, competitiveness, and respect, much like the man.

"He's straight, right?" Liam walked back toward the bed, wiping his hands on a towel. Like Brenden, he'd stripped off the rest of his clothes.

"Yes, he's straight." More entertained than jealous at Liam's pained sigh, he winked. "All the good ones are."

"No." The response was a hell of a lot more fervent than expected. "They aren't." Liam stretched out alongside him. "I would have agreed but then some asshole rocked my world and turned it upside down by telling me he's gay."

"What a jerk." Brenden laughed.

"I agree. Holding himself aloof all those years and for good reason. Trust me, after hitting that, I think I'm spoiled."

"Liam...."

"Eh." His friend cut him off with a finger pressed to his lips. "No regrets, no apologies, no words of understanding. I am a grown man. I know you and I respect you, so if that means you're heading back out after this, I get it. I don't like it, but I get it. I won't be that flaming queer crying all over you." The barest hitch in his voice gave a lie to that statement.

Brenden slid a hand around the back of Liam's neck and pulled him in for a hard kiss. The touch of their mouths offered comfort as much as it stirred the embers of banked passion. "You're a good guy, Liam Gardiner."

"No, I'm a hell of a guy, worth ten of any you might meet.

But I'm a demanding lover and I like commitment. I like—I like knowing someone will be there when I wake up." He rested his forehead against Brenden's. "And now you're thinking, 'great, I banged the dude who cries when he says goodbye.'"

"No." Brenden massaged his neck. "I'm thinking I found my best friend again, and now he's my lover, and how the hell did I get so lucky?"

Liam exhaled a small sigh of relief. "You know, it was hard to let you go before all this. I can't promise not to be a mess this time."

"Don't make me any promises. One of the things I've learned is promises are the best of intentions, but you can't guarantee them. You can't know for certain you're coming home in one piece or several. So you make the most of what you have...." Liam silenced him with another kiss, nipping, licking, and teasing until his mouth opened and their tongues could dance.

"Okay," Liam broke the kiss and whispered.

They were nose to nose, his gaze so close it was all Brenden could see. The intimacy in that moment snuck inside and flipped open the blinds to the blazing heat he always held at bay. "Okay what?"

"Let's make the most of it...." Liam grinned. The last traces of sleep vanished from his expression. "And I have so much to explore...you just lay there and think of guns or something...." He kissed a slow trail down Brenden's stomach and his gut clenched in anticipation.

og

The unexpected dinner party invitation left Liam scrambling. A piece of him wanted to board the plane and fly the thousand miles back to Boston, to get away from the man invading his every waking thought. The rest of him didn't think he could pry himself away with a crowbar. Every day he promised he would go home and then Brenden suggested a movie, a museum, and then the dinner party.

Liam couldn't leave. He juggled his office schedule and took the vacation time he had accrued. He still handled some calls for his clients—including one while Brenden distracted the hell out of him with his mouth, but as long as Brenden wanted him there—he stayed.

He watched him interact with the retired Marines at the party—he wasn't allowed to call them 'ex-Marines,' he already made *that* mistake. But the warning growl in Brenden's voice had been totally worth it.

"Liam?" The feminine voice pulled his attention. Lauren Kincaid stood next to him. Brenden knew the best people.

"Yes, ma'am?" He smiled, trying to not let his distracted gaze wander back over to the gaggle of men laughing together and slugging each other's arms.

"Brenden mentioned that you liked Shannon Fabray's work...." Lauren's comment drew his attention back. A lovely brunette accompanied Lauren. "May I introduce you?"

Gaze flicking to the dark-haired woman, Liam turned all the way to face her and held out his hand. "Liam Gardiner, and a huge fan of your work."

"Shannon Fabray." She shook his hand, tentative and almost shy—no, not shy—wounded. An old wound, but it lurked in her gaze. "And thank you."

"I don't suppose you work on commission?" He lifted his eyebrows.

"Not typically, no, but I might be persuaded." Her smile grew. "What did you have in mind?"

"My own Marine." He rushed the thought, not taking any time to question it. He glanced over at Brenden, his heart squeezing when Brenden turned at the same moment to wink at him.

"I don't know if I can capture that rakish grin quite so well...but I would be willing to try." Shannon held out her card.

"Thank you." He tucked the card into his inner jacket pocket, his genuine pleasure tainted by the bittersweet notion that their time together wouldn't last. Honor and commitment to duty would pull Brenden away.

"And Mr. Gardiner?"

"Liam," he insisted.

"Liam. If you ever need to talk...you can call. I know how hard it is to just say goodbye and then wait to see if they come home." She gave his hand a squeeze.

"That goes for me, too." Lauren touched a hand to his shoulder.

"And me." A third woman joined them—Rebecca—if Liam remembered the name correctly. "Any of us really—though Shannon has more experience with waiting for Brody right now."

The wives and partners of the Marines grilling on the deck surrounded him and Liam grinned. "I appreciate it." It touched him, the ease with which this group included him.

The door opened to the deck and Brenden stuck his head inside and whistled. "Ladies! Your dinner is ready and don't scare off my guy."

My guy.

Liam's grin grew. He had no idea if he was cut out for this life, but he would hang onto it for as long as it lasted. "I'm not going anywhere, sweetheart." He winked and Brenden crooked a finger to him.

He walked out to join him, surprised—thrilled actually— when Brenden slung an arm around his shoulders and murmured, "You're doing it again."

"All good thoughts this time. Trust me." He laughed and leaned into him.

Yeah. He was totally hanging out for as long as it lasted.

WHISKEY TANGO FOXTROT

HEATHER LONG

&

Chapter One

The baby cried again, the pitiful sob's volume piercing the wall separating the captain's apartment from the one next door. He usually cranked up the game to block the intrusion, but the hiccupy-cough punctuating the weeping seized him. Hitting pause on the remote, Captain Joe Cooper sat forward on his sofa and listened. The bawl rose again, and he could barely make out the woman's soothing hums. Stress elongated every sound.

His new neighbors had arrived a few days before, but he barely saw the mother or her baby despite how often he heard them. He didn't know where her husband was or why they were there, but he couldn't ignore the lonely echo in the baby's cries. Not anymore. Setting the remote down, he pulled his wheelchair closer and hit the lock on the wheel brakes. Muscles straining in his arms, he lifted himself off the sofa and slid onto the chair. Six weeks after graduating from the electric to the manual and he was a damn expert in maneuvering into and out of his wheeled shackles. The sparse apartment didn't offer much in the way of a challenge, but he didn't complain. The automated chair limited his physical movements and encouraged his back to heal.

His back twinged but the brace holding him together kept his spine straight. The heavy cast made it harder to maneuver his right leg, and he lifted his thigh to fit the cast on the footrest. His legs and torso suffered from mild atrophy despite constant physical therapy. Only so much his damaged lower body could perform.

Settled, he released the brake, spun and wheeled for the door. Exiting the apartment used to be a bitch. Once outside on the concrete walk, he pulled the door closed behind him and rolled to the next door. The infant's squalls increased—and the little catch hitting in the middle of the scream got longer. His sister's kids sounded like that sometimes—usually when they were teething or gassy—but something was off in this cry. He hesitated; his neighbor might not appreciate the intrusion. On the other hand he couldn't ignore the potential need for help.

Decided, he knocked on the door.

The baby's cries continued, but the door didn't open. He glanced up at the peephole. She probably couldn't see him.

"Ma'am, I'm Captain Cooper, your neighbor. Joe Cooper. I wanted to make sure everything was okay and see if you needed anything." His mouth twisted into a faint grimace, he sounded so patronizing.

The door cracked open and a doe-eyed blonde peeked out. She braced her foot against it, but he could make out her soft silhouette and hesitant expression. Even in the low illumination of the porch light, the sadness in her eyes punched him in the gut.

Joe tipped his head and smiled gently. "Good evening."

Her gaze dropped to meet his and her eyes widened. Yes, he was in a wheelchair. The door opened wider. A big black man in a wheelchair wasn't a threat. He pushed aside his bitterness. *Stop feeling sorry for yourself, you're not a mind reader.*

"I'm—we're fine. Thank you, Captain Cooper." The milk and honey softness in her voice never rose as she rocked the baby. "She's having a hard time sleeping."

"I hear that. Anything I can do? My oldest nephew—he was a colicky thing. Spent one whole leave walking him around my mother's house." And he over-shared, but the skittishness skating across the woman's features forced the confession.

"No—it's—we'll be fine. I'm sorry she bothered you." She withdrew.

"Not a bother. Really, I know she's been having trouble sleeping...." He didn't want to end the conversation. At her swift frown, he motioned toward his apartment. "I'm home a lot and awake a lot, so I hear her when she's not feeling well."

She winced and he sighed. *Way to go, Coop. Make her feel bad because you can hear her baby.* "Not that I mind. Actually it's kind of nice, and you have a beautiful voice." *And that's not creepy at all.*

Her cheeks went rosy and she let go of the door to shift the baby. The cries softened to hiccups. "Thank you." The words cost her, but he'd pay money to slug whoever put that deer-in-headlights look in her eyes. "We're scheduled to be at the hospital tomorrow for another assessment...."

"Is she okay?" He frowned.

"She will be." Her tone lacked the conviction of her words. "The doctors seem pretty certain, and I've heard great things about the physicians at Mike's Place."

She'd heard right. Mike's Place offered a great medical and physical facility for recovering veterans and their families. He was glad the baby had an appointment there.

"They're damn good." What was wrong with her baby? Where the hell was her husband? *And why is any of this your concern?* He ignored the niggling mental voice. Exhaustion rimmed her eyes, light from her living room highlighting the deep shadows underscoring them. He hadn't seen or heard a male voice in the apartment in the week since they'd arrived.

"Thank you. I'm sorry again she bothered you. I'll take her back into the bedroom and settle her down." She started to nudge the door closed, and he put a hand on the wood.

"I'm right next door, if you need anything, Mrs...." The obvious fishing attempt for her name lacked his usual finesse.

"Melody—Melody Carter." She sighed. "I'm sorry. I'm a little muddled right now. I should have introduced myself."

"No worries at all, Mrs. Carter. And I mean it. You need anything, just knock on the wall. I'll come right over."

She gave him another tentative smile and closed him out. He turned the chair around and shook his head. *Yeah, she's really going to ask for a complete stranger to rush over and help. Still....*

He shoved the thought aside. Awareness slid over his skin. She watched him from the other side of the door. The baby had quieted while they spoke, but the back of his neck itched as though he could feel her staring at him, waiting. For what? He wasn't sure. Gripping the wheels, he rolled back toward his apartment. Plenty of time left on the game and it wasn't like he had anywhere else to be.

Standing—pain twisted in his soul—*sitting* watch didn't bother him. He would be sure to sleep in the living room. Sure, she'd knock on the wall and ask his broken ass for help.

Uh huh, and how many beers did we drink tonight? It took a bit of effort to get over the little bump into his apartment, but instead of shifting back onto the sofa, he reclaimed the remote and stayed in the wheelchair.

She might knock.

Yep.

She might.

გ

Melody leaned against the bathroom counter, eyes half-closed. She brushed her teeth slowly and thoroughly. It took every ounce of energy she possessed to keep the brush moving. Focusing on the task, she resisted the urge to slide down the wall because she desperately needed more sleep. Unfortunately, she didn't have time. Libby's next battery of tests was scheduled in an hour.

Peeling her eyes open, she glanced in the bedroom. The light was almost too much and left her tearing up. Squinting, she studied the baby and waited until she saw the slight rise and fall of her chest before letting out a relieved breath. Her daughter never slept well, but sometimes when she did, she stopped breathing.

At sixteen weeks, her failure to thrive left her nearly as tiny as when she was born. The doctors at Mike's Place seemed assured and confident they could repair her angel's broken heart. The apnea monitor helped. It set off alarms to alert her if the baby stopped breathing, but it didn't matter. She needed the reassurance only her own eyes and ears could provide.

Rinsing her mouth, Melody switched to washing her face. She would have preferred a shower, but she couldn't hear Libby over the water. Ten minutes later, she padded into the kitchen and poured a cup of the stoutest, blackest, double-brewed coffee she could stomach then fixed a bottle. She moved swiftly, allowing no more than two minutes to get back to where Libby slept. They had thirty minutes before the shuttle would arrive to pick them up. The lack of a car had bothered her when they'd first arrived, but the continued sleep deprivation made driving unwise.

Bottle ready, diaper bag packed, face washed, hair pulled back into a tight braid, and clean clothes made her feel almost human. The coffee took care of the rest. Every swallow strengthened her resolve and bolstered her against the waves of fatigue. She really couldn't remember the last time she'd gotten a decent night's sleep.

Was there a last time?

Her cell phone buzzed and she pulled it out of her pocket. The text message reminded her she had five minutes until the shuttle arrived. She blinked at her half-empty cup. Maybe she finally mastered the art of sleeping with her eyes open. Draining the coffee, she left the mug next to the bed and slid the diaper bag over her shoulder before scooping Libby up. The infant wrinkled her face but didn't open her eyes. Melody cradled her, snuggling and making sure the blanket wasn't too tight.

Leaving the apartment, she locked up and turned to find her neighbor locking his door. He caught sight of her and grinned.

The curve of his lips deepened the dimples in his cheeks and turned his pleasant face into something positively handsome.

And kind.

"Good morning." His deep baritone hummed over her senses. She appreciated the low-voiced greeting.

"Good morning." She wanted to say something more, but her brain locked up around the words. He eased his wheelchair back until nearly off the sidewalk and motioned for her to precede him. Biting her lip, she found a small smile for him. "Thank you." Her heartbeat accelerated and sweat cooled her spine. She didn't hug the wall, but couldn't help needing more distance between them.

The wheels made the faintest squeaking noise after she passed, and she glanced back to see him following her down the path toward the parking lot. Maybe she should have offered to push. He wore an olive green T-shirt and a matching pair of slacks, though they were cut up the side of the large cast encasing his right leg from mid-thigh to his toes.

He—*Joe, he said his name was Joe*—met her gaze and gave her another easy smile. His eyes crinkled at the corners and the dimple in his cheek deepened. The sidewalk widened and she eased back her hurried pace to let him catch up.

"I'm sorry. I'm not the best company this morning."

"No worries, ma'am. Little ones take a lot out of a body." The buttery softness of his voice washed over her like a soothing balm—like the night before when he knocked on her door and introduced himself. He scared the hell out of her because she liked talking to him. A total stranger and she'd enjoyed five minutes of banal conversation.

I must be tired. I have no idea what I'm feeling from one moment to the next. As if summoned by the thought, fatigue wavered through her and she stumbled. The diaper bag swung down her arm. She couldn't catch it and hold the baby at the same time. Joe stopped the bag's arc, and gave her a chance to catch her balance.

"May I?" He offered, hanging onto the linen satchel. *May he what...?* He wanted to carry it for her and she winced. It was heavy and he.... "I have plenty of room and then you don't have to worry about it taking you off balance again."

The sound logic quashed her natural objections. She shifted Libby carefully and let the strap fall off her arm. Her internal alarms sounded. Giving him the opportunity to help didn't give him some kind of power over her, but her gut tightened at the surrender of her possession.

He settled it against his lap and nodded encouragingly. "Point me to your car...."

"Oh, I don't drive. Well, I do but I'm not driving here. I'm actually only staying here for a few weeks and I'm waiting for the shuttle." She tacked the last on with a grimace. "And apparently I'm as muddleheaded for real as I feel. Sorry. Thank you. The shuttle is scheduled to pick us up here in about...." She couldn't see her watch.

"Two minutes." The captain supplied. "I'm waiting for the same shuttle." His warm brown gaze turned studious. "Are you okay?"

"I'm fine. It's for Libby...they have great specialists here. You?" She could have bitten her tongue for the question. *The man is in a wheelchair for crying out loud.*

"Time for my weekly checkup, ma'am." If he thought her an idiot, he didn't show it. They arrived at the curb where the shuttle would pick them up and waited. The sixty degree temperature offered no chill and only the slightest of breezes to stir the muggy air. Overhead, deep gray clouds hid the sun. In fact, the only real sign of winter lay in the lack of leaves on the tree and the yellow grass.

"It's odd, isn't it?" Captain Joe pulled her attention back to him.

"What is?"

"The weather." He canted his head, following her skyward gaze. "It looks like it'll storm...."

"...but it's not going to." She nodded. "It's been like this for the last couple of days. They keep warning about possible freezing temperatures." She tried to keep the scoff out of her voice.

Captain Joe didn't bother. He snorted. "Yeah, sixty is nowhere near freezing."

"No. It's not. It snowed at home today." She couldn't quite contain the wistfulness from her voice.

"It's a balmy twenty at home today for me." His sigh echoed her sentiment.

She couldn't stop herself. "Where is home?"

"Upstate New York. Been a while since I was there, but I remember the shoveling...."

"Snow angels."

"Snowball fights."

They both laughed and Libby stirred at the muted sound. Melody eased her grip and hummed until the baby's wrinkled face smoothed. "I miss it."

"Me, too. Where's home for you?"

"Philadelphia." Not that she'd spent much time there in the last six years. She moved whenever Tuck received a new assignment, always on her own, always in a new place, never quite fitting in—never daring in case anyone found out. Her brief respite of laughter died.

"Hard to be far from home." He lifted his hand as though about to pat her arm. Her heart froze in her chest and she held her breath. The captain hesitated and tapped the chair instead. She let out the breath slowly.

"Yes." Tremors shook her and it took effort to keep a calm expression. "I'm used to it, I'm afraid."

"Me, too." Of course he was. The dog tags, the Marine green, the tight cropped black hair dusting his rich brown head. The wheelchair and cast didn't disguise the Marine in the man sitting next to her. She stole a glance at his left hand. *No ring.*

Frowning at her thoughts, she stared at the parking lot, relieved—and a little disappointed—when she caught sight of the white shuttle.

"Saved by our ride." His gentle humor eased the bundle of

nerves knotting in her belly.

She still had to survive the ride to the medical center and fumbled for more words, but her tongue seemed to be stuck in neutral mode.

The van rolled up and the driver, a big man, hopped out. He gave Joe a quick handshake. She retreated back a step, keeping her distance. "Good morning, Captain Anderson, Mrs. Carter...."

She barely heard the rest of the words. Plastering a polite smile to her lips took every ounce of her energy. She waited while the driver set her bag inside and loaded Joe's wheelchair with a hoist. Only after the two men were near the back of the van did she ease inside, choosing to sit in the third row closer to Joe's wheel chair rather than the row right behind the driver.

Breathe.... Repeating the mantra helped, and thankfully Libby slept through the whole ordeal.

"He's a friendly," Joe murmured when the van door closed. The driver was still outside.

"I know." Her emotions screeched, denying the words. It didn't matter. It was a ten-minute ride to the center. She could handle it. *I survived eight years with Tuck; I can survive ten minutes with strangers.*

He's a friendly. They're both friendlies. No one is going to hit us....

Chapter Two

*J*oe clenched his hands as the shuttle stopped at one of the medical center entrances. It wasn't his exit, but Mrs. Carter seemed to freeze in place when the driver hopped out to open the door. She paled and kept looking down at the baby. While she didn't quite gnash her teeth, refusal to move was stamped all over her expression.

The van's design allowed for loading wheelchairs and securing the wheels, so patients didn't have to juggle with moving into or out of the vehicle. All the better for his broken back.

"Hey Josh," he called. "Can you come adjust the wheel? I think it's loose."

"Sure thing, Captain." The former corpsman gave Mrs. Carter a quick grin and loped to the back of the van.

Mrs. Carter didn't waste any time. As soon as Josh opened the back door, she slid over the seat and scampered out. The diaper bag banged her legs, but she double-timed it for the exit, still cradling her infant daughter in her arms.

Josh touched the wheel. "Captain, its fine."

"I know. But you made her nervous as hell." Her reaction said a lot about what was going on in her head. "If you have to give her a ride back, just open the door and keep your distance."

The corpsman looked from Joe to the medical center entrance and frowned. "I didn't do anything...."

"I don't think you have to." And he left it at that. It wasn't his business or place to explain, but he couldn't ignore the tangible fear in her eyes or posture.

"Okay." The bewildered driver double-checked the wheels and closed up. Fifteen minutes later, Joe wheeled into the cheerful little room—otherwise dubbed the seventh circle of hell with its blue chairs, donuts, coffee and uncomfortable guests—for his sixth group session since beginning rehabilitative therapy.

He still wasn't impressed.

A number of familiar men and women strolled, limped, and crutched their way through the doors. Three newcomers already occupied seats in the inner circle—two with their own mode of transportation. *Amputees.* A fist wrapped around his heart. The younger of the pair was missing both legs from the knee down, and the other boasted a prosthetic and a crutch.

"Hey, Captain." Gunnery Sergeant Jasmine Winters breezed past his chair, giving his shoulder a light squeeze as she strolled over to grab a blue chair and flip it around. She straddled it, the defensive posture one she assumed every week. Like Joe, she faced a lot of choices in her life and while most of her scars remained on the inside, the faint droop to the corner of her mouth and one eye revealed a deeper, more devastating injury.

"No Logan today?" Joe wheeled himself over to sit next to the Gunny.

"Nope. He's helping Zach out at the field. I had to make up for missing the last group session." She made a face, but the easy humor lit up her eyes. "What's your excuse?"

"Week six. Time to talk." He grimaced and pretended not to see her nod of sympathy. The doc held them to only a few hard and fast rules. The first demanded they listen to every member of group when they talked, whether they had something to offer or not. The second, they show up for their sessions or make it up if they couldn't. The third was that by week six, participation was no longer voluntary.

The last of their group walked in with the doc, a young man with an inner ear injury and a self-confidence problem. The kid needed to lighten up on himself, but the same drive to excel which made for an excellent Marine didn't always communicate to an easy recovery.

"Good morning, everyone." James Westwood followed the circle around, shaking hands, patting shoulders, and meeting each gaze with patience. "How are we today?"

"Running late," Matt McCall quipped. The younger Marine grabbed the empty chair next to the Gunny.

"Well, so am I. But we're here now, so let's dive in. Who wants to get started?"

They began the same way every week. A casual atmosphere, a sense of jittery nerves, and an awkward silence as the newcomers, regulars, and part-timers took each other's measure. Newcomers rarely said anything and today proved no exception.

Still, at week six Joe had a feeling his was the highest rank in the room, so he raised his hand.

The doc gave him an encouraging nod. "Captain Anderson."

"Joe." They were all equals there. They served, they got hurt, they came home and some would serve again—some never would.

"Thanks for kicking us off today, Joe."

A couple of the newcomers winced at the doc's choice of words, but Joe grinned. The best part about the doc was he understood loss and uncertainty, but didn't pander to it. *Kicking it off* was simply a phrase and didn't point to a lack of anything. They needed to get used to it—life sure as hell wouldn't pause for them or pull its punches.

"Hi, I'm Joe." Lame way to start, but it worked.

"Hi, Joe." The others chorused in tones varying from wary to warm. They sounded a lot like an AA meeting, but it was an icebreaker.

"I've been in this wheelchair about six weeks now, and I have another six to ten in front of me, minimum. They are trying to get my leg to heal correctly, and my spine, but no guarantees on either front. They say I might not walk again, to which I say bullshit. I'll walk. I'll run. Then I'll get my ass back to work."

"Oorah," a half dozen members of the group answered. Despite their mixed compliment of services, Marines still made up the majority of that particular groups' numbers.

"It's not easy. I'm still getting the hang of maneuvering, and there's a lot I can't do from this chair." He cleared his throat. "Every day is a new trial. Sometimes, I get really pissed that I can't be more positive about it. I get angry. I get really angry. I know we're supposed to vent that frustration, make it positive, but I can't always do that."

An image of wounded eyes drifted across his mind's eye. Fear tightened their corners, and her nostrils flared. Exhaustion draped around her like a too-large coat. He curled the fingers of his right hand into a fist. "But I discovered today that being in this chair can be a positive for someone else, and weird as it sounds, that's my good thought for today."

"Thanks, Joe." The doc nodded. "Who's next?"

And so they went around the room, to the soldier demonstrating he could walk unassisted on his new prosthetic, to the Marine who shared the challenges of recruiting while injured, to the Naval pilot who'd made it all the way to the cockpit before a panic attack hit him. Progress came in all shapes and sizes.

Unsurprisingly, the new arrivals said nothing. They only listened. Ninety minutes later, the group broke with several hurrying over to grab fresh donuts and coffee. Joe waited. The mad dash amused him—particularly when they always brought in enough for everyone.

"How you doing, Joe?" James Westwood dragged a chair over and sat next to him.

"Not bad, Doc. Not bad." He studied the newer members. Like him, one waited for the crowd to thin around the table. His jaw didn't relax and his expression never wavered from chiseled stone. "That guy will take some work."

"Everyone does."

He recognized that tone, the doc's 'we need to talk' voice. "I'm fine, Doc." Joe transferred his attention back to the psychologist. "Seriously, I'm fine."

"Upbeat is good. Focused is good. But you went from zero, to pissed off, to almost relieved in a few seconds." James tapped his hand against the side of the chair, counting off the ticks in the emotional ping-pong.

He didn't want to talk about his emotional state. "Doc, what facilities does the medical center offer for children here?" It had bugged him most of the night and again that morning. Mrs. Carter wasn't active duty, which suggested her spouse might be. She mentioned being there for her daughter, but the baby was so very tiny. In a facility where they treated war wounds, physical and emotional, could they have a pediatric wing?

"Depends. We have the clinic hours for standard checkups, triage for emergency care and a maternity ward—with exactly three patients at the moment. But that can always change." James studied him. "Why?"

He shook his head, half-thinking to wave away the question but thought better of it. He could ignore a question or refuse to answer one, but lying didn't sit well with him. Too many years of his mother's radar and sharp aim—she could ping him from ten feet away with a wooden spoon. If they gave points for accuracy, his mother would hold the world championship cup, twenty years running.

"Neighbor's baby has something wrong with it. Made me curious."

"Her or her baby?" Doc kept it casual, pausing to shake Jazz's hand as she headed out. And again with Matt and two more.

"Both." Joe answered when they were alone again. "She's a little rough around the edges." How did one fish about her husband? Pursuing another man's wife didn't sit well with him.

I'm not pursuing anything. I'm being neighborly.

"Good." James rose and motioned to the coffee and donuts. "Looks like the horde left us some. Hungry?"

"Nah, I'm good." Maybe Mrs. Carter could use some lunch. He glanced at his watch. They had a great cafeteria in the main medical building. If nothing else, he could hold the baby for her while she ate—if she went for it. "Could you do me a favor though?"

"Name it."

"Make a call and see if a Mrs. Melody Carter is still here at the med center?"

The doc didn't answer for a long moment. "I can do that. Hang out."

"Not going anywhere fast." Joe gave him a quick grin and ignored the fact that his left foot tapped almost impatiently on the wheelchair bar. If she did head home, he could pick something up—course he didn't know what she liked. Maybe they could split a pizza.

Joe. You're a fool. The woman's probably married and exhausted. Why the hell would she want pizza with you? He ignored the snide, little voice. It was nice to have something to look forward to. No reason she might not feel the same.

CB

Libby disliked doctor's appointments almost as much as her mother. The poking and prodding elicited sad little whimpers and sobs. But Melody walked with her back and forth as the physician consulted with two other doctors in white lab coats. Words like mitral valve stenosis, balloon procedure, and valve replacement floated through their conversation. If not for the pair of nurses also present, she might have lost her mind. The consultation room was large, a table for conferencing sat in one corner, a long sofa tucked against the wall and three oversized chairs filled in the intervening space. The room reminded her of a college dorm—without the smell of dirty socks and bad food.

Melody paced, because it was simply easier to keep moving. She cradled Libby as the baby dozed. She slept so much better when Melody walked.

"Mrs. Carter, would you like me to walk with her for you some? That way you could take a break?" the steel-gray-haired nurse offered. Her name was—Noel? She couldn't quite remember.

"Thank you. I'm actually kind of used to this now." And if she stopped moving, she would probably pass out. She needed to stay awake, for Libby. As if she really could sleep with the doctors in the room. The churn in her gut seemed pretty constant now.

"Mrs. Carter?" Doctor Phelps looked more like someone's grandfather than a physician with his kind-eyed, gentle manner. His younger companions failed to set her at ease.

"Yes?" Eagerness crept through her fatigue.

"We're agreed. She's ready to have the surgery now. We'd like to schedule it for later this week. We want to set up a special suite for her intensive care after the surgery."

Her stomach plummeted. *They were ready. Oh God. I'm not.* Her heart slammed almost painfully against her ribs.

"You think she's strong enough for it now?" Every other physician they'd consulted recommended waiting. Waiting, strengthening her, giving her time to grow. Unfortunately, the older she got, the more labored her heart seemed to become.

"We do," Phelps continued. The doctors flanking him nodded. "The defect is correctable. The best part is we may not have to replace the valve so much as repair the area." He walked over to the computer and pulled some images up on the screen. The diagram of the heart included labels for all the functioning parts. "Stenosis is a weakening of the heart valve muscle, but in Libby's case, it's a failure to fully develop. If we perform an intravenous catheterization, we can add small sutures, here— here—and here." He tapped the screen. "These sutures would dissolve over time and will require monitoring, but they will provide the support her valve needs and this should encourage growth, development and...."

"And maybe she won't need another surgery?" Because if she grew and her valves didn't repair, wouldn't they be right back there? *And will she be able to run and play like all other kids or will she be stuck sitting on the sidelines of life?*

"That's our hope. But this isn't a guarantee. She could need one surgery with supportive care for the rest of her life, or we could perform this procedure and she will only need checkups. Ideally—and we are agreed on this," he motioned to his fellows and they both nodded. "Without this surgery, her failure to thrive could lead to further muscle damage in the heart."

She could die. The cold reality wasn't unfamiliar, but it didn't get easier. "Okay." Her voice didn't reflect the quaking inside. "What do I need to do?"

"Exactly what you're doing. We're going to admit her Monday."

Oh, God. Three days. Cool sweat slicked her back and a chill stormed through her system.

Doctor Phelps outlined the details, but Melody barely heard him. She turned her attention to the tiny baby in her arms. She had the weekend to hold her and then they would go in to fix her sweet little heart.

"Mrs. Carter?" Noel stood next to her.

"I'm sorry. I think I faded out there."

The nurse gave her a sympathetic nod. "You did. We want to do a couple of tests—would you allow me to carry her for you? It won't take long and you can have a moment to contact your family?"

She didn't have anyone to contact. Her long marriage to Tuck had left her estranged from the friends she'd grown up with and barely speaking to her mother. As for Tuck's family— she shuddered. She couldn't reach out to them. No, not when they grieved for the son she was so glad couldn't touch her again.

"How long?" She didn't give voice to any of that, but she couldn't bear to let her little girl go.

"No more than thirty minutes, I promise." Noel smiled

encouragingly. "We're going right through there." She gestured to the door to the exam suite. "I want to run an EKG while she sleeps and update her vitals. But you can't hold her during it—"

"—because it messes up the data." They would get her heartbeat as well as Libby's. "That's fine," she lied, barely able to quiet the trembling in her hands as she let Noel take the baby. Her arms felt naked. "I'll get some coffee."

There was an urn down the hall. The best part of the facility was the location of conveniences on every level. Families could stay close to the patients.

"Sweetie." Noel tucked the blanket around Libby, holding her close, but gazing at Melody. "You need to get some sleep. We're arranging for a room right next to hers after the surgery. You can sleep there, close enough to be right on site, but you'll still have time to rest." The nurse's words were an order, not an offer.

Melody nodded, easier than arguing, then watched helplessly as they all disappeared into the other room and left her alone. She checked the diaper bag and her wallet inside. Paced the room twice and glanced toward the smoky glass blocking her from her daughter. Impatience wound through her and she forced her legs to carry her out the door. *Coffee.*

Coffee would give her something to do.

She made it three steps from the room before she realized he sat there. Joe's wheelchair parked right next to the coffee urn, and he poured a measure of cream into one of the to-go cups. For a fraction of a second, hear heart bounced.

"Hey." The word slipped out. She was happy to see him—happy and relieved. It made no sense. She didn't know the man or why he was in the chair. His close cropped hair screamed military, but that didn't mean anything. She knew that better than most.

"Hey." His quick, warm smile wrapped her up in welcome. "I'm getting some coffee. Want some?"

"Yes." She answered without thinking it through, although she had come out for coffee after all. "But I can get it."

"I don't mind." He grabbed a fresh cup, turning the chair with one arm and positioning the cup under the spigot. "Do you like sugar or cream?"

"Yes. But I really shouldn't have either."

"Then how about a little of each?"

"Okay." What the hell was she doing? She walked over and watched as he fixed her coffee, adding one packet each of the cream and sugar before stirring it up and fixing the lid to the top.

"It's pretty hot, so be careful." He held the cup out to her. She didn't know whether to take it or not. Did it suggest something to take the coffee he fixed for her? Or was it just a cup of coffee? *I am so fucked up that I am asking myself this.* Determined to shake off her fugue, she focused on the present and accepted the cup. A tickle of electricity zinged through her as their fingers brushed.

"Thank you."

"You're very welcome. I finished up early, so I thought I'd come over and hang out in case you needed someone to ride back with."

It was a peculiar, if very sweet offer.

"Why would I need someone to ride back with?" She sipped the coffee. It burned her lip, but she embraced the pain. The jolt of heat and caffeine might actually jumpstart her system.

"So you don't have to be alone with the driver." The straightforward response shocked her almost as much as the realization that he noticed her earlier discomfort. Her stomach plummeted again. But Joe didn't seem to notice. He finished fixing his own coffee. When his gaze returned to her, it was open and gentle.

"Thank you. But I can manage." *No I can't. If it's just me and Libby and that huge guy, I'll sit on the curb all day waiting for the right driver.* She'd managed to do that twice already, making some excuse that kept her out of the close vehicle with the larger, more intimidating man. Not that Joe wasn't large—in fact, she imagined he stood around six feet or more when not in the chair. Her gut twisted.

What kind of a monster was she to take comfort in the fact that he sat in a wheelchair?

"Of course you can, but you don't have to. Besides, you'd be doing me a favor." Joe sipped his coffee.

"How so?"

"Most of the drivers prefer southern teams. I'm a Giants fan. They give me sh...er, grief."

She tried to process the information. "That's football, right?"

"Yes, ma'am. You have a favorite team?"

She shook her head, an apology on the tip of her tongue. But he didn't let her utter it because his smile grew and she got lost, staring at the absolute kindness in his eyes.

"Then let me tell you all about the Giants. They're the team to watch...." He launched into a description of the team's challenges and championships. The content didn't quite reach her, but his tone did and the banal chatter eased the jagged edges of her conscience, relaxing her. She sat on the edge of the sofa closest to his wheelchair and told herself it was because she didn't want him to have to keep craning his head up to see her.

But the coil of tension permanently knotted in her stomach began to loosen. *What did he say?* "I'm sorry. I'm not really that into sports."

"No worries. I won't bore you...."

"Oh, please. I don't mind. I liked hearing you talk about them. You sound like you really enjoy it." *Please keep talking.* Something about his voice relaxed her, and she took another sip of the coffee to stifle the urge to beg.

"I do. They're playing this afternoon if you want to come by and watch or something..."

She didn't know who was more surprised when she nodded. "Okay."

"Yeah?" Surprise lit his eyes.

"Yeah. Why don't you come over? I can make food."

"Pizza."

"I'm sorry?" She blinked.

"Let's order pizza. It's perfect for a game and then you don't have to cook."

"Oh. Well—okay." She liked pizza even if she couldn't remember the last time she'd ordered any. Tuck liked his meals prepared, especially when he came home from deployment. She pushed the thoughts aside and covered with another drink of coffee. "But it's my treat."

"Fifty-fifty." Joe countered and a laugh escaped her, the sound almost scratchy, rusted from lack of use.

"Fifty-fifty," she conceded and he grinned again. *What am I doing?*

"Mrs. Carter?" Noel called from behind her and she lurched up from the sofa, nearly splashing herself with coffee. Guilt threaded through her as she spun to face the nurse. *Libby.*

"Everything is fine." Noel gave her a comforting smile. "I wanted to let you know the doctor wants to do a little more blood work, but we have enough from the earlier draw. Do you mind waiting another short bit while I run that down? She's asleep and Tiffany is with her."

The cup trembled in her hand. "Thank you."

"Now sit back down before you fall down, and eat something while you're at it." The nurse glanced past Melody to Joe and gave the man an approving look. "Can you make sure she eats, Captain? She has time and I know she won't leave. But we have bagels and danish here, too."

"Yes, ma'am."

Noel walked down the hall and Melody sat again, fighting not to lose her grip on the coffee. Joe's hand wrapped around hers on the cup and steadied it. She shouldn't let him touch her, but the warmth of his smooth palm blanketed the ice chilling her fingers. She forgot about Libby. For a few minutes, she'd forgotten why she was there. She'd listened to him talk about football.

What the hell kind of mother am I?

"Bagel or danish?"

"I'm not hungry." She needed to take her hand back, but her traitorous arm remained where it was and she leaned on the strength in his grip.

"Okay. But you can still eat and you're pretty pale. You got the coffee?"

Awareness of his regard washed over her and she nodded, easing down from the arm of the sofa onto the cushion. He gave her hand a light squeeze.

"Stay put." Setting his own cup aside, he wheeled down to the end of the table and returned in less than a minute with a plate balanced on his lap. It held two danish and a bagel with a tub of cream cheese. "Eat." He held the plate out to her and took a hold of her coffee.

She stared at the food and then at him. "I don't know if I can." The confession cost.

He tipped his head. "Sure you can. Just one bite at a time. I'll be right here."

Blowing out a breath, she picked up one of the sticky cheese pastries and took a bite. The sugar explosions in her mouth whet her appetite and she took a second one. He passed back her coffee and said nothing while she ate. Before she realized it, she finished both danish and part of the bagel. The cramping in her stomach eased and her hand stopped shaking.

"Good." Joe grinned. "More coffee?"

Her cup was empty.

She glanced down the hallway, but Noel wasn't back. Maybe one more.

"Okay. Please."

"On it." He made her a fresh one, like the first and claimed his own cup. They sat together and she drank the hot, fresh brew with a sigh.

"You must think I'm crazy."

"Nah. I know crazy. You're a mom and you're exhausted. Thanks for letting me help."

She blinked slowly. "Should I be the one thanking you?"

"No, ma'am. You can thank me for the pizza and the game later. Football can really change the world."

She couldn't help it, she laughed again. "If you say so."

"I do."

And he stayed with her until the nurse came back to say Libby was ready. She didn't focus on it too much, but she felt better.

A lot better.

Chapter Three

*I*t was another two hours before Mrs. Carter and her daughter were ready to leave the hospital. Joe stayed with them the whole time. The taut air of fragility clinging to Melody's face lightened when they talked about the most banal of subjects. She liked sports, but she didn't really pay attention to them. She preferred more intellectual activities like Sudoku and crossword puzzles. She'd graduated high school, had a few college credits, but didn't want to talk about why she hadn't finished, or her husband, or anything involving the years leading up to her daughter's birth.

Her wedding ring wasn't on her left hand, but a faint tan line told him that she'd worn one until recently and hadn't spent enough time in the sun to erase the permanent impression. Exhaustion wore at her voice, sanding down any remnants of her Philadelphia accent. Frankly, she could have been from anywhere. He wanted to press her for answers but knew without even attempting it would be a mistake. She reacted to every stranger passing by—particularly male strangers. She withdrew tightly pressing back on the sofa, often turning to focus her attention on him rather than the nurse, doctor, or occasional patient and visitor.

Abuse. Someone—most likely her husband—had created a

well of fear, and she continued to drown in it.

But no matter how battered and bent she seemed, she wasn't broken. The doctors returned to confer with her and they threw out words like laparoscopic, mitral valve stenosis, and valve repair. They showered her in medical terms—none of which sounded good—and her shoulders straightened, her chin came up and the shadows of exhaustion fled from her pretty hazel eyes. She nodded, asked questions, and mulled over their answers. When the nurse passed the baby back into her arms, she gave them a tight smile and agreed to bring Libby in Monday morning.

Surgery. Her baby needs life-saving surgery. Where the fuck is her family?

His would be everywhere. When he woke in the hospital at Bethesda, his entire family, aunts, uncles, brothers, sisters, nieces, nephews and grandparents were all in attendance. His mother stayed with him throughout the first painful days when he couldn't even sit up for fear of damaging his back further. She and his brother flew with him to Dallas, settled him into Mike's Place for rehabilitation, and left only when they'd exhausted all their sick time and vacation leave.

But his mom called damn near every day, and he texted with his siblings regularly. If he didn't check in, they called him.

So where the hell is her *family?*

Outrage and cool fury on her behalf settled in his gut, but he buried it. She needed calm—not anger. She wouldn't react well to it. Call it instinct or observation, but whoever put that fear in her eyes hadn't destroyed her—she was a survivor. However, survivors relied on fight or flight and she was most assuredly a flight risk.

"Captain?" Her soft voice intruded into the tangle of thoughts rioting in his mind and he dragged himself back to the present.

"Joe. Please, Mrs. Carter."

A swift smile lit up her face so quickly it reminded him of twinkling Christmas lights, bright and brief. "Thank you for waiting with me, Joe. We're ready to head back if you are."

"Absolutely." He eyed the diaper bag on her shoulder and held out a hand. "Would you like me to carry that for you?"

Surprise and rebellion argued for purchase in her expression, but she nodded rather than argue. Adjusting the baby, she slid the bag down and passed it over to him. "Thank you."

"My pleasure, ma'am." Settling the bag on his lap, he released the wheel brakes and led the way through the corridors to the exit. He wanted to introduce her to James. He'd bet a hundred dollars for every pastry she'd consumed earlier that he didn't know about her or he would be there providing support.

His gut jerked. If James were there, she might not need or let Joe help out. Still, the psychologist could help. Maybe he could wrangle an introduction. He planned to chew on that thought awhile.

It was warmer that afternoon than the morning. Sunshine and eighty degrees—in autumn. *Strange. Freaky southern weather.* It should be cool and crisp with a bite of chill in the air, leaves turning varying shades. What his mother called hot-mulled-spice-apple-cider weather. Not balmy-why-aren't-people-wearing-swimsuits-weather. The baby made a happy gurgling sound and he glanced sideways at mother and child. Of course, the warmer weather was better for the two of them, so he would keep his complaints to himself.

Thankfully the shuttle driver was an older man, retired Navy from the tats on his arms and had to be close to mid-sixties if not approaching his seventies. Solid white sparse hair and wrinkles in his face told of long hours in the sun. Mrs. Carter barely reacted to him, but she still sat in the last row near Joe.

He didn't mind that one bit.

Libby seemed more active on the ride home. Her eyes opened and her deep blue eyes regarded him as she gurgled and waved her fists in the air. The little one was so damn tiny. Tiny, fragile, and perfect—like her mom.

Whoa, boy. The possessive tinge to his thoughts raced far

ahead of reality. He barely knew her, but his neighborly excuse grew flimsier with every passing moment. Her husband could be deployed and the last thing he needed was to pine after another man's wife. Tension fisted in his gut, but her husband seemed the most likely candidate for putting fear in her eyes.

They were silent as she led the way up the walk. The wavering fatigue marking her steps when they'd left that morning diminished. He wasn't sure whether it was the food or just sitting at the hospital and talking to him for a couple of hours, but she didn't seem quite as exhausted.

At his door, she paused. But he motioned her to keep on going. He could follow her with the diaper bag before going to his place.

"Oh, I thought you might want to change or something before the game." Her eyebrows pulled together in a frown. "When is the game?"

He ignored the internal fist pump that she'd remembered their plans. "We still have a couple of hours. But let's get you two inside and then I can head back until we're ready to start."

"That's silly. The door is a few feet. I can carry the diaper bag." A hint of exasperation decorated her tone.

"Yes, it is, and I like to be useful. So use me." He mulled over all the possible reasons she could call on to push him away.

Her mouth opened and snapped close. Yes, he used his wheelchair to remind her that he wasn't a threat. Not his proudest moment, but worth every second for the easing of the shadows in her eyes.

"Okay. Fair enough." She held out her hand to him. "My keys are in the bag, front pocket."

Fishing them out, he passed them over and tried to ignore the sweet softness of her fingers brushing his when she took them. She unlocked the door and pushed it wide. With his first real glimpse of her apartment—it was a mirror of his own, right down to the coffee table and angle of the television. A playpen sat on the floor near the sofa, and she carried the baby over and settled her down amidst the blankets. Little arms and legs waved in the air, but the infant continued to make cooing, gurgling noises.

Her attention clearly split between him and the baby, she returned to the door to reclaim the diaper bag. "I'll order the pizza if you like, a little before the game starts."

"Sounds good. Order whatever you want. I can pretty much eat anything as long as it's not anchovies." Frankly, no one local made pizza like Bertinelli's Pizzeria at home, but he'd survive. He rolled the chair around and headed for his place.

"Joe?"

Glancing over his shoulder, he found her stepping out onto the sidewalk. *Here it comes. She's already having second thoughts.*

"Yes, Mrs. Carter?"

"Thank you." She exhaled, surprising him. "And please, you can call me Melody."

"You're welcome and I'd love to call you Melody." He liked the way her name rolled around his tongue. His body stirred and he punched the reaction down. He needed to fit her squarely in the friend category, not think about how he'd like to roll his tongue over other parts of her—*just stop.*

Her lips curved upward. It was a little smile, but it didn't seem to take nearly as much effort as her earlier attempts. "I don't think I'm very good at this." She slid a hand into the pocket of her jeans and leaned against the wall next to her door.

Turning his chair around, he studied her. She desperately needed to get some sleep. The deep bruises beneath her eyes practically cried for rest. "Good at what?"

"Small talk. Polite conversation. I don't get to practice it much. Talk to me about medical issues, feeding schedules and symptoms—I'm your woman."

"You don't have to make small talk with me." He smiled. "And if you want to talk medical stuff, we can. But I think taking it easy and cutting yourself a break is fine, too."

"I don't think I know how to do that anymore." She sighed and dragged a hand along her braid, and pulled it free. Combing her fingers through her hair, she cast a look behind her into the apartment, checking on her daughter. "And I have no idea why I'm unloading all of this on you. You probably want to go and take a break from my drama."

He nudged his chair forward and shook his head. "I have four sisters. Trust me, I know drama. You're not that bad."

The dry statement dragged another laugh out of her. She really didn't laugh enough. But at least that one didn't sound so dry and dusty from ill use. "Four? Do you have any brothers?"

"Two." He chuckled. "One older, one younger. Same with the sisters only it's two and two."

"Wow. You're the middle kid." Her eyes widened.

"Yes, ma'am. I kind of like it. Had sisters to spoil me, sisters to drive me nuts, a brother who looked out for me, and one I could do the same for. Lots less pressure that way."

He wouldn't trade his crazy ass family for anything. Not that all of his siblings were actually siblings. Two were cousins adopted into the brood when their parents died young, but his mother never met a child she would turn away from her door. She told them she planned to be swimming in grandbabies and they all had to give her at least one. His sisters were way ahead of the curve with two, two, three and one. His brothers did their damndest to keep from adding to the number.

Until now. The thought crept out of nowhere and surprised the hell out of him. Little Libby would benefit from the zaniness of a huge family surrounding her with love. And his momma loved to shower the affection on.

It wouldn't hurt Melody either.

"I wasn't." Her mouth twisted. "I mean, I wasn't the middle child. I'm the oldest."

"How many siblings?" *And where the fuck are they?*

"Two, both younger and both sisters and both—" A hint of wistfulness drifted across her face. "Both are really busy."

Keep it cool. "And since you're the oldest, they don't check on you. You check on them."

"Yep."

"Do they know you're here?" Yeah, he couldn't keep that question to himself anymore.

She shook her head. "I didn't want anyone to worry. They didn't like Tuck and—"

It was like a window slammed shut, cutting off the words and leaving her expression frozen. Tuck must be the husband or boyfriend. Joe gave her a small smile. "Siblings can be judgy, but I'm sure they would want to know what you and Libby are going through." *And be here to help you out so you don't look ready to collapse.* "Speaking of which, you should go inside and sit down."

Bobbing her head, and not quite meeting his gaze, she pushed away from the wall. "I guess. I—"

"Melody." He went for soothing, burying his irritation with her family because he didn't know the whole story. Not that he needed to know much more than a baby who required heart surgery should be surrounded by love, and her mother should have it every bit as much as that infant. "I'll go clean up and be right back over if you like. We can play some Scrabble or something." *Scrabble? Do people even play Scrabble anymore?*

"Really? I don't know if I have any, but I have cards."

"I love cards." He canted his head to her apartment. "Inside, lock the door. I'll wait right here 'til I hear it click. I'll knock the wall once when I'm on my way back over so you know it's me."

Gratitude flared in her eyes, but she turned away too quickly for him to respond to it. "I'll go ahead and order the pizza then."

He gave her a thumbs-up and waited, as promised, for the door to close. As soon as the locks tumbled into place, he wheeled around and got himself into his own apartment. A bathroom break and a phone call later, he stacked a six pack of beer onto his lap but didn't head out.

Tuck Carter, a private first class, died in Afghanistan seven months before. IED. He left a widow, Melody, and an unborn daughter. Carter's jacket had two citations for conduct unbecoming and insubordination, both kept quiet out of respect for the family.

The information sat like a stone in his belly. He paused, chewing the information over. Fishing out his cell phone, he dialed home and his mother answered on the second ring.

"Hey baby, how you doing today?"

"I'm good, Momma. But I need your advice...." If anyone would know what to do, his mother would.

Chapter Four

*R*etreating into the apartment, her step seemed curiously lighter, the buzz of exhaustion underscoring every minute of the last several months muted. It didn't make much sense, he was a complete stranger. Worse, he was probably a Marine like Tuck—no, not like Tuck.

Walking over to the playpen, she stared down at her daughter. Libby's eyes were open, her little fists punching at the air. She cooed. Heart melting, Melody knelt and brushed her finger along Libby's cheek.

"You're never going to know what your daddy was really like. I promise. He died a hero's death and that's all you need to know. I owe him that much—for you. And I want you to have pride in your father." *Even if I hate him.*

Which wasn't true either. She didn't hate Tuck. The ugly truth of the matter lay in the fact that she still loved him. No matter how many times he'd hit her or belittled her, she never stopped caring about him. It made her heartsick to feel relief over his death. Relief because he couldn't hurt her anymore...and he would never hurt their little girl.

"Okay, you seem happy." She grinned at the wiggling bundle

in the playpen. Libby latched her tiny fingers around Melody's. She stayed at the pen. It was always odd how happy Libby was after a doctor's appointment, as though she knew they were trying to fix her heart.

Satisfied to just be with her daughter, she stretched her hand over for the cordless phone. The pizza place number, along with several other local take out places, was taped to the back of the receiver. The temporary housing took every consideration to make its residents comfortable.

Pizza ordered, she settled on the sofa, one hand in the playpen and watched her baby. She drifted into a half sleep—not quite awake—content to feel her daughter's breathing and playfulness. The quiet knock on the wall followed by a tap at the door barely intruded, but she dragged herself upright and freed her finger.

Peeking through the peephole, she found Joe waiting in his chair patiently. A little flutter of nervousness beat in her chest. She liked the man, maybe too much considering the relatively short acquaintance. But she liked talking to him even more. Another adult, no ties to her former life. He didn't know Tuck, he didn't tell her he was sorry for her loss, and he didn't remind her of the grief she should feel.

Pushing aside the tumble of thoughts, she pulled the door open. "Pizza's ordered."

"Excellent." The warm honey in his voice soothed all the dry, parched places in her soul. He held up a six pack of beer. "Wasn't sure if you would be up for any, but I brought my best."

Uncertain of whether or not she should offer to help him bring the wheelchair inside, she claimed the beer and opened the door all the way. He backed up and wheeled forward, crossing the little bump of a threshold and onto the tiled entrance. He glanced around the apartment briefly, but rolled right over to the playpen.

Libby gurgled up at him and he smiled a soft greeting. "Good afternoon, little one."

Still holding the beer, Melody walked over to him. "Libby.

Her name is Libby."

"Libby. Short for Liberty or Elizabeth?" He turned his attention to her, still wearing the warm smile and she melted a little.

"Liberty. Liberty Belle Carter."

"Philadelphia."

"Guilty." Her face warmed. She dropped her gaze to her daughter. So much safer than staring at the man and the slippery, flip-flopping sensations he brought to the surface.

"I like it."

"Thank you." Oh God, could she get any more awkward? Her tongue seemed stuck to the roof of her mouth. Glancing down at the bottles, she bit her lip. "Do you want a beer?"

"I'm good. I can wait for the pizza unless you want one. In which case, I encourage it." Was he teasing her? Once upon a time she could do that, flirt with a guy without any kind of expectation or second guessing, but apparently that skill was as rusty as her ability to laugh.

"I have a feeling I'll be asleep in five minutes if I drink one. So how about we have coffee instead?"

"Coffee sounds great."

"Okay. I'll put these in the fridge." She studied her daughter, taking a quick, mental inventory of her color, her breathing, her happiness—even the way her eyes tracked their movement. Libby stared intently up at Joe, the sweet, melted chocolate smoothness of his voice captivating her just like it did her mother.

Satisfied she could take a couple of minutes, Melody retreated to the kitchen and stored the bottles in the fridge beside a dead sandwich, three takeout boxes, and fresh formula bottles stored in the door.

Pathetic. She cleaned out the coffee maker and started a fresh pot brewing. "Do you like cream or sugar?" she called. He'd made the coffee earlier, but she didn't remember what he put in it.

"Whatever you have is fine."

She grimaced. No sugar or cream in her barren kitchen, just coffee. It might be time to plan a store run or at least order in some stuff. That could all wait though. Just a couple of nights until Libby's surgery. Panic slithered up her spine.

Three days.

If it went wrong....

She clenched her hands, digging her fingernails into her palms. *Think positive. Focus on what you can fix.* Repeating the mantra four times, she waited while the coffee maker gurgled. A yawn crept up on her and her jaw popped from the force of it.

"Hey...." Joe's voice so close made her jump, and she knocked a coffee mug over. It hit the floor with a thud. Fisting her hand to her chest, she stared at him. He held up both his hands, wheelchair parked next to but not quite blocking the door to the tiny kitchen. "You okay?"

"Sorry. I'm a klutz." She half-feared disappointment curling through his expression, but the patience and kindness in his eyes never wavered.

"My fault. I forget how quiet this thing is on carpet." He tapped the wheelchair arm for emphasis. "Did we break the mug?"

Kneeling, she examined the cup. Not even a chip. "No, apparently it's a lot sturdier than I am." Was her voice as wan as she felt?

"Good. They stocked these places for military, and we don't tend to be easy on fine china."

The lightness in the joke eased some of the tension ratcheting up her spine. Tears gathered in her eyes, and she rose, swinging her attention to the coffee maker lest they begin running down her cheeks.

"And apparently clumsy wives. I guess I was lost in thought."

"I saw that. Look, Melody...I'm going to overstep the boundaries of polite company for a moment and you can tell me shut up and buzz off if you like. No harm. No foul. But I'm afraid I have to say something."

Her gut clenched. "Okay...but could we have the coffee and

pizza first? And maybe watch some of the game? I was looking forward to it." It sounded lame, particularly when she knew next to nothing about the sport. To be honest, she wanted his company, to listen to him tell her about the game.

To not be alone.

"Okay." He nodded. "If you need an ear...both of mine work real well. I can't run or walk at the moment, but I can listen."

A tear splashed down to land on the back of her hand, and she choked on a laugh. "You must think I'm crazy."

"Nah. I know crazy. I think you're beautiful. And I like you. A lot. I'd like to get to know you better, and I'd like to take certain liberties, but I'm good with a game and some pizza tonight." The bluntness of the words greatly underscored by a note of flirting took her aback.

Turning, she stared at him. "I—" What the hell was she supposed to say to that?

He grinned. "Yes?"

She fumbled the words. "I—I don't think anyone's ever said that to me."

"Ah." He nodded and a soft, encouraging smile. God, he was such a beautiful man, from the sexy curve of his lips to the dark warmth of his skin to the sharp intelligence gleaming in his eyes. "That's 'cause most men are stupid where ladies are concerned."

Her lips twitched. "And you're not stupid?"

"No, ma'am. My momma taught me a long time ago that women like honesty and they don't like games. So no games, no pretending. I like you. I want to get to know you better to see how much I do. It's just fair that you know my intentions."

Clearing her throat, she wiped away the trace of tears on her cheeks and reached for the coffee pot. "And if I don't want to pursue this any further than pizza and football?"

"Then it's my job to convince you." He sounded so confident, so easy in his masculinity—but not arrogant.

"Okay." She surprised herself. Picking up the mugs, she nodded toward the living room. "After you."

He backed the chair up and swung around with ease. It

allowed her a moment to watch him. The brace on his back gave him a stiff, rigid posture. Her gaze trailed over his shoulders. His olive-green T-shirt rippled along the muscles of his arms with each roll of the wheels. He was in terrific shape, and terrifically injured.

"Will you tell me what happened to you?" She hadn't meant to ask the question, it popped out before she could catch herself.

He angled the chair near the baby and glanced at her. "If you tell me what happened to you."

"Quid pro quo?" She put his cup on the table next to him within easy reach and circled the coffee table on her way over to the sofa. Her gaze went straight to Libby. The baby was asleep. The radiant, peaceful slumber gave Melody courage. Setting her cup down, she adjusted the blankets, pausing long enough to rest a hand against her chest. Libby's tiny heart still beat.

"What's wrong with her?" Joe's voice softened to a whisper.

"She was born with a heart defect. They thought she would outgrow it, but it's gotten worse. They need to repair one of her valves to make it stronger."

"She's a tough kid then."

"The toughest. They're doing the surgery on Monday."

He blew out a long breath. "You have someone sitting with you Monday?"

She shook her head.

"You do now."

By all rights, that shouldn't have made her feel better.

But it did.

og

He edited the recount of his injuries. She didn't need to hear about insurgents storming through the walls in an armored vehicle, the heavy fire falling on their barracks, or the three men who crashed after a fifteen hour patrol and never woke up again. He couldn't forget the cries of the wounded, the smell of charred flesh, or the pools of blood polka-dotting the ground like sick little lily pads on the pond of death, but he didn't mention it.

"They were under fire when we arrived. We punched through the enemy's line. It was pretty sloppy. We took down the insurgents and went after the wounded. And we had a lot of wounded. My unit only had one corpsman; the unit hit had two, both injured. Air support was incoming and the Brits, too, but in the field, every second a wound is open is a chance for infection and death. I ordered my corpsman to see to our men, and I did what I could."

Melody cradled the coffee mug in her hands, staring at him. "But you were injured, too."

"Yes. But I am the captain. My job is to protect my men and bring them home. My injuries weren't life threatening."

That was his story and he would stick to it. He knew the whole truth and knew his men did. She didn't need the gory details and he would walk, and by God, run again. Shock kept him from feeling most of his injuries at the time. The bullet in his back damaged the bone, but left the nerves. A one-in-a-million injury he thanked God every night hadn't left him paralyzed.

"That's amazing."

She moistened her lips and the glistening lower one tortured him. She was in no way ready for him to go for a kiss. He slammed the brakes on those thoughts and put them in his back pocket. The tight lines of worry around her eyes seemed to have eased, but the wariness hidden in her hazel depths still stared at him.

"It's the job, ma'am." The civilian population didn't understand life in the field demanded courage, fortitude, and commitment. It wasn't about being a hero, but about taking care of the guy standing next in line and letting him do the same. They paid it forward every damn day.

"I've heard that before, but I also know it's different when you're the one in the line of fire. You could have taken care of yourself first."

He smiled. She didn't know him well enough to realize the

insult so he let it slide by. "No, I couldn't. My self-respect, my honor, and my duty rely heavily on the care and keeping of the men under my command. The needs of the many do outweigh the needs of the few or one."

"You're a hero."

Shifting in the chair, he ducked his head and his face warmed. "No, ma'am. I'm a Marine."

Fortunately, his awareness of her let him see the change ripple across her expression the moment he said the words. She retreated, her cheeks paling and leaving her lips almost scarlet by contrast. Her husband had been a Marine, too.

"That—I'm sorry—that doesn't mean as much to me as it does to you." The quiet apology trembling under the fear rent his heart. "Not all Marines are heroes."

"No, ma'am. They aren't. Most are good men and women. But we have our share of bad apples—because every Marine is a person, too." Whatever happened between her and her husband had left scars in her attitude and behavior.

"My husband was a Marine."

He held his breath and covered by taking a quick swallow of the coffee. It was strong, the way he liked it.

"But he wasn't a good man." She damn near whispered the words. He did his best to erase any sense of judgment from his expression and forced himself to listen. The quaver in her voice left him with the urge to deal violence on someone—but that someone was already dead. So he couldn't fight that battle for her. "He wasn't a terrible man either, just—he—" She sighed and rose from the sofa. "I need more coffee. Would you like another cup?"

She glanced at the baby. She did that a dozen times every minute. Looked at Libby, studied her, almost assessing her. The need to check on her daughter—particularly one with a heart condition—must be automatic for her.

He drained the last bit from his cup and nodded. "I'd love one."

"Thank you." She headed for the kitchen.

He'd just turned the wheelchair when a rapid knock hit the door. She jerked and fell back two steps, her wide eyes fixed on the door, and her chest rising and falling. Panic engulfed her features and Joe's resolve hardened.

If nothing else confirmed his suspicions about Tuck Carter, his widow's reactions did.

"It's the pizza." he said, reminding her she wasn't alone. He calmly rolled the chair forward to answer the door. But with one hand on the knob, he waited for her nod. "Go ahead and take care of the coffee. I've got this."

She fled. His heart squeezed. Her fear pissed him off and left him shaken at the same time. He wanted to fix it. He pulled the door open, coordinating the movement by rolling his chair back. The pizza kid couldn't have been older than seventeen, all long limbs and scrawny features. A late bloomer.

"Two pizzas. Mushroom and sausage, and a pepperoni with extra cheese." The kid pulled them out of the warmer packet, and Joe retrieved his wallet from the inside pocket of the chair. He counted out a twenty and a ten and gave them to the kid, accepting the pizzas in exchange. They were hot, but he could balance them on the arm.

"Keep the change."

"Thanks! Have a great night." The kid didn't need any further urging and jogged up the path to his car.

With one hand on the pizzas to keep them steady, Joe eased the chair back an inch, pushed the door closed then nudged forward again to drop the locks into place.

The pizzas wobbled, but he balanced them and with a series of one-armed maneuvers, circled back into the living room. His lower back didn't appreciate the strain, but he ignored the twinge. He was close to getting the damn back brace off. His body could survive a little stress.

Melody stood in the doorway to the kitchen, her pale face giving her eyes a darker, larger appearance.

Holding up the boxes, he smiled. "Mushrooms and sausage is my favorite."

"Yeah?" The single word shook.

"'Yep." He needed to be on his feet. He wanted to wrap his arms around her and tell her nothing would hurt her again. Not without going through him first. But the wheelchair was his key to being there—she seemed to trust his incapacitated state. "Ready to eat?"

"You deserve an explanation."

"Nope, but I do deserve some pizza." He beckoned her over. "If you carry them over to the table, I can grab the paper towels."

"Oh." She pushed away to claim the pizzas from him. "I can do that and get the coffee." She hurried before he could respond, and he bit back a sigh of frustration. She lingered in the kitchen long enough to make him worry, but he forced it aside. *How long does it take to make coffee?* If she needed time, the least he could do was give it to her. She returned with two fresh mugs and the paper towels. Her gaze tracked to her daughter, but Libby had barely moved in her absence. Reclaiming her seat on the sofa, Melody avoided his gaze and studied the pizza slice in her hand.

"Melody?"

She blinked at him almost owlishly. "Yes?"

"The game starts in a few minutes if you want to pass the remote." He swallowed amusement at the baffled expression on her face. "Football game?"

Her quick grimace did manage to draw out his amusement. "I forgot we were going to do that."

"We don't have to, but since we're here, we can watch and you don't have to try and come up with conversation to fill the silence." He meant the offer to be genuine, but her expression crumpled. *Way to go asshole, you made her cry.*

"I am a complete and utter mess."

"So you said, and I disagree. You're a tough mom. You've been holding it together for your little girl and living every moment of every day for her. You've put her needs ahead of your own." The words came out sharper than he intended, but the tears leaking down her cheeks dried up. "Being tough is hard.

Being the strong one is hard. Being the one who has to look everyone in the eye, shoulder all the burdens, and stay positive is impossible. No one can do it twenty-four hours a day."

"I don't have a choice."

"Well, tonight you do. Tonight, we're going to watch football, eat pizza, drink coffee, and relax. I'll even give you a hand with Libby." He didn't take offense at the skeptical frown on her face. "I'll have you know I can change a diaper one-handed on babies bigger and a lot meaner than that."

The declaration worked. She laughed. "You know, I think I do want to watch the football game. But I still owe you...."

He held up his hand. "Nope. You tell me when you're ready and if you're never ready—well, we'll cross that bridge when we come to it. Remote, please."

"Why do you get the remote?" A brief spark of defiance flared in her eyes, and he relaxed for the first time since arriving at the apartment. She wasn't broken.

Bent, yes.

Broken, no.

"Because I am the football expert and I know what channel the game is on." He lifted his eyebrows daring her to challenge him again.

"You could just tell me the channel." The weak effort didn't diminish its existence.

"True. But then how much fun would that be?"

"I'll trade you the remote for two more slices of pizza. This is good and I hate pepperoni."

He threw his head back and laughed, long and throaty. "Deal. I happen to like pepperoni, so I'll fall on that grenade for you." They swapped pizzas and she gave him the remote.

Flipping the television on, he set the volume to low so it didn't bother the sleeping angel, and found the right station. The pre-game rundown flashed the week's stats. The Giants lost. The Jets were ahead. Cowboys didn't play 'til Sunday. They ate their pizza in silence, but it wasn't an uncomfortable one. In fact, whenever she met his gaze, her fleeting smile grew wider and fed the heat inside of him. He liked seeing the shadows fade from her eyes—maybe she didn't know anything about sports, but she relaxed.

Halfway through the first quarter, she'd fed and changed the baby and tucked her back into the pen. He couldn't really tell which of the pair was the most tired, but Melody didn't make it to the third down before she fell asleep. He nudged his chair forward and dragged a blanket over her then settled next to the playpen.

Libby looked up at him with sleepy eyes. "'S okay, kid. I got this. You and your mom sleep."

Funny enough, it was the best college game he'd ever watched. Particularly since he didn't see a single throw.

Chapter Five

She slept for hours. Somewhere between the pizza, coffee, and feeding Libby, she drifted off and woke to a late night talk sports program and Joe cradling Libby in one arm while he fed her a bottle. The alarm on her apnea monitor shrilled, jerking her out of the sleep-blurred state. She reached over and silenced the noise, but couldn't quite wrap around the sight, and a tidal wave of guilt flooded her. Sitting up abruptly, she fumbled for an apology, but the quiet smile on Joe's face arrested the words.

"Hey sorry," he murmured. "I was trying to be careful with that. She woke up about five minutes ago. You had a bottle in the diaper bag, so I changed her and gave it to her. I hope that's okay."

"It's—" *Amazing, wonderful, heart-stopping. Do guys like you really exist?* In the six months since her daughter's birth, Melody had done it all. Struggled through Libby's illness, taken care of her, visited the doctor regularly, fought the failure to thrive, and soldiered through diagnosis after diagnosis.

"Why don't you go back to sleep?" He cocked his head, glancing down at the blonde angel in his arms. "She's fine and I think she's not going to be awake much longer. Her eyes are closed."

Melody rubbed her face, trying to scrub away the sleep. "I should apologize...."

He lifted his eyebrows as though asking, *for what?*

"We were supposed to watch the game and you're—you had to sit here by yourself—and now you're feeding her...and...." She tripped over the words, a yawn splitting her jaw on the last one. Rubbing her face again, she pinched her cheek and fought to focus and wake the hell up. She needed coffee—a lot of it.

"Well, see I don't think we can agree on that." He worked the empty bottle free from Libby and set it on the coffee table before shifting her, almost rolling her onto her side. She let out an indelicate belch, but her eyes didn't open. He settled her back into the crook of his arm and tugged the blanket around her.

For the barest of seconds, she envied her daughter. Envied the safety and security nestled in Joe's very capable arms. *What would it feel like if he held me that way?*

"Melody?"

She dragged her wandering attention back to him. "What?"

"I said I don't think we can agree on that." His gentle voice held a trace of a tease in it and she couldn't contain her smile.

"Why not?"

"Because I wasn't alone, you let me hang out here and it was nice. It's nice to be needed."

The words sent a jolt through her. "Okay, maybe I'm sleep deprived...."

"No maybe about it, darling. You're exhausted." The absolute lack of judgment coupled with genuine sympathy softened the words.

"Yeah, okay. I'm definitely sleep deprived. But I'm not getting how it's nice to be needed...."

"I like being useful. I've been at Mike's Place for weeks, recovering. My family's great, but they all had to get back to their lives and their work, although they call regularly. In fact, I talked to my momma before I came over. My guys are great, too. But I'm the patient here. Folks look after me—they don't let me do the same for them." He glanced down at Libby. "And it's nice...."

"You're a natural with her." Resting her elbows on her knees, Melody stared at him. He was a natural with her, too. She barely knew him. They'd met less than two days ago, not even thirty-six full hours and yet she felt comfortable with him being in the room. Hell, more than comfortable. She liked having him there.

"She's sweet like her momma, and she's smart, too. She's sleeping." Joe studied Melody and heat warmed her cheeks.

"I can't ask you to babysit while I sleep."

"Don't have to ask. I told you, I like it. I like listening to both of you sleeping. It's peaceful. But if you're not going to sleep, why don't you go take a bath or whatever it is women like to do to pamper themselves?"

A shower. She sighed in half-forgotten longing. A shower she didn't have to rush through and could actually enjoy. She bit her lip. The intensity in his expression should have scared the hell out of her, but it fanned the flames of quiet passion—dying embers she thought extinguished a long time ago.

"Go for it. We'll be fine."

She hesitated. Did she really trust a stranger with Libby?

Joe divided his attention between her daughter, the television, and her. Curiously, the lack of staring actually made her feel better. Still....

"Maybe I should wait." Hadn't she already trusted this stranger to be in her home? Trusted him so much she went to sleep. Indecision racked her.

"Melody, I promise your daughter will be fine when you come out. I'm going to stay right here with her to make sure." He patted his chair. "Right here. Not going to move an inch away from her. Go take a shower. Spend a few minutes by yourself. Then come back and play cards with me if you won't go to sleep."

The soft encouragement nudged her and she rose. "Thank you."

"You're welcome."

She promised herself she would hurry, but she didn't. She actually let the shower warm up, brushed her teeth, and found something clean and less wrinkled to wear. Peeking back into the living room, she found Joe watching the television, still cradling Libby. He seemed so relaxed and at peace, her heart warmed up further. Tiptoeing back, she closed and locked the bathroom door. Pressing her ear to the cool wood, she listened but could hear nothing more than the television. *I can do this. The door is locked. He's out there. He's not going to do anything.* Her heart thundered, but she stripped. The faster she got into the shower, the faster she could get out. The hot spray hit her body like nirvana.

The quick shower turned into a thirty-minute spa. She luxuriated in scrubbing her hair, conditioning it, and gave in to the impulse to shave her legs—even if it meant slipping out of the shower wet to find the razors she'd bought and never opened. By the time she re-emerged from the bedroom, she felt like a whole new woman. Wearing sweatpants and an old T-shirt, she padded out barefoot. It wasn't classy, but it was comfortable.

Joe glanced at her the moment she walked out and whistled. "Nice."

Spinning on the ball of her foot, she showed off her blow-dried hair tumbling down her back, free of the earlier pony tail. She'd actually used a little product to soothe the tangles and frayed ends. She desperately needed a trim.

"You ready for me to move her yet?"

"No." He shook his head. "Crazy as it sounds—it's darn nice to hold her."

"I know, kind of like, no matter how messed up the rest of the world is, holding her makes it okay. Like that one perfect moment you can never seem to attain for yourself, you can give it to her." It made every sacrifice worth it and every bump in the road smoother. She brushed a hand over Joe's shoulder. "Thank you, Joe."

He tipped his head back. "You already said thank you."

"That was for taking care of her." The urge to press a kiss to his forehead pushed its way to the surface. "This thank you is for taking care of me—a complete stranger."

He covered her hand with his and she went still. The weight of his fingers warmed hers. "We're not strangers. We're neighbors. And when you're ready, we're going to be great friends."

She admired his confidence. The corner of her mouth quirked up. "That depends on how good a poker player you are."

"I'm sorry, what's poker?" His dark eyes gleamed with mischief and she groaned.

"We'll play for dirty diapers. Winner gets to change them all."

He snorted and gave her hand a squeeze. "How about dinners?"

"Dinners?"

"Yep. If I win, you go out to eat with me."

"And if I win?"

His teasing took on an almost devilish glint. "I'll go out to eat with you."

She ended up owing him a week's worth of meals, but even when Joe finally said good night and headed back to his apartment, her smile didn't fade.

ഈ

She hummed her way through the laundry at lunchtime. Libby sprawled in her playpen, sound asleep. After Joe left the night before, she'd relocated the baby to the crib in the bedroom and crawled into bed, settling her hand on the little one's chest before promptly drifting off into the best sleep she'd had in...well, in forever. Both the drag on her muscles and the unbearable weight always riding her shoulders relaxed.

The gentle knock on the door made her jump but not as bad as the night before. Joe said he would be by after his therapy session, and it was almost two in the afternoon. Running a hand over her hair, she checked her ponytail. She could probably have put on some makeup, but it seemed ridiculous to dress up to do laundry.

At the door, she hesitated and glanced through the peephole. Joe sat in his chair, a warm smile on his face and his head tipped up as though waiting for her to see him. She released the locks and opened it wide, but the greeting died on her lips when she saw an older woman with him. She reminded her of Angela Bassett, only a little heavier and a lot scarier.

"Melody, I'm sorry to spring this on you." He gave the woman next to him a mild look. "But this is my mother. Meredith Anderson—this is my lovely neighbor, Melody Carter." A subtext flowed beneath the words, but she couldn't quite discern whether his disapproval was for his mother or for her.

"Hello." She held out her hand and Mrs. Anderson took it in her own, giving it a firm, warm squeeze before tugging Melody forward for a quick hug. The easy affection startled her even more than the handshake or his mother's presence in the first place. She stared at him over his mother's shoulder and he mouthed 'sorry.'

"You're right, Joe, she needs feeding up." The critical statement carried no censure at all, and if anything, sounded indulgent. "My son says the two of you would like to go out to dinner—"

"Momma." Joe's voice was low, but hard. "I asked you not to...."

"I know exactly what you asked me." She held onto Melody's hands. "And I know you haven't cleaned up since the workout and the removal of your brace. Why don't you go on back with your father and shower? Melody and I are completely capable of getting to know each other."

"You got the back brace off?" Melody stirred enough to walk around Meredith and get a look at Joe. Sure enough, the stiff, white plastic around his middle was gone.

"Yes, ma'am." Joe brushed the side of her hand with his finger. A shiver of electricity skated up her arm. "The bones are knitted. I'll be in the chair a while longer thanks to the leg, but they said in about two weeks I can shift to crutches."

"That's fantastic." Her heart squeezed a little. She didn't wish him a longer spell in the chair, but...no. No buts. A kind man, he deserved to get well and make a full recovery. "Really, it's wonderful."

"Thank you. How's Libby?"

"She's good. She's been really sleepy today, but she had a lot of excitement yesterday and I think you spoiled her a little last night." Which had nothing to do with anything, but she appreciated the time and the patience he showed to both of them. "And I really don't want to intrude on your family time."

"Oh honey, you're not intruding." Meredith threaded her arm through Melody's and turned her back to the apartment, the move so smooth she was halfway inside before she realized what had happened. "In fact, I'm the one intruding. My son is going to shower and change, and then he'll be over to take you out on a proper date."

"Momma." Joe sighed. "She doesn't want to go out tonight. The baby has surgery on Monday."

"And that's exactly why the two of you can take an hour and go have a meal by yourselves and I'll watch the baby. Now. Go."

She closed the door and Melody was left alone with the force of nature.

"Um...Mrs. Anderson...."

"Meredith. My children call me Momma, and you can when you're comfortable, but for now let's settle with Meredith. Joe will be a bit. His father has orders to keep him occupied." The woman's stern features relaxed, echoing the gentleness Melody already adored in Joe's demeanor. "I wanted a chance to talk to you. Joe says you have no family here and you've got a little one. And before you get too worried, I know I'm a bit overbearing. It's a part of my charm. You'll learn to love that about me. Do you have time to sit down for some tea or coffee so we can chat?"

So far beyond the wheelhouse of her own experience, Melody nodded. "I was folding clothes, but Libby's napping." She glanced at the playpen. Despite the chatter and the new voice, Libby hadn't moved. Frowning, Melody stared until she caught the barely perceptible rise and fall of the tiny chest. The deep sleep was another symptom, but it could also be a result of the overstimulation from the day before. She could never be too careful.

Meredith watched her quietly, her kind expression sober and intent. "Yeah, you been alone too long, baby. Come sit down and let Momma make you some tea and we'll talk."

"I don't have any tea." She didn't have much of anything.

"I brought my own. Never travel without it." She bustled Melody over to the table, sat her down, then busied herself in the kitchen.

Embarrassment crept through her. The kitchen was clean, as were the dishes, but the barren cupboards and the desolate refrigerator didn't offer many prospects. Meredith didn't slow down. Putting her purse on the counter and coat on the chair, she set up two mugs with tea bags and filled the kettle.

After setting the pot on the stove, she pointed a finger at Melody. "You stay right there. I'll be back in a moment."

Without waiting for a protest, she slipped out and Melody could almost imagine her marching next door. His mother would likely give him an earful about strays and pathetic homemakers who couldn't even keep fresh milk in the house. She tried to formulate an apology, but Meredith blew back inside with a small box of sugar, a carton of milk, some bread and lunch meat. She started to stand up, but the woman gave her a firm look.

"Sit."

She sat.

"Mrs. Anderson...."

"Honey, we'll be much better friends if you just call me Meredith, and I told you, I know I'm overbearing and pushy. But you look hungry and I don't believe anyone should go hungry."

She wanted to protest, but the meat turned out to be honey-baked ham and at the first whiff, her stomach gurgled. Joe's mother grinned and prepared sandwiches. Apparently she'd stolen Joe's mayonnaise, cheese, tomatoes, and lettuce, too. The generous sandwiches smelled delicious. In a few minutes she had a plate in front of her along with a steaming cup of tea, and the milk and sugar at the ready. Taking the chair opposite Melody's, she nodded toward the food.

"I really don't know what to say, Mrs...Meredith." All good manners seemed to have failed her.

"Then eat and let me talk. I'll say my piece and when I'm done you can say, 'thank you, Meredith, but I'm okay,' and I'll leave you be."

The words filled Melody with trepidation and her stomach cramped.

"Honey, you don't need to be afraid of me. I promise. I don't bite. I just want to tell you a story, okay?"

Nodding, Melody reached for the sugar and added a single teaspoon of it along with a splash of milk to the tea and stirred it slowly. Meredith nodded with approval and doctored hers.

"My sister, God rest her soul, was a good woman. She was loyal to a fault. The kind of woman you could rely on to take anything life threw at her—even when the one doing the throwing was her husband and what he used were his fists."

Ice latched onto Melody's spine. Everything inside her went still.

Meredith took time to cut her sandwich in half and when Melody still hadn't touched her own, she reached over and cut hers in half before nudging the plate back toward her.

"She believed in her marriage, she believed in her vows, and she believed in her loyalty. So it didn't matter what her husband did or how afraid it made her, she protected him even from her own family. From me. I'd like to say I knew what was going on, but I didn't catch on for a while. She was very good at covering for him. But loud noises, they bothered her. Knocks on the door would make her jump, and God forbid she broke anything—even by accident." Meredith sighed and took a sip of her tea.

Melody knew how the woman's sister felt. The description echoed her life too closely. The fear in her gut gnawed at her spine. She dropped her gaze to the sandwich. She wanted to eat it.

But she feared throwing up.

"The problem with abuse, you see, is that it isolates the victim. It makes them think they have no one they can go to, especially when they're embarrassed by what happened and they still love their abuser. Took me a long time to reconcile with that idea, particularly when he got into a rage one night and drove my sister off the road in his car and killed both of them. The police say it was an accident, but I've never been convinced.

I took their babies in and I raised them like my own and I learned about abuse—so I could help others the way I couldn't help my sister." Meredith cleared her throat. "And when Joe called me yesterday, I knew I needed to come here to meet you. And you don't have to say anything or tell me about it. Joe says your man died, and I'm sorry for you and your little one."

Why was his mother telling her all this? The fear turned to guilt and soured in her belly. Melody's hands shook and she put the tea cup down. She pressed her lips together tightly. She wouldn't cry or scream.

"My son has a heart as big as a house, and he wants to help you. So do I."

"You don't know me." Melody finally got the words out. "He barely knows me. We met less than two days ago...."

"Don't matter, honey. Some people, they meet and know right away what they want. My Joe, he's never called me about a woman. Not ever. But he called me about you."

She didn't know how to respond to that. Frustration welled up. "I—he is wonderful and very sweet. But my focus is my little girl. She's everything and...."

"Exactly how it should be." Meredith nodded. "Which is why I think you and Joe need to go have that dinner. Joe's daddy can drive you and sit somewhere else, and I can keep the baby for a bit...."

She didn't want to go out to dinner. She didn't want to be away from Libby. "Libby has a heart condition."

"Joe said as much. So you'll pick a place to eat close by, I saw a lot of restaurants out there on the way here from the airport. I have raised my fair share of babies, so you can tell me anything special I need to watch for and I'll be vigilant as a hawk."

"I can't." Melody pushed away from the table and stood up. "Mrs. Anderson, I appreciate the offer...really I do. But I don't know you. I barely know Joe. I can't do this right now. I need to be here for Libby."

"Would you consider a compromise then?" If Melody's rejection bothered her at all, Meredith didn't show it.

The exhaustion returned all at once. She looked at his mother patiently.

"Have dinner with him next door, and I'll keep Libby here. You won't be more than a dozen steps away."

Sinking back down, she propped her chin in her hand and stared at the woman. She couldn't detect any deception or malice in her manner. She genuinely seemed to want to help.

"I'm sorry. You told me about your sister and now you want me to go eat with Joe and it all seems very rushed...I'm confused."

"Mommas need time, too. You've been alone so long, you're used to being alone. You've learned to fend for yourself—protecting the world from your fear and your pain. You bottle it and hold it close and it eats at you, like a cancer. You're not broken, you've got spine and you just stood up to me and told me what you weren't going to do. I'm glad, but I'm worried, too. I want to help, and if all I can do is sit and make a fuss of a beautiful baby so you can have a meal with my son, then I'd like to do that."

It all sounded so utterly reasonable. "You can't possibly want someone as damaged as I am for your son."

"It's not about what I want. It's what Joe wants. He likes you. See, I know my son. He sets his sights on something, he's not going to go anywhere. But he'll treat you with kid gloves, gentle as a lamb, because he wants to protect you."

"And you want to protect him?" Wariness surfaced through the tangle of guilt, fear, and frustration.

"Now don't go putting words in my mouth. If you'd been

some meek little mouse, I'd tell my son he could help you better by letting you get help elsewhere. But you're not. You're tough. I can see why he likes you. 'Course, if you don't eat that sandwich, all that chewing you up inside is going to make you sick."

Meredith sat relaxed as a queen in her chair, sipping her tea and nibbling on her own sandwich as if to show her how it was done.

"I'm a wreck." If his mother wanted bold honesty, then so be it. "I'm a fraud. I'm taking charity from people who want to help a fellow Marine's child when I'm not sorry he's dead...." She sighed. "That isn't true either because I am sorry he died. I didn't wish Tuck dead.... It's a mess. Joe and you are very kind, but I think it would be better if I finished folding my laundry, took care of my daughter, and got ready for her surgery in a couple of days."

"Like I said, you have spine and now you have people, too. So eat your sandwich and I'll help you with the laundry and I'll even make supper this evening."

"You don't have to do that—" Why was the woman offering to do that? Hadn't she said no? Melody frowned and took a bite of her sandwich.

"Of course, I do. My son is a Marine, tough and resourceful just like you. He sits in that wheelchair and doesn't complain, doesn't let on how much it bothers him, and he focuses on the task at hand. But he needs his momma and so here I am. If I'm not mistaken, he needs you, too."

He'd said something about that the night before—needing to be needed. But wasn't going out for food and letting his mother bully her into a dinner because he needed to be needed wrong?

"You've managed to completely confuse me, and now I feel bad for wanting to say no. How did you do that?'

"A mother's secret gift. You'll master it in a few years with your little one. Trust me. As for feeling bad—don't. Joe should have to work some, but I like that you aren't intimidated by me. Yes, I do." Meredith smiled. "And you feel better."

Oddly enough, she did. She took another bite. "You're sneaky," she said after swallowing.

"Thank you, dear."

Chapter Six

"I'm sorry about my mom." Joe couldn't figure out how to make it right. The last thing he'd expected when he called to ask for her advice was a drop in from both his parents. *No, I should have expected the visit, but Mom taking over and wanting the chat?*

Melody sat across from him, a hint of amusement on her face, the expression so at odds with the few he'd glimpsed, he wasn't sure what to say. "You don't have to apologize for your mother. She's very sweet—in a velvet tank kind of way." The corner of her mouth twitched and Joe laughed.

"I think that's the best description for her I've ever heard." He toasted her with his beer bottle and took a drink. The dinner was simple, but tasty. Burgers and fries from a local restaurant along with a cherry cola for her and a beer for him. They sat in his apartment, with the front door wide open to the cool breeze. Seventy degrees in October...didn't Texas know how to have an autumn?

"I like her and it's okay." She raised her Styrofoam cup and touched it to his beer bottle.

"It's a little weird," he teased. But having his parents right next door while he considered all the ways he might seduce his dinner date if she didn't have emotional hang ups, a lifesaving surgery for her daughter, and his wheelchair in his way, definitely qualified for weird.

Her gaze slid to the right and she laughed. "Yes, it is a little weird. I feel like I should walk over and check on her."

"You can you know. I don't mind." He missed the little bit, too, but he was confident his mother could handle her and they were right there.

"I know and you're amazing that you don't mind my distraction—"

"Hey, she's your baby. That's not a distraction, it's a higher calling. Don't ever apologize for thinking about her." It came out crisper than he meant it and he regretted the tone. "Sorry, I shouldn't snap."

Her expression didn't waver. "You didn't snap. You were very authoritative."

"That's called snapping." He grimaced. "And now I'm correcting you."

She propped her chin in her hand and pulled a foot up onto the chair. She looked sixteen with her blonde hair pulled back from her face. He loved the relaxed smile on her face.

"You're funny and you don't have to handle me with kid gloves. I'm not going to break."

"Who said—" *My mother*. He sighed. "Melody...."

She shook her head. "No. It's okay. I think I needed to hear what your mom had to say, and I think I have enough courage in me from sleep, food, and velvet tanks to say what I need to say now."

"Okay." He tossed the napkin onto the table and tried to sit back in his chair. He could give her space and respect her wishes.

"We just met." She licked her lips and the quick brush of her tongue distracted the hell out of him. "Realistically, we're barely acquaintances. You know almost nothing about me and I know almost nothing about you—except maybe some of the important stuff. But I'm messed up, Joe. I made some mistakes, and I've been hiding behind a lot of lies for a long time."

He didn't interrupt or say anything. Each word seemed to be a struggle to push out.

"I met Tuck in high school. We were crazy about each other—or maybe I was plain crazy about him. He wanted to join the Marines and I wanted to go to college. When he asked me to marry him, it seemed really natural, you know.

"My parents—they were furious. They wanted me to wait at least until I finished school, but I said four years of college can't change my mind. And I knew he had basic and then training and might be deployed, so us getting married didn't mean I couldn't go to school. It wasn't really any different." Mouth twisting, she laughed a humorless sound. "It's amazing the things you tell yourself when you think you know everything."

Joe allowed a slow nod. She wasn't the first girl to regret a speedy marriage or a too-young one.

"And it seemed great, you know? We got married the summer after graduation, he left for basic in July, and I didn't see him again until almost November. I went to college locally, a good school. I could have gone somewhere else, but I like Philadelphia and wanted to be close to our families. But I had tests the day he came home and I wasn't there to greet him and I'd been carrying a pretty heavy load in classes—so I was really tired and I forgot to throw a party. It seems so stupid and trivial now, but he was really disappointed and I felt bad. He only had the week and I had so many projects due. He went back to base right after the holiday was over and suggested that I move there in January and change schools." She stirred a french fry in the ketchup on her plate. "We talked all the time and he said how much he missed me and how tough it was and how much he enjoyed it. He promised we could get a little apartment near the base and be together. He still had his work and I could still go to school. So in January, as soon as the semester was over, I moved."

"I can make a lot of excuses and say I was young, but we weren't there two months when his orders came down for his assignment. He didn't tell me that the base we were at wasn't his final destination, and when I said I'd need to stay to finish at this new school, he said I couldn't because we were in base housing and they wouldn't cover it. So I had to withdraw and I can tell you what that did for my credits. It was too late in the semester to start again so I thought I'd wait for summer. Then he was deployed, and I was living in North Carolina and didn't know anybody."

Marrying a Marine could be hard on the spouse. "Didn't any of the other wives or spouses reach out to you?"

"Yeah, but I was pretty focused at first and didn't really seem to fit in. Tuck was always worried about what impression I gave and used to tell me it was better to let people think I was a little slow, rather than open my mouth and prove it."

Joe's fingers curled. *Dick.*

"His first deployment was a few weeks, well—like twelve—for training and then he was back. I was in the middle of trying to get accepted back at school. He insisted that I put it off again because he needed me. He was only home for three weeks then went on his first deployment to Afghanistan. Nine months, four days, and twenty-one hours. I managed another semester, but my grades struggled. It was weird, Tuck's emails were short and grew terser the longer he was there and when he came home...." She blew out a breath. "When he came home, I made the mistake of doing homework instead of fixing dinner one night, and he threw my books in the trash. When I tried to get them out, he yelled at me. He'd said hard things before—but not like that."

She went silent for a long time.

"He grew abusive." Not that he didn't sound abusive before, but something in the way she held herself told him that was the first time her husband had hit her. "A hand grab here—bruises on my arm—or a broken plate and I got cut—nothing really mean, but when he came home from his second deployment, he was a stranger." Her voice remained remarkably strong despite the quaver he could hear beneath the words. "I was still in school and I asked teachers to help me advance, finishing the semester early when he let me know he was coming home, because I didn't dare have any homework in the house. I thought it would be better if he didn't think he was competing for my attention."

"But it wasn't. Sweetheart, why didn't you talk to his commanding officer? Or someone on the base? We know some men come home changed—and they need help."

"I couldn't do that to him." Her eyes widened and she shook her head. "The first time he hit me, he didn't mean it. I know he didn't. He actually seemed stunned. I chipped my tooth and my nose was bleeding. He apologized and promised it would be better and it was, for a long time. But his nightmares never went away. I had to slip out of bed after he was out and sleep on the floor because he-he attacked once. And he didn't mean it...."

He wouldn't argue with her, not when she shook her head so hard.

"But when they wanted him to deploy again, I told him he should stay and see about getting help and...."

Joe sighed. He'd seen cases of it—too many. Combat was hard on everyone in the family, harder still when the Marine struggled with it.

"That time, deployment lasted eighteen months and I finished my degree. I got a job and was ready for when he came home, ready to take it on and fix it, but nothing got through to him. He only understood sex, food, and when he got upset he would just lash out. He always promised to get help, and sometimes we could go a whole week and then it would start over again." She sat up, slid her foot back to the floor, and rubbed her face. "God, I sound like some *Lifetime* movie."

"No, you sound like a strong woman determined to stay with the man she loved even when he didn't treat her well." Understanding that combat and stress damaged the man didn't make him want to beat him any less for taking it out on his wife.

"His unit was reassigned, and he didn't get a promotion he thought he was due, and when his contract came up for renewal, he signed it and volunteered to go back. The night he told me was the same night I found out I was pregnant. He was shipping out in two days—" She bit her lower lip and dropped her attention to the plate. "And for the first time I was a coward, I didn't tell him. I made sure the meal was perfect, I didn't argue or give him lip, I took his insults and I let him—we had sex—and I kissed him goodbye when he left. I was glad that he was deployed because it meant he wouldn't hit me while I was pregnant. I hoped the baby would be there by the time he came back and...."

"And everything would be different." Joe rubbed a finger to the side of his nose. The little act kept him from clenching his hands into fists—fists that would only scare her.

"Yes. I told him in an email about the baby and he was really excited. He got a chance to Skype me and for a few minutes it was like talking to my Tuck again. He was so full of plans—"

Joe knew what was coming, he'd gotten the report.

"And then he died. An IED and we didn't have a body to bury." She exhaled and lifted her gaze, staring at him as though she stared into the eyes of a firing squad. "And I was relieved."

He sat forward and held his hand out to her, resting it on the table and waited. She looked down at his outstretched fingers and back up with far more trepidation than he thought he could stand before resting her fingers on his. "It's okay."

"But it's not—he died. The man I was supposed to love, the man I defied my parents for, I gave up all these things for—he died. The father of my baby, a Marine, serving his country and I was relieved. Now I'm here and taking the charity of all these fine men and women because Tuck was a Marine, and I'm a liar and a fraud and a...."

"A survivor." Joe held her hand gently. "You're a survivor, Melody. You didn't wish him dead, and you sure as hell didn't kill him. You suffered and you are allowed to feel relief at the end of your suffering."

"But he's dead...."

"He died doing his job. Right, wrong, or indifferent, he died leading the life he chose to lead. We all know what can happen to us over there, we all know that we may come back in pieces, if it all. You married your high school sweetheart and lived in hell to stay with him. You didn't leave him, didn't walk away, didn't report him or ask for help even when you had every right to it. Do not be upset with yourself for being relieved. Hell, I'm relieved for you." *Because I don't have to kill the son of a bitch.* He could rationalize that getting the man help would have been sufficient, but a man didn't beat his wife.

Period.

"I told you, I'm a mess."

"Okay." Joe brushed his thumb along the side of her hand. Her skin was soft. "Well, as you can so readily see, I'm one-hundred percent tip top perfect."

"Well...." Her weepy smile turned up. "You kind of are."

Masculine pride bloomed in his chest, but he kept his focus on the prize. "We're all damaged, sweetheart. Some scars you can't see. I like you. I can live with messy."

"I don't know if I can."

And there was the kick in the gut. He half-expected it. "Well, like you said, we just met. And we have a lotta time to work on it."

Her laugh was a breath of fresh air in the dark conversation. "You're a bit of a velvet tank, too."

"I learned from the best. But I tell you what, I know someone I want you to meet, and I want you to seriously consider talking to him—about everything. Libby. Tuck. You. Hell, you can talk to him about me. We can put anything back together. We only have to want to." He'd heard that enough over the last few weeks, maybe he finally could believe it.

She squeezed his hand and the sensation went all the way to his heart. "After her surgery."

"Okay." He would give her all the time she needed.

Chapter Seven

*M*elody couldn't have been more prepared for Monday morning. She slept hours at a stretch. Meredith and Joe took turns sitting with her and Libby, making sure she could shower, eat meals, and watch more football—although the night before, Meredith insisted on a movie and Melody had fallen asleep on Joe's arm watching an old black and white film noir. The Marine captain and his parents took her and her daughter under their wings and as profoundly grateful as she was, she didn't want to get used to it.

What happened when Joe got better? Or if she couldn't be more than friends? Her attraction for the man overwhelmed her, and she constantly had to remind herself he was still in recovery and she should be worried about her daughter, not thinking about what his lips would feel like.

But while standing in the surgical waiting room as her daughter disappeared behind the heavy doors for a procedure that could improve the quality of her life and end it in the same breath—everything crashed in on her. She couldn't move. Her rigid muscles cramped, her chest hurt, and spots danced before her eyes. Joe's voice came from so very far away she struggled to hear it, but the spots blurred together and blackness swallowed her whole.

Sound came back first, a steady thump echoing in her ear. She opened her eyes and stared up at Joe. His cheer pushed back the dark curtains shrouding her mind.

"Hey, there you are...."

He caught her hand.

"You hyperventilated and passed out. But you're okay." A doctor appeared over his shoulder. At least she thought he was a doctor. He wore a white coat and a stethoscope.

"You're going to be fine, Mrs. Carter." The doctor echoed Joe's words. "But we'd like you to rest for a little while longer, and we want to check your blood pressure again."

Uncertain, she glanced at Joe, but he watched her steadily— not sharing his thoughts, whatever they might be. She nodded to the doctor. The pressure on her arm increased and she realized it was a blood pressure cuff. Closing her eyes, she burrowed her head against Joe's shoulder. *Wait.* Her eyes opened wider. They were in a room, Joe sat on the bed and she sat on his lap.

"Your back—" She fumbled with the mask, but he caught it and pressed it back into place.

"I'm fine. I caught you and I figured if I had to hold you for a bit we could sit here. Okay?"

He caught me.

His chair sat parked a foot or two away. The cast on Joe's right leg was barely visible in her periphery. He'd gotten out of the chair and caught her. What if she'd hurt him?

Lips pressed against her forehead. "Shh. Just breathe."

"Libby?" Her voice sounded wildly muffled.

"Still in surgery, you were only out a few minutes. But breathe, okay?"

She tried to relax and ignore the pressure on her arm, the coldness of the air filling her lungs, or the decided emptiness in her gut. She couldn't lose her little girl.

Leaving her alone with James was one of the hardest things Joe had ever done. The psychologist arrived and asked for a few minutes. He waited until Melody nodded before letting her go.

His pride forced him to limp the steps from the hospital bed before putting himself back into the wheelchair. His back ached from catching her, but he embraced the pain. James gave him a mild, reproving frown, but he ignored it. The wonder in Melody's gaze satisfied him.

Or it had, until he took up his post outside, back in the damn wheelchair again. A warm, feminine touch closed on his shoulder, and he reached up to grasp his mother's hand. He wasn't too proud to admit that her presence provided a balm to his soul.

"She's not going to stay, Momma."

"No baby, not yet. She's not ready."

It was bad enough to believe it, worse to hear it from his momma. "Did I do the right thing, calling them?"

"You did. The psychologist fellow, he'll know what to recommend. He can find her good people to help her help herself."

"I never believed in it before." A muscle twitched in his jaw, and his leg ached from his ankle to his hip, like it had been shredded with bullets all over again.

"Believed in what?" Meredith Anderson stared at him with patience and wisdom—both of which he wished he possessed right then.

"Love at first sight. Always thought it was a lot of hogwash for romance fairy tales."

"Of course you did." She brushed her fingers across his forehead, as though straightening his close-cropped hair. It was military perfect in cut, but the familiar gesture comforted him nonetheless. "You've never fallen in love before."

"Or lost the girl." He frowned.

"You haven't lost her."

"Momma, she doesn't want me...."

"Joseph Cooper Anderson, you should be concentrating on getting well. You've saved her. You braved that firefight and got her out, and now she's where folks can help her. You also gave her a lifeline to hang onto while that sweet baby gets surgery. It's time to trust her to get well while you do the same." She turned the chair around and knelt so she could gaze into his eyes. "You have good instincts, solid, honorable, upstanding instincts and you make me proud every day to call myself your momma. Now you trust those men and women who've been helping you to help her. You want her whole, yes?"

"Of course...."

"And you want to be whole yourself, yes?"

He bowed his head. "Yes, Momma."

"All right then. One step at a time. Have faith, baby. God doesn't let you find love to take it away like that."

"Yes, Momma." He'd have to trust God. Life hadn't been particularly kind of late.

The hours dragged by, but Joe stayed with her. They played more cards, ate the food his mother brought by, and drank coffee until Melody thought she might turn into a cup of it herself.

The psychologist gave her a lot of options and introduced her to another psychologist, a woman named Claire Rogan. James Westwood recommended Doctor Rogan highly—even if she was Navy. The camaraderie between the two set her at ease, but it wasn't until James left and Claire sat down to talk to her that she realized how hard she clenched her hands.

Joe covered her fists and brought her back to the present. His touch didn't bother her. Just a few days before, she'd been terrified to open her door to him. It baffled and delighted her. "Thank you."

"You're welcome." He smiled. "For what?"

"For being here. For being my friend. For knocking on the door because you heard Libby crying and for not running away when you discovered what a train wreck I am."

He chuckled and lifted her hand to his lips. The kiss he pressed to her knuckles sent a flutter through her insides. "Thanks for answering the door and letting me in. And you're not a train wreck; you're a work in progress."

"Claire told me about a program they have—for women like me." She chewed her lower lip. "Do you know the story behind the founding of Mike's Place?"

Joe shook his head. He cradled her hand in his and kept stroking her palm. "No, I don't think so."

"The man who founded it—"

"Captain Dexter." Joe's lips quirked. "I know him."

"Of course you do." She grinned. Joe probably knew everyone. He was that kind of a guy, trustworthy, honorable—gorgeous. "Anyway, he had a friend in the service and I don't remember all the details, I don't think I really absorbed it all."

"'S okay. Just tell me what you can remember." The constant petting of his fingers on her skin muddled her thoughts.

"They were in the same unit, but when Mike came home, he was suffering from PTSD, or at least they believe that was the issue. He hurt his wife, killed her and then himself." She wanted to say it never occurred to her that Tuck might have done that to her someday, but she couldn't lie—not to herself, not anymore. "Captain Dexter decided to start this facility, in part to help guys like Mike and other veterans and to help their families."

It surprised her, how accepting Claire had been.

"Sounds like Luke. The facility is relatively new, but it's gained quite the reputation. I know a lot of the men working here, or at least have a passing acquaintance with them. Good people."

The endorsement made her feel better. "They have a program for spouses like me." She didn't want to say abused. She hated the label and the connotations. "Claire said that when Libby was ready, she would recommend me into it. They'll offer counseling, relocation, and support to get back on my feet. It's also close enough to here that Libby would still have access to her physicians and...." How could that sound to him? Her going on about leaving and he would still be there?

"I think it's a great idea if that's what you want to do."

"I don't know if want is the right word." Between the fainting, the confusion, the jumping at loud noises, and the crazy flutters in her belly every time he touched her—want, need, and should got mixed up in her mind.

"Okay." He tipped his head to the side, studying her. "What's the right word?"

"I think I need to do it, for me and for Libby. I want to be a whole woman again. I never stopped fighting—even if my rebellions were little things." *Like my degree.* "But I have poured everything into getting through each day."

"I think that's great. What can I do to support you?"

Her heart melted and to her horror, tears filled her eyes. "You just did."

He cupped her cheek and she bent her forehead to his. She wanted to kiss him—but not with all the confusion swirling through her. It wasn't right. Not yet. "I want to be here for you, too. Your leg and your recovery...."

"Shh. I got this. You need to focus on you and Libby. I can take care of me." He looked like he wanted to say more.

"Is it wrong that I know I need to do this and I'm terrified to go and leave—but I'm more terrified not to?" *Am I even making sense?* She needed help to sort out the morass of guilt and pain she wallowed in, but she'd just met Joe. What if he found someone else? Someone not damaged?

But didn't he deserve that?

If only the doctors would come out and tell her everything went great. That Libby would be fine and her heart would heal normal. Then Melody could focus on her own heart.

"Whiskey tango foxtrot, Melody."

The words threw her and she leaned back to stare at him. "What?"

"Exactly. We're whiskey tango foxtrot. You need to heal, so do I. I *want* you to heal. I *want* to be there for you, too. But that's not what you need. So right now, we focus on getting Libby through this and being together. And whether it's tomorrow or next week or next month, you go with Doctor Rogan and you get the help you need. We clear up the whiskey tango foxtrot and then we take it from there."

"You're a little too perfect," she admitted with a watery laugh and he pressed a kiss to her palm.

"Only the best for my girls."

His girls. It had a nice ring to it.

"Mrs. Carter?" The doctor's voice pulled her around and she stood, clenching Joe's hand tight as she did. The surgeon walked toward her in his dark green scrubs. "She did great. Real great. We're moving her to the PICU and you can go in to see her shortly. We're not out of the woods, but we can definitely see the light."

Relief soaked into all of the cracked and splintered places in her soul.

"She's going to be okay?"

"I think so. We'll know more in the morning, but she's a fighter."

"Of course she is, she's like her momma," Joe murmured and squeezed her hand.

Chapter Eight

Six months later....

The warm April evening melted off the snow and teased a hint of green from the trees on the historical street. The cab slowed and Joe leaned forward to check the address. The Grand Hotel. *This is the place.* He read the total on the meter and slid a twenty through the payment box to the driver.

"Thanks, man. Keep the change."

"Thank you, sir."

The muscles in his right leg clenched as he slid out of the cab and stood. Even after months of therapy and recovery, he still led with his right leg and always experienced a brief moment of doubt that it would hold. His dress blues earned some attention from passersby on the street. Pulling his cover off as he stepped inside the lobby, he tucked it under his arm. He was a few minutes early, but he scanned the lobby for a familiar blonde head.

In the months since Libby's surgical success and Melody's transfer to another facility, a day hadn't passed where he didn't think about her. Melody didn't say a lot about herself that first month. Emails came first—little notes—progress reports about her daughter. He wrote her back, always happy to hear. And then she included pictures.

Libby sitting up.

Clapping her hands.

Beaming her cherubic smile at the camera.

The baby flourished.

The cast finally came off his leg and the doctor's agreed—he would regain full function in his leg. Intense rounds of physical therapy got him back on his feet. He traded her pictures of Libby pulling herself up with pictures of him doing the same thing. He hesitated at first, but he wasn't ashamed of his vulnerability.

The first standing-up picture earned him a phone call.

Her voice poured over him like liquid gold. Gone were the tiny catches and quaver under the words. Like her daughter, she thrived and began to come to terms with the choices and direction in her life. It wasn't long before their weekly phone calls turned into twice a week and sometimes three times. The emails became text messages.

The day he checked out of Mike's Place to return to active duty, he received a teddy bear dressed like a Marine in the mail. The note told him his girls were thinking of him and they sent a Bearine Honor Guard to watch over him. The bear had a place of honor in his bedroom on base.

He walked calmly through the lobby, not seeing her. The invitation to meet had surprised the hell out of him. They'd agreed to wait a few months, to heal, to stay in touch—but when she said she was in the city and wanted to see him—yeah, no way he would miss the opportunity.

"Joe?" Her voice washed over him.

Pivoting, he blew out a long breath and drank in the sight of her, barely noticing the green dress or the pair of heels—except that they gave her calves definition. What he saw were warm hazel eyes, a soft smile, and color filling her cheeks. Gone were the hollows and shadows and pinched lines holding her hostage. Her golden hair spilled over her shoulders and down her back. His body throbbed and peace flooded through him.

She's here.

One step toward her and she wrapped her arms around him. He closed the loop, half lifting her up. Her breath feathered across his neck, and the clean, fresh scent of her hair filled his nostrils. He closed his eyes and savored the feel of her in his arms. A tension he barely remembered unlocked and relaxed in his soul. The hardest thing in the world had been tucking her into that cab at Mike's Place and watching the yellow-checkered vehicle carry her and Libby away.

But to protect her, he'd needed to let her go. He pushed the empty, lonely moments away. She was there.

He leaned back. "Where's Libby?"

"Across the street—at the other hotel with your mom and dad."

His parents were there? He frowned then laughed. Of course they were.

"I hope you don't mind—I wanted the chance to see you—and let you see the new me. By ourselves." Her smile never faltered.

He brushed the hair back behind her ear, marveling at the change in her. She was still the same, beautiful woman who'd captivated him all those months ago. The air of fragility, however, was gone.

"Of course I don't mind. I can be greedy with my girls one at a time." Was she still his girl? The increasing wattage in her grin eased that concern.

She held up a key. "I wanted to invite you out to dinner—but how do you feel about room service?"

His body pulsed at the suggestion. But he wouldn't leap to any conclusions. "I could eat on a park bench with you."

Melody tossed her head back and laughed, the full, throaty sound echoing with genuine mirth. She had changed—and all for the positive. Her shell cracked wide open and revealed the beautiful woman underneath. He shifted and offered his arm. She tucked her hand in the crook of his elbow, and his chest puffed out with pride as they walked across the lobby to the elevator.

"How long are you here?" He wouldn't press for more, not yet.

Inside the elevator, she pushed a button for an upper floor. "A week right now. I have some job interviews lined up, and if they work out, I could be here longer."

He nodded, ordering his inner excitement to calm down. "Let me know if I can help. I have connections, you know."

The doors opened and they strolled out together. She motioned to the left and he turned. "You didn't even ask what kind of job I'm looking for." Her grin turned impish.

"Don't care. You'll be amazing and anyone who hires you will be damn lucky if you agree to work for them." Few things in life were so certain for him. This was definitely one. "But since you brought it up, what is your degree in?"

She giggled and slid the card key into the door. He pushed it open and held it for her and she strolled inside. God, she was so amazing. The confident, sassy sway to her hips drove most of his good intentions toward a cliff and tossed them off the edge.

Dropping the card and her purse on the dresser next to the flat screen television, she pivoted to face him. "Accounting."

"Ugh." He made a face. "Accounting?"

"Oh yeah. I'm the sexy accountant. I think numbers are hot." The playfulness took his breath away. Walking up to him, she settled a hand against his chest. "Like the number of times you held my hand—"

He heard the suggestion in the words and set his cover on the closest table before capturing her hand on his chest with his own. His heart thumped.

"Or how many times I thought about how gorgeous you were." She rolled her pink tongue across her lower lip and the last of his good intentions. "Or how often I wished I'd kissed you—"

He slanted his mouth over hers. Electricity sizzled through him, like coming home and flinging himself into a hurricane all at the same time. She wrapped her arms around his neck, and he stroked his hands down her spine. She fit him perfectly, her soft, sweet contours molding to his body.

The plan to take her out to dinner, maybe a little dancing, spoil her with presents and lavish her with attention fizzled out. Gliding his tongue along the seam of her lips, he sought and received access. Her mouth opened to him like a flower drinking in the sun. She tasted of honey, sweet tea, and lazy summer nights. A man could get drunk on the flavor of her.

When they came up for air, he panted. "That's one."

She blinked at him slowly. "What?"

"That's one kiss. I have so many others I want to try." He nuzzled her cheek, the warm skin so soft beneath his lips. She dug her fingers into his shoulders and laughed.

The seductive sound went straight to his dick, rousing a whole new collection of thoughts and wants—like stripping the dress off and kissing every inch of her sensuous body. He wanted to hear her sigh and more. He wanted to feel her come. He wanted to chase away any lingering shadows and fill them with pleasure until they were both drunk from it.

"I have a plan," she said and went to work on the buttons of his jacket. Yes, this was definitely a plan he could appreciate.

"Yeah? I like plans." He found the zipper on the back of her dress and nudged it downward.

"I'm going to find a job." She pushed his shoulders back so she could strip the jacket down his arms. He let go of her long enough to lose it and set it aside.

Her dress gaped over her shoulders and gave him a glimpse of her breasts filling out the lacy cups. His tongue stuck to the roof of his mouth. She stepped back and let the dress slide down her arms and pool at her feet. His brain short-circuited. She wore a delicate lace bra and a pair of matching boy shorts. Every inch of her was creamy smooth and sweet as sugar. "And a nice place to live. Something not too expensive, but in a nice neighborhood."

"Uh huh." He allowed the luxury of tracing a finger along the lip of her bra, just barely touching her skin. The nipple puckered beneath the fabric.

She went to work on his belt. "And I want to date—a lot."

He flicked his gaze up to her face. "I'm sorry."

"I want to date *you* a lot. I want to go out to nice dinners, to movies, dancing, social functions...."

She unbuttoned his fly and his cock tensed at the nearness of her hand. He nudged off his shoes and slid one finger under the strap of her bra. A smile curved her lips, and she pushed the pants open and down his hips. He let her go and stepped out. Their underwear was all that stood between them.

She wore confidence like lingerie—and damn she could rock it.

"So just dating?" he asked, closing the distance between them. He wanted to see her breasts.

She ran her hands up and down his chest, and he traced his fingers along her spine. She'd filled out in the intervening months. All soft curves and glowing skin.

"And other—recreational activities." A hint of shyness veiled the boldness in her eyes.

He grinned, tugging her bra away until her breasts came free. "I like recreational activities."

He wasn't sure if he should slow down, but he took his time. Touching her arms, gliding caresses over her shoulders and back, finally circling one breast. The stiff nipples beckoned him, but he listened to the inner voice urging patience.

She mirrored his touches, running her palms over his chest. Her eyes widened and she stared at him. He knew she focused on the scars from the bullet wounds or the pale skin around the line of a surgical incision. The field work hadn't been pretty.

"I'm really interested in embracing the recreational activities." She lifted her gaze to meet his and leaned into him until her breasts brushed his chest. His cock gave a little jerk and she laughed. "I know it might seem fast."

"No." He stroked his hand through her hair. "It doesn't seem like anything. It's perfect. What happens after the dating and recreational activities?" He focused on the conversation because his body was already four steps ahead and wanting her on the bed, straddling him, riding his cock until they both pitched into bliss.

She pressed a kiss to his collar bone, the tender gesture spearing through him. "Well, I thought we could take an inventory every six months or so. See where you were and I am and maybe in a year, you would propose and we would have a big wedding and in a couple of years—give Libby a baby brother or sister." Her teeth grazed along his throat, little nipping kisses that drove all the blood out of his brain and south.

Closing his hands on her ass, he tugged her closer and tortured himself with a slow grind against her. She groaned and then their mouths fused. He lifted her, his back letting out the tiniest of protests, but he ignored it. Sitting on the bed, he pulled her onto his lap until she straddled him. The fabric of her panties and his briefs kept his cock contained, but the languid roll of her rubbing along his length threatened the last shred of his control.

"So," he murmured between kisses, "find a job. Find an apartment. Date. Make love. Propose, Wedding. Baby. That's the plan?"

She let out a shaky breath and stared at him. The first trace of uncertainty filtered into her eyes. "If you—if you're okay with that."

He groaned softly. "Baby, I'm okay with anything that means I get to be with you and you're happy. I love you."

Tears sparkled in her eyes. "I love you, too. I don't know when or how—but not a moment goes by when I haven't thought about you or wanted to be here—right here—just like this. But I also wanted to be whole for you, for me, for—" She choked on the words.

He kissed the tears trickling down her cheeks. "For our little girl. I know and it's why I waited and worked on me. No more whiskey tango foxtrot."

"No. No more—just us."

"Us. I'm going to make love to you now." He cupped her breast, caressing the nipple between his thumb and forefinger.

Her mouth opened in a silent gasp, and he caught her lips in a long kiss. She surged, straining against him.

"Okay. That's skipping ahead in the plan."

Her shaky laugh deepened with a husky note and he lifted, flipping her around until she lay on the bed and he loomed over her. Hooking his fingers into her panties, he stripped them down.

The sight of the blonde curls between her thighs damn near made him come on the spot. He wondered if she understood the depth of how much he wanted her. "Then let me eat first—so we can call this a date...."

Nudging her thighs apart, he pressed a kiss to the inside of her leg, and she let out a moan that rolled over him like a physical caress.

"Joe—" she whispered.

"Yeah, baby?"

"I missed you."

"I missed you, too." He licked her sex in a gentle kiss and groaned at the sweet flavor bursting on his tongue. He teased her with soft licks, and long pulls on her clit. He wanted to be inside her, and that thought sobered him. He lifted his head, fighting for control. *Son of a bitch.*

"What's wrong?" She pushed up onto her elbows.

"I didn't think to bring—" He could do this—he could give her pleasure.

"My purse."

"What?" It was his turn to blink.

"There are condoms in my purse."

"I love you." He pressed a kiss to her clit and sucked hard until she thrashed.

"Oh my God. I know—but get the condom...."

He laughed, pushing free of the bed, then flipped open the catch on her bag. And there they were, waiting like the best prizes in the box—three condoms. He admired her faith in him. Sheathing himself, he all but fell into her waiting arms and thrust inside her.

Her kisses grew more eager and their tongues dueled. Her fingers became frantic as she pulled at his shoulders. They surged together until he forgot all the long months keeping them apart. Her orgasm triggered his and he came with a force that took his breath away.

They lay together, drowsy and replete. He cradled her. She was so pale to his darker skin, and so perfect in the complement. She'd taken his heart the night he'd knocked on her door and she opened it with such caution and trepidation. It hadn't been easy and they still had a long road to travel.

She opened her eyes and he lifted her head to look at him. The adoration in her face filled him with the most extraordinary glee. It didn't matter that it hadn't been easy.

"Would you mind if we amended the plan to six months of dating and then moving in together?" He grinned slowly. "I promise you'll still get a romantic proposal."

"I think I'm open to negotiation."

"Excellent." He caressed her hip. "It could take us several rounds to hammer out the details."

She stretched against him and kissed his jaw. "Are you up to the assignment, Marine?"

"Oh, yes, ma'am." Scorching heat licked along his flesh and his cock twitched. "I'm definitely up for it."

"You're easy." The lighthearted note in her voice made his soul sing. *She* made his soul sing. God knew their lives hadn't been about the easy moments—but she was a survivor, they both were.

"Only for you." With her by his side, he could handle anything.

**If you are being abused, you are not alone.
Call for help:**

National Domestic Violence Hotline –
1-800-799-SAFE (7233)

Military OneSource –
1-800-342-9647 (To locate a victim advocate in your area).

Defense Centers of Excellence Outreach Center –
1-866-966-1020 (Helps you find resources in your area)

Department of Defense (D.O.D) Child Abuse Safety and Abuse Hotline –
1-800-336-4592

Or visit **Real Warriors** "Domestic Resources for Military Families"

COMBAT BARBIE

HEATHER LONG

❧

Chapter One

The music playing via her earbuds kept her running apace. Mary, Stormer to her friends in the Corps, jogged through the streets, weaving in and around the businessmen on their way to the office. Some people liked to run on the beach, others preferred the park or the hiking trails. Mary liked the city streets—the thrum of traffic building up, the throb of drums and steel guitar on her iPod, and the road rising up to meet her feet. She ran steadily, her clothing soaked with sweat, but even heading uphill didn't slow her down.

It wasn't like she carried a rucksack or wore combat gear. In fact, her shorts and tank top were as close to naked in public as she'd been in months. California breezes washed over her sweat-slicked skin and a wild grin hovered around her lips. It felt good to be home. It felt better to run. The tension at home had reached unbearable levels after just three days back in Los Angeles. Her mother wanted her to opt out of her contract and go civilian while she still had her looks.

Flames of resentment burned through her. *Breathe.* Three days on leave at home and she wanted to board the first flight for Dallas, but she planned a full week with her parents.

I miss them so much when I'm away, but I forget that most

of the time, distance is what we need. I should have just gone to see Jazz. She can sex up her hot fiancés anytime she wants when I'm not around. Fiancés. Stormer snickered. Hard enough to believe that the tough gunny was getting married, even more difficult to wrap her mind around the fact she intended to marry two men.

Dropping her pace to a fast walk, she pressed two fingers to the pulse point on her neck. Four-count breaths brought her heart rate down. She paused at the corner to wait for the traffic light, and took the time to stretch. The area seemed vaguely familiar. It took a moment, but she realized her favorite coffee spot sat a block up.

The temptation of a rich, foamy pumpkin latte on the cool California winter morning verged on perfect. Pleased, she walked across the street and began a light jog toward The Orange Rind. A completely ridiculous name for a coffee shop, but since it sold fresh-squeezed juices and Slushies, she forgave them. Their coffee was unmatched.

The music track rolled over to a personal favorite and cranking the volume up, she moved at a more sedate pace by the time she reached the shop. Waiting in line patiently wasn't a hardship, not with the rich coffee scent to tease her palate and solid tunes in her ears. She fought the urge to dance in place, settling for tapping her fingers against her leg.

The line in front of her moved and a tall guy with a thatch of thick black hair brushing his neck and a rumpled appearance that cried, 'just rolled out of bed,' stepped to the side and leaned against the counter—clearly to wait for his order.

He glanced back at her and she gave him a quick, polite smile as their gazes collided. She shouldn't be staring—or judging. Just because the man wore a polo and khakis and seemed ready to walk out to the golf course at seven a.m. on a weekday didn't make him a lazy bastard or wealthy dilettante. Hell, she'd jogged in an exclusive section of the city, about to order a cup of eight-dollar coffee just for the thrill of it.

Looking him over again, she found him checking her out. He

stared at her hard, the tiniest of frowns wrinkling his brow. Lifting her eyebrows in challenge, she waited for him to look away but he didn't. Thumbing her music off, she pulled out the earbuds to ask what the hell his problem was, but the barista waited on her order.

"What can I get you ma'am?"

"Double tall pumpkin spice latte, with extra foam." She pulled a credit card out of her back pocket and slid it across the counter. Despite having received his drink, her gawker still stood at the counter when she walked around to wait.

And he still stared.

Maybe it was years in the field or maybe it was just her sour attitude after the argument with her mother the night before, but she wasn't in the mood to have some stranger undress her with his eyes.

She whistled between her teeth. "My eyes are up here."

He glanced up and amusement curved his lips. "I know. I wanted to see if you had a tattoo."

"Is that some new form of pick up line?" Damn, she must be rustier than she thought if she didn't know the latest techniques. But then, she hadn't lived in California for years, and her last trip home hadn't included any kind of dating or introductions. After attending her grandmother's funeral, she went back to base and off to deployment. She hadn't spent seventy-two hours straight in the state since she enlisted.

"No." He shook his head and laughed. The barista called out her order and slid the coffee cup over.

Claiming it, she gave him a half salute. "Have a good one." She turned to leave, but rather than accepting the brush off, he followed her and grabbed the door.

"Sorry, not trying to go stalker creepy on you, but you remind me of someone I used to know—hence wondering about the tattoo."

The unabashed flirting rolled over her and she tipped her head back. If this guy thought her an easy mark, she couldn't wait to disappoint him....

Still, the longer she spent with him the more familiar he seemed. *Definitely not a Marine.* He didn't carry himself that way and wore his hair too long. So why did it feel like she recognized him? "What kind of tattoo?"

"A purple butterfly—on her calf, just behind her right ankle—tiny, delicate thing. I used to think it was a fairy, but she corrected me. It was a butterfly." He cut himself off, perhaps realizing he'd gone to unnecessary lengths.

"I used to wear one in high school, but it was a press on. I had hundreds of them. If I'd gotten real ink, my mother would have had a coronary." *High school.* "Kyle?"

"Mary?" His eyes widened and his grin grew with delight.

"Oh my God." She opened her arms and they hugged, a quick, firm embrace. And despite her joking thoughts earlier, he was hard bodied beneath the polo and khakis. Retreating from the hug, she studied him. "It's been...."

"A decade, yeah. You look fantastic."

The affection- laden compliment buoyed her pride. "You're looking pretty good. I'm sorry I didn't recognize you."

He snorted. "I grew three inches between graduation and my freshman year at college and all my acne cleared up. I would have been shocked if you did recognize me."

Now that he mentioned it, he did seem taller than she remembered. He easily topped her five foot nine. Of all the people to run into—she'd liked Kyle in high school. He hadn't been a douche about her looks, and he never tried to feel her up or ask her out. He actually noticed she had a brain.

Glancing around the rapidly filling street, she motioned to a table. "You have time to...?"

"Hell, yes." He grabbed a chair and pulled it out for her. It was a sweet, genuine gesture. "How have you been? You moved back here?"

Setting the iPod and earbuds on the table, she said, "No, just a visit."

"Ah, the reunion." A hint of bitterness creased the words.

"Yeah, no." She shook her head. "I know it's happening this

weekend, but I'm not going. You?"

"Thought about it, but...." He shrugged. "You should go though. You had a lot of friends in high school."

"I knew a lot of people and a lot of people wanted to know me because of—" she grimaced and twirled her finger in the air. "You know, the thing."

"The beauty pageant thing? Oh yeah. I remember."

The Marine in her cringed and she swallowed back her embarrassment with a long drink of the latte. "Yeah, that thing."

Of all the people in the world to run into at The Orange Rind—Mary Phillips—deluxe senior goddess with a soul. Yes, she had won the genetic lotto, a gorgeous blend of her African-American father and Asian mother, and yes, he'd had more than a few fantasies about her through their four years together from freshman to senior years. For him, she remained the one who got away—not that he'd ever managed to cobble together the courage to ask her out.

They were in most of the same classes together, and he loved her as a lab partner. She'd never shrugged off the work to hang with her friends or get a pedicure—she actually did the work. Including the single most awesome detonation of a soda bomb their high school had ever seen. Beauty queen or not, hot bod or not, her smarts turned him on. He couldn't quite keep the grin off his face. "So what have you been up to? Didn't you enlist in the army or something?"

"Marines." Her lips twitched with amusement. "And I'm a career grunt. I work for a living and I like it. What about you?"

"Built a company, sold a company, made a few million, and now I'm bored." Which sounded terrifically lame when compared to her job. "You stationed here or overseas?"

"Overseas mostly. I'm on leave currently."

He didn't know a lot of military personnel or whether it would be rude to ask where? Or what? Scratching his jaw, he skipped the question in favor of.... "Got any plans while you're home?"

"Not really, just seeing my parents. It's been about five years and I was getting the 'notes.'" She delivered the last right down to the air quotes. Not even the Marines could take the California out of his girl.

Clearing his throat, he stuffed that thought into a dark closet in his brain and shut the door. They were having coffee, not happily ever after, and he wasn't a horny teen with a hard dick and a desperate desire to jack off to her text message about explosive equations. "You're parents can't be that bad."

And he would know that how?

Scratching his jaw again, he blew out a breath and leaned back in the chair. He needed to relax. She'd been happy to see him and he no longer worried about some dumbass pantsing him while he talked and leaving him standing there half-naked, effectively killing any chance he might have had to impress her. These days, the same dumbasses who gave him shit back in the day now called him sir and hoped he'd talk to them about a new lucrative venture.

"You'd be surprised. You forget that for my parents, image is everything and I hardly work in a glamorous enough field." She didn't sound like she minded their disapproval. "So you built a company? How do you do that?"

"You get a good idea, make it work, patent it, and then start selling it. I worked out of my mom's garage all the way through college, and made my first million before I finished my bachelor's degree." He chuckled. "I honestly hadn't even realized how much I made until Mom insisted that I hire a real accountant. She was like my secretary, slash manager, slash billing department."

Mary grinned. "And you made a million bucks?"

"Yeah. She apparently got behind in the bookkeeping that year. I was buried in classes and design and didn't notice. She took a long weekend and caught it all up and then gave me an earful about being more on top of what I was doing. We got a lawyer and an accountant the next day."

His mother was the best thing that ever happened to him.

She worked two jobs and put herself through school. She bought a house for them during junior high just to get him into a better school and the mortgage half killed her. Paying off that house was the first thing he did with his income and buying her a better one came next.

"That's—funny as hell actually." Mary laughed. "I can't imagine having a million bucks and not even realizing it."

"It's never been about the money. I like designing software and I always tried to make the next one and keep my grades up. People actually liked them and apps got popular in the last few years—that made a huge difference."

"Okay, tell me a program you wrote. Let's see if I know it." She propped her chin in her hand and stared at him, her deep black eyes like pieces of the starry sky plucked down to glimmer at him.

He considered it and took a long drink of the coffee. "VerifyIt."

"Fact-checker software—you wrote that?" *How hot is it that she actually recognizes the little program that could?*

"Yep. Started off as just something I wrote for myself to help with papers, later it turned out to be pretty lucrative. I modified it last year after all the reports about bad facts in the news and political speeches. You input a statement and it looks it up, runs a Boolean search on about four different search engines, collates the data and gives you results."

"But how does it know that it's found 'facts' and not just an op ed piece or a fauxpedia entry?"

Her tongue skated across her lower lip and his blood drained south. It actually took him a minute to remember the answer.

"It has an algorithm. It compares the websites it locates to a table of data from location to meta entries, to number of visits, to sources used by the page. For example, if it's a dot org, because most of those are far more regulated than a dot com, it will give it more weight. If it's a dot edu it will give that more credibility, too. It can't tell you that a fact is absolutely true, but it can tell you where to find the information that supports or debunks it."

"No wonder you made a fortune on that. That's so cool. Go you." She drained the last of her coffee and stood. He rose with her and sighed. She probably wanted to return to her run, but he could sit there and talk for hours.

"Thanks. Hey, before you go—" He pulled a card out of his pocket and handed it to her. "Call me before you leave? Maybe we can grab dinner and catch up some more."

"Got a phone on you?" She took his card and slid it into her sports bra. Yeah, that didn't help his scrambled thought process any.

He pulled his phone out and she rattled off a series of digits. "That's my cell. Call it and not my house and yeah, I'd love to get dinner." She pressed her fingers to her throat and slipped her iPod back into its snap at her waist. "It was good to see you, Kyle."

"You too, Mary." Uncertain whether a hug would be appropriate, he held out his hand and she gave it a quick squeeze. Electricity sizzled through his nervous system. She winked, tucked her earbuds into place and jogged off.

She didn't have her cell phone on her...so he dialed the number. He listened to the quick message that answered as he watched her run down the street. "Hey, Mary, it's Kyle. What are you doing tonight?"

Chapter Two

"So he called you before you were even out of sight?" Jazz's tinny voice echoed from the speaker phone. "Not sure whether that's creepy or sweet."

"Sweet." Mary checked her appearance in the mirror. The buttercream silk dress drifted against her skin like heaven. She skipped jewelry completely, preferring to wear a watch. But she gave a concession to the dress and chose a gold watch. The overstuffed jewelry box on her dresser offered her a wide selection. She didn't recognize several pieces. Her mother had been shopping again. "Definitely sweet."

Smoothing a hand over her hair, she shifted sideways to check her silhouette. She'd bought the dress three years before on another leave, but never had an excuse to wear it. The sleeveless top and gathered bodice made it an ideal evening casual dress. Fortunately, it seemed she'd lost a few pounds rather than put any on. Not that she dressed to impress anyone.

"You like him." Masculine laughter burst out in the background and faded as though Jazz moved away from her fiancés—*two of them*. Just the idea made Mary laugh. She would settle for one guy, and her best friend had two.

"Yes, as a matter of fact I do but it's not a kink thing. It's a he-was-a-decent-guy-in-high-school thing." She chewed her lower lip. "Lipstick or no lipstick?" She couldn't quite decide.

"You planning to kiss him?" The bed squeaked and Jazz let out a sigh. She still went to physical therapy three or four times a week. She didn't have all of her mobility back and occasionally her calls were punctuated with swearing about her leg, but if she didn't bring it up, neither did Mary. Jazz lived—that's all Mary cared about.

"No. It's two people getting together for a meal and to catch up, not one of your sex dates." The prim note in her voice reminded her of her mother and she winced.

"Hey, my sex date turned out freaking awesome and you asked me for all the details. And if you're not going to kiss him, wear lipstick so he wants to kiss you."

The advice made sense, and the laughter in the other Marine's voice warmed her. "Yes, your sex date was awesome. But this isn't the same thing."

"You can still sign up. I have all the info and the referral if you want it." She must have covered the phone, because her words muffled. "Out, this is girl time, boys. We can play strip poker later."

Another soft burst of laughter washed over the end of her words.

"Sorry about that. Anyway, what was I saying?"

"You were trying to hook me up. Maybe you'd like to share one of yours—you know since you have two," she teased.

"Yeah, no." Jazz replied, cheerfully. "And I mean it. I know it sounds weird, but that 1Night Stand lady—she knows what she's doing."

"I'll keep that in mind. In the meantime, I'll settle for my vanilla dinner date with the hot millionaire who knows how to treat a lady—" She cleared her throat and glanced at her watch. She ran well ahead of time. She'd told Kyle she would meet him, but he really wanted to pick her up. Capable of getting herself from point to point, his insistence flattered her. *And it doesn't hurt that having a man pick me up will get my mother off my back.*

"Millionaire? I thought you said he sold his company."

"Hence the millionaire, although I have no idea how much money he made." Mary crossed over to the frilly window seat and sat down. She eased her feet into strappy sandals. She hated heels—she'd spent too many years strutting across a stage in stilts. She'd prefer to wear her boots, but they definitely didn't go with the dress.

"You don't care either." Ever practical, it was one subject she and Jazz agreed on wholeheartedly. Money made life easier, but it sure as hell didn't make a person worth knowing.

"Nope. He's really cute—I tried to find my yearbooks to see if he showed that potential back then. I mean he was always smart and polite and sweet, but *dayum*. He got fine."

Jazz laughed. "Well then get off the phone with me and go knock him dead. Are you wearing lipstick?"

She lied. "Yep."

"S'okay, let him kiss it off. I bet it looks better on him anyway."

"Bitch."

"I love you, too. Oh, fine. Logan, don't turn on the football game. Anything but that."

The mock horror in Jazz's voice sent another ripple of laughter through Mary. The phone disconnected and she sighed.

After damn near losing her to that IED, she liked hearing Jazz's voice on the other end of the phone. She would love it more when she got a good look at her in person, and in two weeks she would. She glanced at her watch again...ten minutes until he picked her up. Would he be punctual or annoying?

Kyle turned the car in a quiet U-turn to slide up to the valet stand in front of the Nucleus. It was a blues-meets-jazz-meets-modern club that had opened the year before. The laid-back mood inside seemed perfect for chatting and they often featured local musicians, but the food—yeah, he chose the place for the food.

Mary studied the blue electric lights illuminating the club name. "I don't remember this place."

"It's new." The valet opened her door and another came around to take his keys. She waited on the sidewalk, looking better than a million bucks. "But I think you'll like it. You remember that old drive-in that used to host Freaky Friday movies?"

"Oh, the Gemini. Yeah, I heard they shut it down." The last of a dying breed, the lingering holdout to a bygone era couldn't compete with the move to digital and multiplexes with their one hundred-and-twelve screens. "Which is sad. The sound quality sucked, but it was a great place."

"Exactly." He grabbed the door of the club and opened it. She gave him a bemused smile and strolled inside. "The guys that own this place? Owned the Gemini."

"Oh, God." She stopped. "Please tell me they serve—"

"Green chile chili fries? Oh yeah, baby. Yes, they do." Her delight made the surprise completely worth it. The fire hot chili fries tasted beyond excellent and the most popular item served at their little snack shack on the Gemini property.

Mary put a hand over her heart and beamed. The wattage in her smile sent electricity zinging through him. "I think I love you."

"Just wait till you eat them. You'll be mine." He winked and her laughter buoyed him. They didn't have to wait long. As soon as he'd decided to ask her out, he called in a reservation. The club décor—like the music—mingled classic with the modern. They had a booth near the stage and she slid right in, scooting around so they sat near the center of the horseshoe.

They gave their drink orders to the hostess and Mary reached for the card on the table advertising the evening's entertainment. "This is nice."

"I like it. When I heard they planned to open it, I checked it out for nostalgia. But I come back because it's worth it."

She ran her finger down the center of the card. Her teeth scraped across her lower lip and for a moment, he envied their ease of contact. What would it be like to kiss her? His dick stiffened and he shifted.

"So, tell me about you and life in the Marines." *Yes, remember she is a Marine and can kick your ass with a hand tied behind her back.*

"Well I—" She paused while the waitress delivered the drinks, wine for her and a rum and coke for him. Since he drove, it would be his only drink of the night. "Do we want to order or wait?"

"I think we can agree the green chile cheese fries are a must." He lifted his eyebrows at the gleam in her eyes. Her thumbs up made him chuckle. He looked at the waitress. "Double up the order if you please."

"And napkins. We'll need more," Mary tacked on. She crossed her legs under the table and his gaze dropped to the flash of cocoa thigh and he sighed a little. Glancing up, he met her bemused gaze. "See something you like?"

"Very nice muscles. You can probably crack me like a walnut." Ten years ago, he'd have probably turned redder than ketchup saying something like that, but now he just smiled.

Her very inelegant and unladylike snort cracked him up. "We may yet have time to test that theory."

"I can hardly wait." And he meant it. "But you were going to tell me about the Marines."

"What do you want to know?" She sipped her wine and amusement crinkled the corners of her eyes.

What did he want to know? "Not to be blunt but Marines seems a little butch, all things considered."

"Absolutely and part of the appeal. I wanted to be more than the sum of my parts. I wanted to engage my brain and be used for more than just a pretty face strutting across a stage." Her mouth twisted. "Don't get me wrong, you can raise a lot for charity and put the spotlight on a lot of worthwhile issues when you have that tiara on, but I got tired of being 'just that girl.' You know, the one who won that beauty contest."

He nodded. "I'm guessing rocking a swimsuit didn't help your bid to enlist?"

"They didn't care. Oh, they gave me crap in boot—I was Combat Barbie for years—but, I didn't care. I proved myself. They had my back, I had theirs."

His rum and coke went down the wrong windpipe at the

Barbie comment. "Okay, forgive me, but I can't picture you in uniform."

Twisting, she opened her purse and brought out her phone. Flipping through the images, she held it over to him. She stood in front of a sandstone building, the yellowish landscape a barren backdrop to the three women in the center, all dressed in fatigues, helmets and carrying very big guns. He enlarged the image with a swipe of his thumb and forefinger. "Wow, it's hard to tell which one is you, but I think you're the tallest one."

"Yep. That's Jazz on my left and on the other side of her is Roxy. We were part of the same FET."

"FET?" He passed the phone back reluctantly, curious about what other pictures she might have stored on it.

"Female Engagement Team. We work with the women and girls in the outlying villages and in the cities. We offer them opportunities, listen to their concerns, get them feedback and answer their questions. We're liaisons for the U.S. forces there and do our best to help them get the aid they might need." She thumbed across the camera and held up another image. "Those are some of the girls now enrolled in one of the schools we helped build."

"Cool." It deserved far more than just a 'cool,' but bowing down with an 'I'm not worthy' seemed like overkill.

She flicked to another one. "And these are their mothers." Pride and respect filtered through her voice. A quiet sense of awe slipped through him. "They're enrolled, too. And that was no easy task, let me tell you. This one here? Sovra is studying education so she can actually teach the children in her village as they get older, and Johnara wants to specialize in women's medicine. She's already a midwife, so it's actually just a matter of giving her access to more information."

"That's—amazing." The word didn't do her story justice. "You're changing their worlds."

"No." Mary shook her head slowly. "They are. We just plow the row. They take the seeds and make it grow." She smiled down at the picture on the smartphone and his heart squeezed.

Yeah, he was toast.

Chapter Three

"*Y*ou did not." Mary snorted.

They'd talked for hours, listened to some beautiful bluesy horns and a jazz trio before paying the tab and driving down to the beach. Home a week and she hadn't even made it down to the blue waters.

"I did." Kyle laughed and skimmed another rock across the water. "School email was still in its infancy, but they used it to keep score in their sex game. So I sent it to all their dates, figured it was the least I could do."

The wind turned chilly off the Pacific, but she didn't care. They'd left their shoes at the car and walked along the water's edge. The sand retained a hint of the day's earlier heat, and the ocean rolling in offered a beautiful accompaniment to their stroll.

She laughed. "I would have paid money to see their reactions." Had she been on their score list? The thought sobered her. "Hey, was I...?"

"A gentleman would never tell." He nudged her around a seaweed covered board, leftover debris the ocean carried home. "Of course, I'm not much of a gentleman, but yeah, you were on there with really sweet odds against anyone ever getting the points."

"I dunno whether to be flattered or offended." She touched his elbow and pulled him closer when the chill water raced up toward his feet. He bumped her and linked their arms.

"Be flattered. It would have netted the winner some ridiculous number of points because the odds were a thousand to one anyone would even make it to second base with you."

Amusement drifted through her. "What a bunch of idiots."

"Yup. Course, I think they should have given points to the guy with the balls to ask you out." The water pushed in farther. They danced out of reach and she let out a squeal of laughter as it froze her toes.

"God, I forgot how cold this gets sometimes. Beaches are supposed to be sunny and warm."

He gave her a dry look. "You grew up here, right?"

"Yes. Course, I've been living just south of hell so the Caribbean is probably cold to me at the moment."A song drifted down on the breeze and she canted her head up. "Oh, I love Pink."

"Are you sure that's Pink?" Kyle guided them toward the hillside overlooking the beach as though to get a better earful. "Sounds like Lady Gaga."

"No, I know Lady Gaga. Roxy listens to her nonstop. That's Pink." She started moving to the beat. Kyle shot her another skeptical frown, but the corner of his mouth twitched.

He held out his free hand and she took it and then he spun her out and tugged her back and they were dancing. They danced a half-waltz, half-so-very-not, and she held onto his shoulders as he guided her through the steps. The music faded in and out, louder at times and softer at others.

"Probably a party up there and people are going in and out the doors."

He twirled her again and she let herself float on the imaginary music. She knew the song well enough to fill in the gaps.

"Probably." She rested a hand on his shoulder as he drew her close again. He was solid muscle beneath the crisp shirt. It made her double glad he'd shed the jacket along with his shoes before they walked down. Petting the fabric, she studied him. "So why didn't you ever ask me out in school?"

"Because I was the geek and you were the beauty queen." He spun her around, and the lightness in his words didn't make the sentiment any easier.

"So? You were a fun guy." She would have gone out with him—maybe. Frankly, she hadn't dated all that much. Most of her free time got sucked up in practicing for pageants and training her skills for talent contests when not on parade for her mother's friends. "I think I would have liked a date with you."

"Well, that makes two of us." Kyle waggled his brows. "So you want to be my date to prom?"

She snorted. "I didn't go to prom."

"I noticed." Something in his voice wiped away her amusement.

"Yeah?"

"Yep. I worked up the courage and told myself I'd ask you to dance—just one. But I waited all night and you never showed. I figured your date skipped the dance and you two just got a room." The crestfallen note softened with apology. "And I should probably say sorry for that thought. I found out later you didn't go."

"Nope. We had to be in Sacramento for the preliminary Miss California run." Leaning back on his arm, she stared up at the sky. She could make out a few stars. He dipped and spun her again. The lack of music didn't stop their dance.

"Want to know a secret?" His voice lowered.

Straightening, she wrapped an arm around his shoulder. She should have taken Jazz's advice and worn the lipstick. She wanted him to want to kiss her. "Yes."

"I watched that pageant on television. You looked great." No self-deprecating snark marred the compliment.

"Thank you."

"You're welcome." He leaned closer and they were dancing, chest to breast, hips brushing. His mouth hovered so close. "So...."

"Yes?"

"About prom..." The warmth of his breath teased her cheek. His smile faded and his expression grew somber. "Reunion is day after tomorrow. Be my date?"

The reunion was the last thing on her mind. She had zero desire to catch up with all the jocks, cheerleaders, nerds, or stoners and everyone in between. But she did want to spend time with Kyle. "On one condition."

"Name it."

"I want a corsage and a limo ride."

His brows rose and he laughed. "I think that can be arranged."

"Then in that case, Kyle, I would love to be your date for 'prom.'" She rose up on her tiptoes and kissed him lightly, the barest touch of her lips to his. A tease for him and a promise for her.

She so planned on wearing lipstick for their date.

A bemused expression fell over his face, and she pulled slowly out of his arms but twined her fingers with his. "That does leave us with one quandary." She started walking.

"What's that?"

"What are we going to do tomorrow night?"

Sadly, they didn't do anything the next night. Mary's mother ambushed her with a dinner party. She should have expected it, but calling to let Kyle know she couldn't make it disappointed her more than she cared to admit. She sucked it up and made herself pretty and played the part of gracious hostess under her mother's stern eye. After boot camp, her mother shouldn't be able to intimidate her—on the other hand her drill sergeant could have taken lessons from Mrs. Phillips on how to freeze someone in place with a simple stare.

By the time their dozen guests ate, drank wine, made small

talk and finally left, all Mary wanted was to strip down to her PJs and pass out. The tedium actually made her miss Afghanistan. She crawled into bed before she saw the text message from Kyle.

How was the party?

Fluffing a pillow, she picked up the remote, turned on the television and texted back. *Boring as hell. How was your evening?*

Finished reading the Steve Jobs biography and checked out the fashion channel. Thought I should brush up to be your man candy.

She laughed, exhaustion evaporating. *So what tips do you have for me? High skirt or low? Shoulders bare? What's the new black?*

Scrolling through the channels, she waited for his response. Her movie options were sad, sadder, and *please kill me now.* She scanned the regular stations. *Space Marines* it was. Nudging the volume up, she waited for the commercial to end to see how far into the movie they were.

Wearing clothes in public is a good plan. I like a little thigh, so high skirt. Bare shoulders work for me. And why does there need to be a new black?

Another snicker escaped. *So, mini dress with cleavage, and basic black.* Biting her lip, she hesitated a moment before finishing the thought. *Where will I wear the gun?*

Yes, giving into Freud. Is it a big gun?

She had to stuff the heel of her hand into her mouth to stifle the guffaw rumbling through her. *Big enough.*

Her phone buzzed. She hit answer and laughed her greeting. "Good evening."

"So, big enough…. Does that mean big enough for a sexy thigh holster tucked into a garter or 'make my day,' bigger?"

"Big enough like a Glock nine. But I'm thinking I don't need to carry for a dance. I mean, unless you're planning something." She snuggled down into the covers and tucked an arm behind her head. Marines blowing away bugs on the screen and Kyle on the phone. Life was good.

"I am totally planning something. You should probably ask your mom if it's okay to stay out all night. I promise, we'll be good." The man definitely knew how to flirt. Her body hummed from the lighthearted teasing.

"You know, I discovered a long time ago that with my mother, it's better to ask forgiveness than seek permission. So what are you planning?"

"That would be telling." He sighed. "And I think I want to use a little shock and awe."

"Are you trying to sweet talk me, military style, Brainy Smurf?" Her lips pursed with the effort to hold back the laughter.

"I dunno, Smurfette. Is it working?"

"I'll make you a deal. I won't bring up Smurfs again if—"

"Sold." He laughed, a warm, low masculine note. "Hey, do you have a sexy nickname? Marines always have some call sign in the movies."

Grimacing, she chewed her lip. "Stormer."

"Oh, like the superhero?"

She stretched under the covers, tension winding through her. "No, that's Storm. I'm Stormer—as in storming the castle."

The bare sound of his breathing filled the silence. "Not seeing the connection there."

Yeah, he wanted her to tell the story. "During training exercises post-boot, we broke into six-person units trapped behind enemy lines with heavy fire. Our goal was survival and return to our division. My team took the flag before we went back." She chuckled. "I stormed the castle and drew fire so that my unit could come in from all sides—"

"You took point? Isn't that the most dangerous spot?"

"A, it was a training exercise and B, my idea, my unit, made it my lead. She who gives the orders leads the charge. It worked. We took the flag and prisoners and made our way back to base." But the nickname stuck. It suited her direct attitude. When he said nothing, she frowned. "Kyle?"

"I'm still here. Just trying to wrap my mind around what you do. Part of me hates the idea of you in any kind of danger."

Well, if that didn't dampen the ardor, she didn't know what would. "And the other part of you?"

"Is blown the hell away by the idea of talking to such an amazing woman—Marine—and maybe just the slightest bit intimidated."

The overwrought feeling relaxed. "Thank you, but I'm not that special. I need you to understand—this is who I am, and what we're doing right now....it's fun and I am enjoying the hell out of you and the flirting, but I'm not going to change." Moment of truth time. Some men couldn't handle the idea of a woman comfortable in full combat gear. She liked him in high school and he'd been a great guy then, but what kind of man was he now?

"I wouldn't dream of asking you to change. Frankly, it makes you even sexier than you already were." He waited a beat. "On the other hand, how do you feel about jotting down a few names to kick their asses for me?"

Her smile grew. "I got your back."

"See, I feel safer already."

She yawned and snuggled deeper against the pillows. "Good. I'll see you tomorrow night?"

"I'm counting down the hours." They talked for a few more moments and rang off. Mary glanced at the TV screen but didn't see the gore or the flying body parts. Her mind drifted over Kyle's words. *It makes you even sexier than you already were.*

Yeah, she definitely had his back.

Chapter Four

"You're acting like you're in high school again." His mother leaned against the door to the kitchen, a cup of coffee cradled in her hands. "The tie looks fine, just the way it is."

Kyle smoothed down the navy tie. It was boring, hardly as much fun as the character-driven ties housed in his closet, but he thought sedate seemed the better way to go on this date. "You sure?"

"Yes, I'm sure. I put the orchid in the refrigerator so it didn't wilt while you fussed with your clothes. So who is she?"

In her mid-fifties, Florence Stewart stood a full half foot shorter than her son, not that it prevented her from reining him in when he got obsessed. Which, considering his line of work, was more often than not.

"Maybe it's a he." He grinned slowly. Somewhere around his sophomore year in college, his mother broached the subject of his sexuality because married to his work and studies, he didn't date. It had been embarrassing for both of them, but worth a few laughs now.

"Uh huh. Who is she?" She padded forward on her bare feet. Her toes were painted eggshell pink to match the little hearts on her kitchen window curtains. He'd moved her into a nice neighborhood, paid off her house and she still made her own curtains, painted her own nails and treated herself to a cup of standard coffee. Just because a body had money didn't mean she had to spend it. Someday he'd figure out what frivolous thing she really wanted and spoil her.

"Mom, I came by to fix the sink because you asked me to, and I brought the suit so I could change—"

"And the corsage, and I heard you discussing when the limousine would pick you up so you could pick her up on time." She patted his chest.

"That's eavesdropping you know."

Her eyebrows raised. "If you wanted privacy, then you shouldn't have taken the call in the middle of my kitchen."

She had a point. He slipped his hands into his pockets. "Her name is Mary. We went to high school together, and we're going to the reunion tonight at The Grand."

"Mary Phillips. Well, you don't let the moss grow on you. It only took you ten years to ask her out."

The cheerful glint in her eyes roasted his ego, but Kyle laughed. "Yes, but I still asked." He winked. "Even better, she said yes."

Florence waved to the table. "Sit down, I'll fix some sandwiches and you can tell me all about it before you rush off."

"Mom, there will be food there—" He swallowed the words at her stern stare. "Yes, ma'am." It didn't matter that he was a multi-millionaire or a decade past being a minor. If his mother wanted to take care of him, the least he could do was do as he was told.

Pulling out a chair, he sat and didn't offer to help. She wanted to fuss, better to let her get it out of her system.

"How did you two meet again?" His mother knew him too well.

"Ran into her at The Orange Rind a couple of days ago. We chatted and swapped numbers, and I took her out to dinner." He kept it casual, played it cool.

"And now you're going to the reunion together?" She spread

a thin layer of mayo onto bread slices and added a combination of turkey, ham and swiss, his favorites.

"Yes, ma'am." He cleared his throat.

"I thought you decided against going to the reunion."

"Things change." His evasion techniques left a lot to be desired.

"That they do." She carried the plates out and set one in front of him. "Kyle, do you really think I don't remember who she is?"

"One could only hope that even if you didn't remember, that you'd let me make my own mistakes."

She ran her fingers through his hair as though straightening it. "Now, why would you think it's a mistake?"

"Because she's the one, Mom. The one I really liked and never could ask. But I'm not that nerd anymore. Well, to be fair I'm a nerd, but I'm damn proud of it, and she seems to like me just fine. So get your coffee and your sandwich and let's talk about something else." The key to dealing with Florence meant giving her the sense her questions were answered and then moving on.

"So where has she been? I'm assuming she moved away because otherwise you two would have run into each other." She walked away and missed his rolled eyes. Sure, because in a city of four million, running into each other happened all the time.

"She joined the Marines."

"The Marines?"

Ha. Got her with that one. He leaned back in the chair and took a healthy bite of the sandwich.

His mother carried the coffee cups out and set his in front of him before taking the chair to his right. "A Marine. Her mother must have had a coronary."

Determined not to snicker, Kyle managed to hold onto a solemn face. "But she's been doing great. She works with women in Afghanistan and is trying to help them get education and more. I think she's seen combat, but she hasn't talked about it. And if it's possible, she's even more gorgeous now than she was then—still—with her brains, she didn't need the beauty."

"Only a man could say that." His mother beamed at him. "When do I get to meet her?"

"In a year, when I'm positive you won't ask her about potential grandchildren."

Florence laughed and slapped his arm lightly. "You are a terrible son."

Widening his eyes, he gave her his most contrite look. "It is a burden for you, I know. I'll try to do better."

Her inelegant snort reminded him so much of Mary's that he couldn't help but grin.

"Fine, I will leave you alone about it. But you must promise to get me a picture of the two of you together, and I want that corsage on her arm when you do it."

"Okay." He frowned. "Why?"

"Because I never got the prom picture you wanted, and I still have the frame we bought for it—"

The donkey kick to the gut evaporated his humor. They had picked out a frame. When he finally confessed he wanted to ask a girl out, his mother coached him on how, used her gas money to rent him a suit and bought the frame that complimented it. When he hadn't asked Mary, she never once gave him hell about it.

"I'll get you your picture, Mom. I promise."

"Thank you." She picked up her coffee cup and gave him another smile.

He sighed. She won. "What do you want to know?"

"Do you still like her?"

"Very much." Enthusiasm filled his response. "She's a hell of a woman and one I want to get to know a lot better. But—" He held up a hand. "She's on leave. So I don't know how long we have before she goes back to work overseas. You know, a few thousand miles away."

"That part doesn't matter." His mother continually surprised him.

"No?"

"No." Putting the cup down, she covered his hand with hers. "Moments, Kyle. Remember that. All we have are moments. When you make the moments count—that's what matters. If you like her, then you go for it. You enjoy your date, you dance, you laugh and you talk. You make it a great moment. Tomorrow will take care of itself. After all, you waited ten years for this tomorrow, didn't you?"

"I love you, Mom."

"I know, dear. Now eat your sandwich."

တ

Wrapped in a towel, Mary stared at the contents of the closet with her hands on her hips. Reunion meant fancy dress. Asking for a limo and corsage meant she better damn well wear a spectacular dress but nothing in the closet appealed to her. Half the dresses hung there still had their tags and the others were mummified in dry cleaner plastic. Shoving one organza peach nightmare to the back, she tried to arrange the other dresses in order of acceptable to no-effing-way.

Very few made it to the acceptable spot. She'd had a basic black number the last time she visited. She left it behind because she deployed a week after returning to base. *So where is it?* Sorting through the dresses one more time—because shifting them back and forth on the rack might make the dress reappear, she glanced at the clock. Less than an hour until Kyle arrived. No way she could make it to a shop and back with the right dress, even if she found her mother's magical dress genie locked up somewhere in the house.

"Mary, a letter arrived for you today from your—what *are* you doing?"

Gritting her teeth, she looked over her shoulder at her mother, all four-foot ten of her. In her late fifties, Lianne Phillips maintained her figure well and dressed in conservative silk pants and jacket. A pair of peep-toed heels peeked out from beneath the hem of her trousers that had to be hemmed exactly right to fit whatever shoes she purchased to match.

"I left a black dress here on my last visit. The one I wore to the opening of the Kensington." Mary impressed herself that she even remembered the event her mother dragged her to during that leave. Fortunately, the Kensington hosted an opening of a local photographer—a man who spent years photographing war zones. His images were stark, devastating, and left her moved.

"Hmm. I remember that dress. Too short for you. Wear the sienna, it's far more flattering and it has a lovely slit that will allow you to accentuate your legs." Setting the manila envelope down on the dresser, she strode across the room and sorted through the closet. The dress she pulled out didn't boast of any bustle or frills. It gathered tight at the bodice and fell in a straight line to the floor.

Completely unremarkable.

Unconvinced, Mary stared hard at the closet. She really liked the black dress.

"Mary Elizabeth Phillips, the black dress made you look like a hooker. This dress is elegant, and I wasn't sure it would fit after your last visit. But your lines are cleaner now than they were at eighteen. Put it on." She thrust the dress at her and Mary chewed her lip.

"It's for a reunion, Mom. I don't really want to arrive dressed as the Great Pumpkin."

Her mother didn't dignify her with a response, merely pointed to the oriental divider Mary used since junior high to change behind when her mother came in to help her pick out clothes.

Grabbing a pair of panties and a bra, she walked behind the divider obediently and hung the dress up. Stripping off the towel, she pulled on her undergarments and then frowned. "I don't have a strapless bra."

"You won't need it." Her mother opened another door on the closet and pulled out a pair of three-inch heels in the exact shade of the dress.

I'd bet money she has an army of personal shoppers, all

outfitted with swatches to find the right match.

"Just to be clear, you're advising me to go out bra-less." Her poker face held out.

"Don't be indelicate. The dress is designed to cup and shape your bosom. Even the sag from the lack of a good bra should be corrected easily enough."

Sag? Mary gaped. Did her mother just say her boobs had gotten saggy? She glanced down at herself. They looked the same. Okay, maybe they hung a little lower, but she worked out regularly and her chest never developed much beyond a B-cup anyway. Grumbling she unzipped the plastic wrap on the dress and slid into it. It hugged her from breast to flat midriff, flaring just over the hips and falling to the tops of her feet.

Perfect length.

Walking out from behind the screen, she studied herself in the mirror. The color was outstanding against the rich, warm cocoa of her skin. If anything, it almost gave her a golden sheen. Her mother walked over and set the shoes down in front of her. Sliding into them, it took her a moment to adjust to the height and the feel. She pivoted and the slit played peekaboo with her leg. Damn the shoes made her calves look fantastic.

A moment later her mother beckoned with a gold choker and she slid it around Mary's neck. Patting her hair, she twisted it into an elegant knot and fixed it up in two quick gestures, pinning it in place with another gold hair clip.

"The hair up emphasizes your neck and you've always had a beautiful one. The necklace is perfect, and I have a bracelet in here that should match."

"No." Mary declined, finding an apology because her mother was right—the dress did suit her. "I mean, no thank you. I asked Kyle to bring a corsage."

"Hmm." Tapping a finger to her lips, Lianne nodded. "Give me one moment." She hurried out of the bedroom and left Mary to study her own reflection. She looked good. Elegant, but good. Turning sideways, she ran a hand over her stomach self-consciously. She'd put on muscle weight, but the dress didn't emphasize that. It smoothed her out—'better lines,' her mother said.

Lianne sailed back in with a gold cuff and wrapped it around Mary's right bicep. "There. Wear the corsage on your left wrist and don't forget the gold earrings I set out. I have a clutch bag that would match this but do you prefer a strap?"

"Sure. Whatever you have, I bet it's perfect." Impulsively, she leaned forward and hugged her mother. "Thank you."

"You're welcome. Now, go do your makeup. The cake should always have a fine frosting on the top." Lianne waved her off and disappeared down the hallway again.

Stomach fluttering, Mary laughed and walked over to the vanity. She added a light touch of eyeliner and a dusting of eye shadow. Inheriting her mother's fine skin and her father's complexion eliminated the need for base. She just applied a shiny gloss to her lips by the time her mother returned. Approval radiated the air around her.

"He must be a worthy man." She set the purse down on the dresser.

"What does that mean?" Mary met her gaze in the mirror.

"It means exactly what I said and a car just pulled up out front. I imagine he's here. Shall I have your father meet him?"

Was her mother messing with her?

"I think I can handle it." She smiled.

"Good. Call if you don't plan to come home. You know I worry." And with that, Lianne sailed out of the room again. Yes, her mother did worry.

Putting her keys, mirror, lipstick, a credit card and a couple of condoms into her purse, Mary glanced at the envelope.

Her new orders had arrived.

Wrinkling her nose, she patted them. They would be there tomorrow.

Tonight she had other plans.

Chapter Five

Kyle's tongue felt permanently stuck to the top of his mouth. He always forgot how close to Beverly Hills her parents' house sat and the fact that they had staff. Reminding himself money didn't define a person sounded a lot better when a housekeeper didn't answer the door. Mary descended the stairs, her thigh flashing with every step. Ten years of success melted away. The words *I'm not worthy* echoed in his mind.

"Hey." Her mouth curved around the word and all the blood rushed from his head to his cock, then bounced back up again.

"Hey, you look—" He needed an adjective. "Fantastic."

"Thank you. You're pretty tasty, too." She lifted her chin. "Is that for me?"

Following her gaze to the corsage, he chuckled. He'd forgotten all about it. "Yes, ma'am. As requested, one lovely flower sacrificed for the pleasure of being against your skin." *Okay, lay off the poetry, you are not Shakespeare.* He opened the box and took the corsage out. The orchid was a lovely enough flower, but it truly did not come close to matching her.

She held out her wrist. "The sacrifice is duly noted and I will honor it."

Sliding the band over her hand, he fastened it and caught her fingers with his. "Thank you."

"For what?" Her brows lifted.

"For being you." He pivoted and swept an arm toward the limo with a half bow. "Your chariot."

Taking one step forward, she brushed her lips to his cheek and murmured, "Marines are infantry, not cavalry."

"Then would you like a lift?" The kiss, the teasing words, and the ease of her manner relaxed him. He flashed forward from awkward teen to accomplished adult again.

"I would love one."

Inside, she crossed one leg over the other and leaned back. "This is nice."

"It's not bad." A closed partition separated them from the driver. Since he was about to share her with their entire graduating class, he wanted the privacy for the ride there. "I don't do this that often."

"Me neither. Usually it's a MRAP that's roasting us alive or freezing our private parts to death." She rubbed her palms against the soft leather seats.

"Does it ever bother you?" He shifted, sitting so he could rest an arm along the back of the seat and look at her. "Spending so much time in a battle zone like that and then coming home to this?"

"Sometimes." Her bare shoulders lifted in a shrug. "But you have to remember this is what we're fighting for—not a limousine ride, obviously—but the right to achieve your dreams. To be you, to have fantastic ideas and turn them into a fortune, or to be my mom who hosts her tea parties and luncheons and receptions for a hundred different causes and be obsessed with shoes. It's not easy, but I didn't sign up for easy."

"You okay?" A distant air of melancholy seemed to hover around her.

"Yeah, I was—I was thinking about my mom. She said something when I was getting ready and it's—it's playing a loop in the back of my mind. Sorry." A tight smile dragged at the corners of her mouth.

Going with his gut, he reached over and caught her right hand in his and interlaced his fingers. "So talk it out. I'm really good at listening."

Surprise creased her brow then she grimaced. "It might be a little heavy for first date conversation."

"Okay, then let's call it an old friend's conversation while we're in the car and when we get there, we can pretend we're on our way to prom, play it up and forget about everything else." Hell, they could forget about the reunion entirely if she wanted. He preferred to erase the shadows in her eyes.

"Deal." She squeezed his hand. "I give my mom a lot of crap because she was obsessed with the beauty queen thing and dresses and shoes, and she's always after me about my appearance. The other day, she said something about me getting out of the Marines while I still had my looks. It pissed me right the hell off. But tonight she asked me to give her a call if I wasn't coming home because she worries."

"And maybe all her comments about you getting out are more because she worries about you being in danger?" He hated the idea of her being over there, facing potential fire. The reports of casualties and injuries didn't seem to have the impact they once did, not when they came every day. The reality turned into the second donkey kick of the day. He didn't blame her mother for worrying.

"I'm a bad daughter." She castigated herself in word and tone.

"No, you're not. My mom would say that parents worry—period. They worry when we learn to walk, when we go to school, when we cross a street: it's how it goes. She loves you. I'm thinking that it's a good thing for you to know rather than resenting the way she shows it."

"Does it sound completely stupid that I was surprised she felt that way?"

Knowing everyone had self-worth issues at some point and time or another and seeing someone as amazing as Mary express them were two completely different things. "No. And I don't say that lightly. I've learned that we don't always value about ourselves what others value in us. Parents are tough because they're supposed to love us, but they're people so they don't always show it well. Case in point—" He took a deep breath. *In for a penny, in for a pound.* "I totally had a thing for you in high school."

Bracing himself, he tossed that kernel of information onto the fire.

"Seriously?" She blinked slowly and studied him, as if seeking the truth in his expression.

"Swear to God. I wanted to ask you out a hundred different times. But every time I opened my mouth to do it—I couldn't. I didn't know how to say, 'Hey Mary, want to get a cup of coffee? And you know you're really smart, want to come check out this game I designed?'" Tracing the line between her thumb and forefinger with his thumb, he concentrated on that contact and not the sinking gut feeling he'd given into when he was a teen.

"I'm not going to lie and say I would have gone out with you." The blatant honesty drew his gaze up. "But I didn't date anyone. Little known fact about Mary Phillips—the jocks thought I was a tease and the others thought I believed myself better than anyone else."

"I never saw you act that way." He frowned. "Did your parents not let you date?"

"No, my mother wanted me to meet a nice boy—preferably one who would get a medical or law degree and move me into a big house just down the street from her. But I wanted—I wanted more. I wanted to get out of high school and Carlysle and the pageant circuit. It took going Marine to make me grow up and realize that what I really wanted was to be me, and I didn't think I could be in high school." She bumped his shoulder. "Except with you. I didn't have to pretend when I was with you. So, maybe I would have broken my rule for you."

"Kind of glad you didn't." Self-realization was a quirky thing; it always hit when a body least expected it.

The limo swung into the car port of The Grand Hotel. Mary

glanced out the window and then back to him. "Before we dive into our Back to the Future prom date—why are you glad I didn't?"

"I lacked the confidence to follow through in high school." The driver opened the door and Kyle slid out first and held out his hand to her. She glided out as graceful and elegant as any ballet dancer. He kissed her fingers once and then tucked them into the crook of his arm.

"Does that mean I might get lucky on this date?" She murmured against his ear.

He grinned. "I might let you get to second base, if you play your cards right."

She'd laughed away her earlier melancholy by the time they walked through the main doors. He wished he could say the same of his apprehension for the evening.

The party was in full swing by the time they signed in with the welcome committee and picked up their name tags. She refused to stick a pin in her mother's pretty dress so Kyle volunteered to wear both name tags.

"And if they ask, I'll tell them I got a sex change." He winked, making her laugh. He probably would, too. His confession in the car surprised the hell out of her and left her a little wistful for what might have been. *Realistically, you would have had a couple of dates and then left him for the Marines anyway.*

The practical side of her nature couldn't be less interested in making excuses or speculating on the past. The ballroom was done up in black and silver with streamers and balloons everywhere. Kyle surprised her by navigating right over to the decorated arch and posing for a couple of photographs. Waiters in white suits carried trays of champagne flutes, and he snagged two for them and then they were in the crowd.

"It's so great to see you!" Mimi, former student body president-turned aide to a city councilman, oozed earnestness when shaking their hands.

"Babe, you turned into a real looker." The very-married Chad

Murray, former prom king, point guard for the basketball team and the owner of a car dealership in Fresno, was already well on his way to being blitzed.

"I totally bought every one of your games." Vapid little Marcy Cates cooed at Kyle. "You think maybe we could get a drink and talk Code One Red?"

Poor Kyle seemed completely flummoxed, and Mary threaded her arm through his and gave little Marcy a hard stare. "I'm sorry, his dance card is full for the foreseeable future. Ta ta." She gave him a light tug and they were off. She bypassed the next set of land sharks and they glided out onto the dance floor. "Kyle is the hot guy on campus now. I shall have to keep my wary eye out for possible ambush."

He snorted. "I'm not worried."

She looped her arms around his neck and drifted to a song she barely recognized. "No?"

"Hell no." He leaned in close and murmured. "I have a Combat Barbie on my arm. She can kill them and not even break a nail doing it."

Mary gaped, speechless, before throwing her head back and laughing. "I will so get you back for that."

"Challenge accepted." He winked and spun her around the floor. "Besides, I didn't design the game she mentioned. That's an EarthBWare product. Not a Kyle Stewart."

"Tsk tsk. Shot down in flames by flubbing the nerd. However will Marcy survive?" Not that she cared.

"Don't know. Don't care. Heads up—Jones Briggs just walked in." He maneuvered them around another pair of swaying couples and turned so she could survey.

Jones Briggs. NFL linebacker, MVP three years running and all around son of a bitch in school. He studied the crowd, sweeping his gaze back and forth across it—passing right over them. Her relief was short lived however when he zeroed in on her and Kyle and made a beeline for them.

Would the joy ever end?

"And he's coming this way." She gave Kyle's shoulder a

squeeze and considered putting herself right between the two men. She knew the kind of hell the jerk had heaped on him in school. Rites of passage be damned, it seemed like the man had made it his mission in life to treat Kyle like crap.

Linebacker or not, she'd dropped Marines far bigger—and better—than him. On the other hand, she didn't want Kyle to think she didn't believe he could handle himself. So she chose her position carefully, taking up right at his side.

The football player arrived, gave them a quick, hard grin and stuck his hand out. Kyle didn't show an ounce of reluctance in taking the offered handshake.

"Jones. Congrats on winning MVP again." Smooth as silk and utterly polite, he didn't even twitch delivering the compliment.

"Thanks. It's good to see you, man and no hard feelings, you know?" Suddenly, Jones seemed uncomfortable and took a step back. "Probably not the time and the place. But I'm sorry for all the crap I gave you in school. I had some anger management issues. I got it together now and one of my assignments is making amends. I'm sorry."

"No problem, man. It's in the past. Let's leave it there." An uncomfortable silence stretched out between them and Jones gave them another nod and walked away faster than he'd approached.

"Okay. That was weird." Mary stared after him.

"Nah. He rated MVP, but he's got issues and I heard his team is considering trading him—which could mean a lucrative new contract or a move to a less successful team. Apparently his 'anger management' issues cause problems in the locker room, and the coaches ordered him into therapy."

"Well, check you out knowing all the dirt."

They wandered away from the dance floor, sharing polite nods here and there.

"Nah, I did my homework after we agreed to come here." He rubbed a hand against the back of his neck. "Besides, Jones' issues are all over the sports news network. I actually thought he wanted to come over and ask you for a dance."

"No, I'm not the one everyone is paying attention to tonight." She watched a cluster of girls she vaguely recognized from Lit class murmuring excitedly to each other and gesturing at Kyle. "Of course, if they overstep, I'll make sure they notice."

He grinned. "How much longer do we have to endure this torture?"

She mimed looking at her watch. "Five minutes?"

"Sold."

Chapter Six

*I*t took them almost thirty minutes to negotiate their way through the crowd. It surprised Kyle just how many people recognized him, shook his hand, and seemed genuinely happy to see him or Mary, or both. He and Mary separated briefly when a man in a deep blue uniform wheeled through the door. He seemed vaguely familiar, but Kyle couldn't place him. He exchanged business cards with Fisher Thom, another nerd-made-success-story and his former co-captain of the AV club, and made plans to meet for a round of golf sometime—the vague niceties observed, he made his way over to rejoin her.

The wide, warm grin she flashed him threatened to stop his heart. "Kyle, do you remember Boone Stevens?" Despite the introduction, he couldn't reconcile the name to the boy he remembered. The close-cropped military cut and the uniform, didn't match the high school memory. They shook hands and he stepped back to rest a hand on the back of the chair Mary claimed.

The clues snapped an image in his mind—long blond hair, scruffy beard, board shorts year-round and a surfboard secured to the back of his jeep. Boone was one of those guys who coasted through high school, friends with everyone and belonging to no particular group. He preferred the waves to the classroom and his grades often reflected it.

"He doesn't." The officer laughed. "But I think it's the lack of shaggy hair and a surfboard."

"Holy shit, no I almost didn't. But how the hell are you?" The minute the words left his mouth, he could have kicked himself. The guy sat in a wheelchair.

"Not bad. Enjoying shocking the hell out of people. You?" The corners of Boone's eyes creased in easy humor.

"I can't complain and I think I've shocked my fair share. Navy?" It didn't surprise him—he could easily picture Boone as a sailor—particularly with the clean-shaven appearance he sported.

"Yup. Mary here was just telling me about a rehab center in Texas. But you two look ready to get out of here...."

"We can hang out if you want back up." Mary glanced at Kyle when she made the offer, but he nodded in agreement. He'd tutored Boone through most of their junior and senior years. In turn, Boone taught him to surf. A skill, he let drift away after those couple of years, but he still enjoyed the memories.

"I'm good. You two get the hell out of here, especially if you're deploying again in a few weeks. You need the break. I'll check out Mike's Place though. The docs are planning to get me fitted with a prosthetic that doesn't chafe."

The words dragged Kyle's gaze downward. It wasn't noticeable at first, but Boone's left pant leg draped a little different than his right. The third donkey kick of the day left him a little sick to his stomach.

Boone gave him a patient look. "It's cool, man, seriously. Accidents happen. I'll be on my feet in no time."

"Good for you." He reached into his suit jacket and pulled out a card. "If I can do anything or you need a job or just want to grab a beer—gimme a call." He didn't have a company to hire him with right now, but a new idea began to form in the back of his mind. He'd have to let it ruminate, but he had over two hundred million in the bank.

I could do some good with that.

"You got it. Watch your back, Mary." He and Mary shook hands and the image of the two vital people exchanging such a private salute and mutual respect shook Kyle to his core. He was still trying to wrap his mind around it all when they strolled across the lobby ten minutes later.

"You got quiet. You okay?" They held hands as if it was the most natural thing in the world.

"Yeah, I'm just—" How did he put his thoughts into words without sounding like a complete jackass?

"It's okay to be a little fucked up over seeing someone you knew stuck in a wheelchair." She paused next to a column. The lobby bustled with evening activity, but she chose the one quiet corner. Her dark eyes softened in understanding and he sighed.

"You've seen that a lot, haven't you?" How close had she been to ending up like that? Would she yet if she planned to deploy again? The sobering thought gnawed on his soul.

"More than I like to think about, but it's the price we're willing to pay. My best friend got hit by an IED a few months ago—I was thirty feet away? Forty?" Dark emotion clouded her voice. "She was talking to a kid. It was a routine day, and one moment she's standing there and the next she's running, pushing the kid out of the way and blowing into a wall. People make jokes about the bone-crunching noise you make when you slam into something, but I heard the crunch and then she was down and bleeding."

He crowded closer to her and slid an arm around her. He didn't know what to say, but he wanted to give her support at the same time. "I'm sorry."

"She's okay—now. But it was touch and go for a long time, and I couldn't do anything about it except pray and hope. She's at the rehab facility I told Boone about, and I'm going to her wedding in a week or so. They had to postpone the official ceremony last Christmas for one more surgery, even though Jazz swore it gave her two honeymoons." Tears glimmered in Mary's eyes, and she swiped a hand against her face.

"I'm glad." And he was. Glad her friend was okay and beyond grateful it hadn't been her. He closed the distance between them, his mouth hovering close to hers. She stopped him with a hand on his chest.

"Kyle—"

Dammit, here comes the rejection. He could handle it. "Yeah?"

"I'm a Marine." She met his gaze steadily. "It's not just what I do—it's who I am."

"I know."

"That means I could end up like that, I could end up not coming home, and—"

He pressed a finger to her lips. "Life is about moments, Mary. This is our moment. Let's worry about today and let tomorrow take care of itself."

"Okay." Her breath tickled his finger, and he traced the soft skin of her lower lip.

"I'm going to kiss you."

She smiled. "Okay."

He wasn't sure which one of them moved, but she was in his arms and his mouth slanted over hers. Her tongue met his in a fierce dance. She tasted as sweet and strong as she looked and fit against him perfectly, supple steel and utter femininity. He cupped the back of her neck, caressing the skin with his thumb. The cascade of worry inside him parted for the pleasure of just holding her close.

The slow heat building in the kiss soothed the fist of tension in his gut. Over and over again their mouths came together, the kiss taking on a life of its own—playful and intense by turns. Heart hammering in his chest, he lifted his head and gazed down at her. "You need to call your mom."

She laughed and nibbled his lower lip. "I should, especially if I'm not going home tonight."

"Yeah." Sliding an arm around her waist, he fished his phone out of his pocket and unlocked the screen. "Here, use my phone."

Her orchid corsage tickled his wrist as she took the device and punched in the number without looking away from him. She held the phone to her ear, her free hand stroking the hair at the base of his neck. Her mother answered.

"Hi, Mom. Just wanted to let you know I'm going to be out the rest of the night. I'll see you tomorrow, okay?"

His heart kicked against his ribs.

"I will Mom, love you, too." She hung up. "All good."

"You will what?" He tucked the phone back into his pocket.

"Have a good time."And their mouths came together in another kiss. They needed to walk over to the elevators, but Kyle contented himself with the intoxication of her kiss and the sweet spice of the moment.

The perfect moment.

"You were that certain I'd be a sure thing?" She teased.

Kyle let her go long enough to slide the card key into the door. They were on the top floor of The Grand, and he pushed open the double doors to reveal a hedonistic suite done in sweeping white with gold accents. Candles decorated the sitting room, along with flowers, a bottle of champagne chilling in an ice bucket, and a table with warming lids over a meal laid out next to a panoramic view overlooking Los Angeles.

"Let's say I like to think positive." His ears actually turned a faint shade of pink. He delighted her. He was so real and despite his success, managed to hang onto what had made him so awesome in high school. Sexy, sweet and smart. *God, I'm lucky.*

Dropping her purse on the table, she let him draw her into the room and close the doors. It was beautiful and romantic—and unmistakably sweet and thoughtful.

"I wasn't sure what you'd like to eat, so I ordered up several different dishes...." He paused halfway to the table and glanced at her. "If you're hungry."

"Not particularly." She crooked her finger at him, beckoning.

He pivoted slowly and walked back toward her. "No?"

"Nope." She flattened her hands on his chest and rubbed her

palms over the fabric. "Not for food at least."

"Well, okay then...." And their mouths came together. She didn't need words or long conversation, but this? This she needed. The electricity skating over her nerves kindled a deeper heat in her belly. They glided across the room. She loosened his tie and pushed his jacket free. He pulled the clip from her hair and combed his fingers through it. Their tongues twined, rubbing along each other, and she tasted a hint of the champagne they'd drank downstairs and the intensely masculine flavor of him.

They made it to the bedroom door. Leaning back, she panted for a breath and gazed up at him. The quiet heat of him pressed against her raced through her veins like a fever. She didn't want the moment to end. Everything he'd done since running into him three days before collided through her in a wealth of intimacy.

He dipped his face to her throat and inhaled deeply. A raw shudder of need trembled through her. He drew his tongue along her neck, tracing small circles around the pulse point, and she wanted to go up in flames. The feel of his hands over her breasts made her hate the dress. It separated her skin from his.

"The zipper is on the side," she whispered breathlessly, and God bless him, he took the hint and peeled it downward. The dress fell, pooling at her feet, and he eased his way along her body, breathing fire across her skin until he captured a nipple in his mouth. The point ached with want, and she clutched his hair, holding him to her as he lavished attention to her breasts. So lost in the pleasure of his tongue and teeth teasing her nipple that his fingers slipping under the waistband of her panties shocked her.

A moan wrenched free and she banged her head on the wall. The tiny bite of pain just enhanced the pleasure throbbing in her center. Every hard pull of his mouth teased the liquid heat in her core higher, she burned from the want of him. And the man had way too many clothes on. He slid his hand around and cupped her ass. Accepting the invitation, she ground against the erection tenting his pants. The door opened and he ushered her backward. They tumbled onto the bed. He lay across her and she parted her legs to keep them touching.

"You have too many clothes on." She pulled off the corsage and worked her hands between them to unbutton his shirt. He laughed softly and caught a nipple between his thumb and forefinger.

"You don't." He kissed a path to the other breast and lavished it, every motion pressing him against her, and she arched her back. God, the man had a beautiful mouth and he knew how to use it. He continued to slide down her body, pulling free of her hands. He hooked a finger into the scrap of fabric and peeled her panties down, then stood over her staring down.

"Damn—" Panting, he seemed to be struggling for a breath. He smoothed a palm over her belly. "Stay—right there."

Going to his knees, he pulled her legs until they slid over his shoulders. Rising to her elbows, she met his gaze down the length of her body. Pure lust and deep affection collided in his eyes and she felt beautiful.

"I told myself I'd lick you everywhere if I ever got the chance. I'd taste you, stroke and explore every inch of this gorgeous body." His breath teased her sex, and she clenched her thighs at the promise in his dark voice. He pressed a kiss to the inside of her thigh and she moaned. She didn't have to imagine the sensation because he moved his mouth to her sex and drew a long lick up from her entrance to her clit.

Her mind locked up. Every stroke of his tongue, every light bite of his teeth enchanted her and she writhed under his mouth, spreading her legs wider and digging her heels into his back. The pressure mounted, and when he slid a finger to test her entrance and pushed inside, she came with a shout. He didn't back off, driving her past one orgasm and straight into the tumbling force of another.

When she floated back to earth, he stared up at her— fascinated.

"Get naked, mister—now."

He grinned slowly and pulled free of her. Stripping out of his clothes in short order, he lowered over her, covering her chest, belly and thighs before taking her mouth in another searing kiss. The musky spice of him filled her nostrils and the wild need he unleashed within her roused.

"Condom," he murmured and she broke from the kiss to bite his shoulder.

"Hurry up." The order turned into demand, and he laughed at her before rolling over to grab the foil package she hadn't even seen him drop on the bed. His cock rose hard and proud, jutting up toward his belly. She rolled onto her side and traced a finger from his pectorals to his abdomen. He wasn't ripped like a bodybuilder, but no spare flesh marked his tan skin. Watching him sheath himself had to be one of the sexiest things she'd ever seen. Impatient, she rose up and straddled his hips.

He looked up at her and his mouth quirked teasingly. "Hello there."

"Hello." She stroked her hand down to cup his balls and massage the soft skin. He sucked in a hard breath, delighting her. "You're a beautiful man, you know that?"

"No, but I'll take your word for it." He didn't lay there idle, instead rubbed her sides, then under her breasts, teasing the swell before tracing caresses across her nipples. She firmed her grip on his cock, adjusting him to her entrance and easing onto him. He pushed into her, inch by glorious inch. She didn't pause or slow, just one long relentless thrust until he filled her. God, he was so huge and stretched her.

She couldn't catch her breath. It was perfect—she wanted to feel him deep and know he belonged to her. Pride filled her at the adoration in his gaze, a thrill that he wanted her—her—the woman and the Marine with a mind and a desire to do good in the world. She impaled herself on the last of his hard length and shared a groan with him. He fit her.

Surging up, he wrapped his arms around her and kissed her until the dizzying feeling threatened to carry her away. "You're really here," he murmured against her mouth, the sensual words unlocking another tidal wave of pleasure and then they moved together, a coordinated dance that took her breath away with every thrust.

He flipped her over and every nerve pinged to life. She gave him the control and the pace, locking her legs around his hips and meeting his kisses with fervor. The world faded and she and Kyle existed in a cocoon of pleasure. He filled her over and over again and she rode the flash of sensations bursting through her body. Each wild kiss and frantic moment drove her closer to the edge and she urged him on, digging her fingers into his back and the pleasure spiraled out of control.

Hot sensations exploded through her—strafing fire like a hundred rockets taking off at once. She barely heard his shouts, but the lock of his muscles increased the friction, and she clenched him, holding him fast through his orgasm. He jolted and they shook with the force of it. When he collapsed, she cradled him close and tears floated in her eyes.

Chapter Seven

𝑀orning came too soon and Kyle stared with a sigh out the window at the rising sun. Mary sprawled next to him, pillowed on his chest. She'd fallen asleep sometime around three, exhausted and happy, but sleep eluded him. He felt raw—everywhere—inside. Spending the night with her filled him with such an incredible sense of rightness, and his heart longed to not let her go. But he couldn't keep her chained to his side and that meant accepting she would go back to work—go back to a war zone.

Glancing down at her, he sighed again. He loved the sight of her darker skin next to his, the taut muscles illustrating her strength. He wanted to capture the moment forever, and keep her safe, but he refused to lame up their night by getting needy.

Moments. Hang on to the moments and let tomorrow take care of itself.

"Morning," she whispered, her breath feathering along his chest. Her eyes were still closed and he smiled.

"Good morning." He stroked the hair away from her cheek. "How are you doing?"

"I'm good." The lazy sweetness in her voice stroked him.

"But you're worried."

Was he really that transparent? "Pensive, maybe," he conceded.

She shifted, settling her chin on his chest to look at him. "We can talk about it now, if you want."

"Don't want to spoil the day." He rubbed her shoulder.

"It won't." She seemed so certain. But then she always did. It was one of the most fascinating parts of her—that determination to make the world the place she wanted to be in. Hell, he wanted to be in that world she made, even in some small way.

"I'm worried I won't be able to let you go when you deploy again." The confession tweaked his pride, but he preferred honesty.

"You don't have to let me go," she murmured. "You just have to be here when I come home."

His heart thudded, squeezing with the pressure of saying goodbye. "How is that different? Doesn't one have to happen for the other?"

She chuckled. "It's hard. I'm not going to lie. I see it all the time and I've never been in the position to have to say 'until I see you again.' But you're a smart guy, we can do this."

"You know, I'm not going to worry about that right now." Decision made, he tightened his arms around her. She was there, in his arms, and they were together. "Tell me something you've always wanted to do—"

"Yeah?" Her eyebrows lifted, her gaze softening on him.

"Yeah. See I can't change everything, but name one thing you've always wanted to do and let's see if I can make that happen."*Moments.* He couldn't change her orders, her determination, or her service, and he didn't want to. He wanted to make moments for her though, moments they could share.

She sucked on her upper lip and he could almost see the thought occurring to her. He waited.

"You're going to think it's silly."

"Okay." She eased over to sprawl across him, their legs tangling. "I want to go to Disney World."

If he didn't know better, he would have sworn she blushed. Truly intrigued, he traced a path down her back and waited.

"I want to wear mouse ears and ride the rides and get pictures with the characters and stare up at the fireworks as they go off every night-I want to feel the magic...."

"Done." He didn't even care what it involved.

"Yeah?"

"Honey, I'll buy you an entire hotel and throw in a cruise if that's what you want."

She tilted her head, her smile turning playful and coy. "I always wanted to go to Disney World-I know we have Disneyland and it's great, but..."

"You don't have to sell me. I'm in."

"I adore you." Her eyes widened.

"Right back atcha." Pulling her closer, he kissed her. "You let me take care of it, and I'll give you a vacation you won't forget."

Her sigh pierced him to his soul. "You already have."

And they didn't need any more words.

~ABOUT THE AUTHOR~

Heather Long lives in Texas with her family and their menagerie of animals. As a child, Heather skipped picture books and enjoyed the Harlequin romance novels by Penny Jordan and Nora Roberts that her grandmother read to her. Heather believes that laughter is as important to life as breathing and that the Easter Bunny, the Tooth Fairy and Santa Claus are very real. In the meanwhile, she is hard at work on her next novel.

You can visit Heather online at:
www.heatherlong.net

www.ingramcontent.com/pod-product-compliance
Lightning Source LLC
Chambersburg PA
CBHW071137170626
46809CB00002B/656